NIGHT DREAMS

Germaine Kaub Fraley

Ironwoman Publishing

Germaine Fraley/Ironwoman Publishing
Printed in the United States of America

Publisher's Note: This is a work of fiction. Names, characters, places, and incidents are a product of the author's imagination. Locales and public names are sometimes used for atmospheric purposes. Any resemblance to actual people, living or dead, or to businesses, companies, events, institutions, or locales is completely coincidental.

Night Dreams/ Germaine Fraley. -- 1st ed.

ISBN 978-0-9983668-0-7 Print Edition
ISBN 978-0-9983668-1-4 Ebook Edition

To my Aunt Diana,
Love,
Germaine

Enjoy!

Chapter 1

It started with an argument, more violent than any we'd experienced before. My uncle Boris rarely visited, but when he did, there was almost always discourse between him and my father, King Phillip Hamilton. On this particular day, their voices rose so loud, we could hear them echo through the stone walls of the castle. We were going about our various activities until the argument sharply escalated, at which time we spontaneously gathered in the foyer one by one. We whispered in low worried voices. Even Mother seemed more concerned than usual. We could hear the escalation of their voices and objects shattering. They were in my father's office on the second floor, and although we couldn't hear what was being said, we definitely felt the tension. It was the worst fight yet.

Our castle is small compared to others, but much bigger than our family requires. We live in one wing with seven bedrooms, a formal dining and sitting room, a large rustic kitchen with a maple wood table and chairs, a big old stove and oven, a cooling bin, a sink, and lots of shelves and storage space. Then there is a living area for the servants. We have a beautiful, cozy circular wood and stone library with one stained glass window reflecting lilies, poppies and vines, and another very large clear window that looks out over our vast property. The room has a vaulted ceiling made of decorative brick in a spiral design, built-in bookshelves stuffed with books on all kinds of subjects, a desk, a divan, two overstuffed chairs, a fireplace and my telescope. We are fortunate enough to have deep, fresh well water, easily pumped to each of the bathrooms that are equipped with a tub, sink, and a toilet with a pull cord to flush. Our bedrooms are large and comfortable, each with a fireplace and decorated to our individual taste. The rest of the castle is closed off and maintained just enough to keep it from crumbling and decaying. When we were younger we used to love to play in that part of the castle, an imaginative child's play house. But it was cold, dusty and empty except for old musty furniture covered with sheets, and creaky floorboards. A couple of the rooms were so creepy feeling that we stayed away from those, sure that if we entered or lingered too long, the wispy arms of a darkened entity might try to grab us and disappear through the cold stone fireplace, never to be seen again. My parents had considered renting out that part of the house, but the discussions never seemed to amount to anything, and so it sits empty.

Before we left we had a few servants and maids and four kitchen ladies. All personnel had their particular jobs and we had no one extra. My father paid them well and we treated them as family. Most of our employees have been with us since before I was born, which was seventeen years ago! The castle grounds are beautiful with rolling hills, creeks, olive and fig groves, wide meadows and old wooden bridges. There are cherry, apple and pear orchards on the other side of the berm, where Mother spends a good deal of her time. We have lots of trees and gardens tended to by three gardeners, and a stable with six horses that are cared for by a stable master and his assistant. We have an abundance of wildlife on our land, including rodents and reptiles, birds, bears, deer, wild pigs and turkeys, peacocks, coyotes and small lions, porcupines, beaver, and much more. Some of our land in the hills is leased to sheep and cattle farmers.

My father inherited his title and the kingdom from my grandfather. Our family ownership goes back for many generations. We rule just eight small towns and villages and one larger city with a population of 150,000. The largest town of Zap has a population of 15,000; the smallest, Nicwic, has 250 people. My father has ruled by intelligence and trust, and takes a hands-off approach, allowing the people to rule themselves justly and fairly. He only gets involved when there is a land or water dispute, or a conflict that can't be resolved by the people themselves, or the mayor or sheriff. Our family takes trips to the nearest town of Bellingham frequently. We love the life of the small city and the people, who are friendly and welcoming and treat us like regular folk. There we can pick up necessary supplies, maybe catch a street show and visit with neighbors and friends.

My uncle Boris is my father's only sibling; they had another brother but he died of typhoid at the age of three. Boris is a large, intimidating man who smells of rat piss, straw and dirt. His breath usually smells of stale whiskey and cigars, and he has wild, unkempt hair and a beard hanging down to his rotund belly that is prone to collecting debris from his last gluttonous meal. I often imagined a small rodent or insects making a nest in there without the slightest notice from the landlord. Boris's teeth are yellowed and he sports a number of dark, sinister tattoos on rough, leathery skin. He had always been jealous of my father's inheritance and stature, and although Boris is the elder of the two, he was never in line for the throne, as he was the bastard stepchild of my grandfather, the result of a tryst with a servant, who died in childbirth. My grandmother reluctantly raised the child as her own, and the brothers didn't know any better until my grandfather wrote out his will. Boris bitterly resented my father and picked fights whenever he had the chance. He lived in the valley outside of the kingdom and rarely showed up to visit. When he did it was usually to ask for some favor, money, a letter needed for some questionable business he was investing in or such. He'd bring us children small gifts that were always questionable as to their purpose and meaning, and were mostly inappropriate. Once when I was seven, he brought me a rather ratty, satin stretch band with a limp, dirty pink bow on it. He told me I could wear it on my arm like a bracelet or in my hair. It was too thick for a hair band and fell off my arm as it was much too wide, and it was just plain ugly. When my mother saw what he had given me, she snatched it away and glared at my uncle. Later, I realized that it was a garter he had received as a gift from one of his ladies of the night. Another time he brought my brother Phillip the skull of some animal, maybe a deer, which still had tufts of fur and remnants of flesh on it and had a very rotten smell. Again my mother grabbed it away and removed it far from the house. He brought my sister and younger brother faded and worn pamphlets for vacation travel, and café menus. He thought it would help them become worldly.

When my father and uncle argued it seemed to be mostly about the ownership of the estate, or money. Boris was always broke, always gambling his money away and making poor investments, living beyond his means and spending extravagantly. He felt my father owed him a sizeable stipend, since grandfather only left him with a farm and some land, over in Huntsville on the other side of the realm. My grandfather thought he could make a good living leasing the land and raising livestock, but Boris squandered it all in poor business dealings. The arguments always ended with my uncle leaving in a huff and putting my father in a dark mood. My mother explained it away as sibling rivalry; fighting just like us kids do from time to time. But this day, after the loudest, most contentious and the worst argument of all, he stomped down the stairs and swept an expensive vase off a small table in the foyer, shattering it to pieces, brushed right past us and left, madder than ever before. We secretly hoped he would never come back.

My mother went to my father's office and they shuttered themselves in and talked for long hours. Father tried not to let the incident bother him, but I could tell it weighed heavy on his mind. He became particularly preoccupied in his den, writing initiatives and memorandums and sending them off by courier to who knows where.

Ten days later, as we were going about our chores on a cold Saturday, we saw in the distance a cloud of dust and snow following a large group of men on horseback. Boris had arrived with a band of rebels, and they had weapons! My siblings and I ran into the castle yelling for our parents, who had also seen them from a distance. Father told Mother to take us and leave, *"Now,"* while he frantically grabbed his rifle and called for his guardsmen. Boris's army came faster than we could prepare for and stormed the castle, setting off a series of explosions and lighting fires. The patches of snow still on the ground hissed and sputtered in response to the hot torches. My father and his soldiers were able to mount a decent defense and fought skillfully and very hard. The servants, cooks and groundsmen took cover or scattered from the fray. My mother and siblings and I ran for the cellar, then through a tunnel to the back stable. We began throwing supplies in our old caravan and readying the horses with the help of the stable men. The horses were frightened and not easily calmed. They were neighing and bucking, instinctively wanting to run. We could hear screaming; there was smoke and bloodied bodies, and loud percussions that rocked the castle. Without another thought my mother nearly threw Jeffrey and Emi into the caravan as Phillip and I scrambled aboard. Mother took the reins and let the horses loose; they took off so fast it threw us against the back door in a pile of bodies. I was sure we were going to flip and all die, or the wooden gate would break and dump us all out in a tumble on the road, only to be trampled to death by my father and his comrades. We untangled ourselves and looked back at the commotion of horses and riders. I could see and hear a barrage of gunfire following my father and his men as they galloped as fast as they could away from the castle. We were all crying and extremely frightened; Jeffrey was bawling like a little girl until Phillip smacked him hard on the arm.

A couple of miles later, Mother slowed the horses and tried to calm them with a soothing voice, she herself dropping her head, taking deep breaths. We were wet with sweat and tears, cold and dirty from the road dust. My mother brought the caravan to a stop in a snow-dusted field near a stream. My father and some of his men caught up to us, breathing heavily. We jumped out of the caravan and hugged and cried. The caravan had scant supplies and a few blankets. Our only clothes were what we were wearing at the time of the siege, my mother having the good sense to grab a couple of coats hanging in the stable before we left, and nothing else. Suddenly we were alone, helpless and very poor.

CHAPTER 2

My name is Blue. I am 17. My sister Emiline is 10, my brother Phillip is 13 and Jeffery is 9. We are a dark-haired clan of beauties with strong, sharp features and clear, smooth skin. I have dark blue eyes—almost purple, thus my name. My hair is a bit curly and leans toward brown tones, while Phillip has dark eyes like my father's, and wavy hair as black as obsidian. Jeffery's eyes are more hazel colored, and he has thick dark brown hair with lighter tones that show through when the sun hits just right. Emi's eyes are also hazel with specks of red and blue in her irises, striking in contrast to her lovely smooth, deep sable-colored hair.

For the first few weeks after we fled, we wandered without the aid of maps or compass, relying on my father's geographic and informational knowledge. We lived like gypsies out of our caravan and tents and moved further south, from place to place, trying to stay ahead of the wintery season and live as best we could. The first week was the hardest, as we had no idea what our future would be. All at once we were torn from our home and routines and thrown into a life of uncertainty. Emi and Jeffrey took it the worst. They cried frequently and it required a great deal of comforting from Mother to soothe their fears. Phillip was an adaptable kid, easy-going and not prone to opening up to his emotions. He watched, observed and anticipated. I tried to be strong but was equally worried. I tried to be as helpful as I could, not really knowing what to do but taking directions for camp set-up, meal prep and caravan tending. I kind of like organizing so enjoyed playing house in the caravan, cleaning and straightening up, putting things in their proper places, trying to make it more comfortable for six people to live in and work out of.

My uncle was a powerful man in his own right and had amassed a number of soldiers and dedicated ne'er-do-wells. He'd come in and out of money from his gambling habit and at times seemed to have significant wealth (none of which he spent on his own hygiene). He was therefore able to keep my father's truth from being known by paying his men to invent stories about our whereabouts and spreading the lies across the land. One story had us all dying in a fire at the castle. There was even a memorial service in our honor. Another killed us off by drowning while on a family vacation to Lake Isideron, on which our small boat capsized. Another was that our father left us for another woman and my mother took her children to live with her parents far away, leaving my uncle to mind the kingdom. The stories were rampant and varied, many humorous or shocking. Father felt it best not to let on who we were, or to contradict the tales until we knew more about Boris's motives and intent. For all we knew, he might indeed try to find and dispose of us. For now, we must make the best of it, stay together as a family and support each other.

My father was strong of mind and character and very smart, but he cared most for the health and safety of his wife and children, so would not risk a conflict to regain his position. Instead he took trips on horseback and would be gone for days, sometimes weeks, on "business." When he returned, he often brought my sister and brothers and me a small gift or clothes, and for my mother, a new frock or nice hat, and always some food. Occasionally he would show up with a large leg of lamb or a turkey.

Late at night when we had cozied down in our beds of straw and tattered blankets under the canvas tents, I could hear my mother and father in the caravan whispering in the candlelight about his travels and adventures. Now and then I could hear him comforting my mother and telling her that he was making connections with the right people to help us get back home. He had many friends, some of whom were courtiers and soldiers from his kingdom, who would impart important information to help him plot to overthrow my uncle. Most of my parents' conversations I could not hear clearly, but I always fell asleep comforted and knowing that one day we would be back home.

As time went by our days were filled with work, school studies and play. My sister and I would try to sell our needlework and crafts at the nearby markets in the towns and villages close to where we camped, then return to help my mother and the boys with chores. My mother suffered the worst those days, as she tried so hard to keep a clean and neat home in our tents and caravan, but she was constantly dismayed to see her children in tattered clothing, forever in need of a good bath and having to sleep on the ground. Filling our stomachs with a hot meal was always a challenge. The caravan had some essentials like old pots and pans, a few blankets and some tools, so we had to make do with what we had or barter for items when we passed through towns. When we lived in the castle, we never went without a proper meal and clean clothes. We were "moderate" royalty. Never wealthy, but our needs were met. We had few servants. Unlike upper royalty, we dressed ourselves, and did chores, and occasionally my mother would attempt to help in the kitchen and learn to cook a recipe or two. The boys were always made to help in the stable, in and around the castle and buildings on the grounds, or to run errands. My sister and I helped with cleaning and sewing and many other household duties. We were self-sufficient even at home.

We moved about every three weeks or so and tried to settle somewhere near a village or town, but far enough away so as not to raise the eyebrows of the authorities or residents. We tried to remain discreet and didn't want to create any confrontations, much less a lot of questions.

In July of the year we were banished, we found a fine place to camp near a wide river. The water was shallow and gentle but fast enough to carry a mild current. It was clear and clean and the banks were lined with a few short willows in bunches. We settled on a wide and long swath of meadow east of the river. On the other side there was a railroad track, then more meadow, and further beyond was a dense forest of pines and birch and wild fruit trees. The railroad track wasn't used much and when a train did roll through, the rumbling sounds would mingle with the gentle rippling of the river and create a symphony of lulling sounds, clicks and clacks, and an occasional bellow of the horn.

Our camp was near some birch trees and large boulders, about fifty yards east of the river. The area was beautiful. The meadow grasses were green and thick up to our calves, soft and breezy. Colorful summer wildflowers in large masses filled the meadow. As the sun set, the stream sparkled like millions of tiny shiny diamonds, and the meadow turned to soft ambers and muted colors. The road we had arrived on was several yards to the east and beyond that was more forest. Further to the south, about a mile away, was a town of good size, maybe 2,000 people, called Iznot. It was convenient and we could replenish our supplies there.

Chapter 3

In the months we lived as nomads, my father would occasionally gather us up and take us into the local town or village, and surprise us with a stay at the local inn or hotel. There, we could take a bath with soap and hot water and wash our clothes. When we were clean and dressed, he and my mother would take us for a delicious meal in the tavern. We were a wonderment of the establishments, as we displayed discipline and manners like no one in the village had seen. Here was a family of seemingly homeless and likely uneducated waifs who were very polite, with exceptional manners, courteous and articulate, and knew how to use their utensils correctly. We always won the respect and friendship of those people, who in turn often gave us one more night at the inn for a pittance or for free, and often would not let us leave the next day without a basket full of bread, cheese and fruit.

After supper we would stroll around town, or my father and mother would leave us to do as we may (as long as we were back at an appointed hour and wouldn't get into mischief), and retreat back to the inn to have some privacy without us children for a while.

A couple of evenings after setting camp near the stream and getting organized in our new location, my parents took us into Iznot for our special treat. After we bathed and dressed and our bellies were full, my sister and I strolled down the boardwalk of town, looking in the shop windows and delighting at the beautiful and sparkly things. My brothers had met some other boys and were whooping and hollering off in the distance, probably playing street ball. As Emiline and I were commenting on a hat in a window that we thought would look nice on Mother, I felt a strange and unnatural sensation, as if I wasn't alone in my thoughts. When I turned and glanced up, I noticed a young man across the road holding a bucket and a brush, standing stock still like a statue, watching as my sister and I passed by. My sister noticed him and began to giggle. "That man is looking at you," she said with a singsong voice as if she and the stranger had a secret.

"He is probably just curious about the new strangers in town. People take notice in small towns like this," I said in huffy retort; however, I did feel a little different about the way this person looked at us.

That night, back at the inn, warm in my own comfortable quiet room with a fire flickering and snapping in the stone fireplace, shadows dancing on the stone walls, I lay under a loft of fresh, clean linens and quilts that smelled like lilacs, just thinking. The stranger on the road popped into my mind, and I fell asleep dreaming of him wrapping me in his arms and whispering words of love in my ear.

The next day, we left the inn with our basket full of fresh goodies and headed back to our camp at the edge of town to begin our chores as usual. Since it was summer, we were given a reprieve from our studies, although we were still expected to read books and continue to learn. My mother gave us quizzes now and then on arithmetic, history, geography and spelling, but upkeep of the camp was our priority. My father left on another excursion, waving and blowing kisses; as he galloped away he said he loved us and would be back soon. I always worried about and missed him when he was gone.

On the day before Father left, the local sheriff and a couple of other men came riding into our camp on horseback. He was tall and lanky and was wearing denim trousers, boots, a crisp white shirt, a leather vest with a badge attached to the left side, and the kind of hat I had read cowboys wear. He had a big scruffy handlebar mustache, and thick, wild eyebrows. He looked to be in his sixties, a bit weathered but with friendly eyes. I could see the look of worry in my parents' eyes, but the sheriff dismounted and took just three long steps forward with a big smile, an outstretched hand, a friendly demeanor, and introduced himself as Mr. Jacobson. My father introduced himself, his wife and us children, and we nodded politely.

Mr. Jacobson said he had heard a new family was in town and he wanted to check on us, see who we were. "Can't be too careful around here," he said with a drawl. He was very kind and open, but had several questions he wanted answers to, like where we came from. "From the west, near Bellingham." What was our business? "Planning on visiting relatives over in Cataract." How long were we staying? "Not sure yet, but we won't overstay our welcome, maybe a few weeks if that's okay and we'll be good tenants." Any others joining us? "No." Any word of news on the road? "We really didn't run into many people."

Mr. Jacobson said he'd heard about a rash of bandits out west who were stopping travelers and robbing them of money and goods. We kids deemed him safe and harmless, and went about our duties while Father and Mother spoke with him for quite awhile. He offered any help he could give or questions he could answer, and told us a little about what was offered in the town and resources for our use. He said if we kept the area clean of trash and debris, watched our horses and cleaned up after them and acted responsibly, we could stay through the summer. Soon he bid us farewell, tipped his hat and rode back toward town with the other men.

After he was gone, I asked Mother a little more about the part of the conversation I missed. The only thing she offered me in private was that he had heard about an overthrow of a kingdom far off. He asked if we knew anything about it. My mother and father feigned ignorance, saying we were traveling to Upshot to visit an ailing relative before heading home, but Mother said she could tell that he suspected we might be the royal family, as we certainly fit the profile. My parents sat us all down and talked to us again about the importance of keeping our identities secret, as it could compromise our return to the castle.

Late one afternoon, the train tracks suddenly came alive and began to vibrate and grumble, and way off in the distant south we could hear a train whistle. Minutes later, people from town were coming our way. They were on horses, in wagons, on bicycles; children and adults were walking briskly and running toward our camp with a sense of excitement and anticipation. The banks of the river began to swell on both sides with townspeople and our little camp was suddenly in the midst of a mass of excited people. They respectfully lingered a distance from our camp but couldn't help eyeing us, some with disdain and judgment. They knew some strangers were in town but didn't know where we were staying, who we were or what our business was. Because we looked like gypsies with our dark hair, worn clothes, caravan, tents and a fire pit, the mothers kept their children near to their sides and quietly warned them to stay away from us—gypsies were known to steal things and kidnap small children to roast and eat them in stews. Amongst the crowd we overheard talk of a circus coming to town. The adults discussed the arrival of new supplies and goods. Soon our presence was ignored or forgotten. Everyone was smiling and chattering happily, the kids running around, jumping up and down and giggling. We joined the crowd and were prickled by the contagious excitement and anticipation.

Suddenly someone was touching my shoulder and talking to me. I turned around and looked into the deep, reflective brown eyes of the strange young man we had seen in town. He was handsome and tall, with a bush of curly dark-blond hair down to his shoulders, a kind face and a day's worth of whiskers on his chin. I figured he must be around 20. I nearly melted and felt a little embarrassed, recalling my earlier thoughts of him. He asked me if I would be going to the circus. I hadn't even had time to think about it and stammered out an answer: "Sure, maybe, I think so, probably, I don't know." I sounded like an idiot. He politely introduced himself as Anton and I returned the pleasantries. "Hi, my name is Blue." He said, "That must be because of your blue eyes," which threw me a little as I looked into his radiant brown ones. I dropped my gaze and looked around to see my mother and siblings in faded and drab clothing, our caravan and horses, our little canvas tents. Over the fire was a steaming pot of soup and our laundry was hanging about on ropes and poles for drying after washing in the stream. I was suddenly, utterly, embarrassed and ashamed. We must have looked like a very poor family of orphans abandoned by a mean father and left to survive on our own. What did this boy think of us? I quickly and rather rudely made an excuse to leave, turned and walked away without another word. He must have thought I was a real snob, and I regretted it immediately.

Sitting on a rock away from camp that night, I cried. Mother came to comfort me. Sitting on an abutting stump, she put her arm around my shoulders and said nothing. I told her of the handsome boy and of my embarrassment when he saw how we lived. She cradled me gently, lightly stroking my hair, and reminded me that although we had to live like this for now, the day would come when we would be able to return home. She assured me that while my father was away for those many days and weeks at a time, he was making contacts and gathering information useful for displacing my uncle and regaining the kingdom.

I felt very selfish, for I knew my father would return us to the castle and restore our royal status. I was really very proud of both my mother and father, and should the truth be known, this was all a new adventure, something I could imagine looking back on in the future with fondness. After a while, I didn't even have the desire to set people straight on the outlandish stories they had heard about our flight and family. The stories were interesting and often humorous, something to talk and laugh about in the evenings. My parents also kept the secret, as they did not want to arouse suspicion should my uncle have supporters in this part of the country. My father insisted that we remain quiet and humble. My sister always looked up to me and followed what I did, so she didn't let on. I think my brothers kept quiet because they had found new friends and lots of things to occupy their days, places to explore and games to play. I doubted they wanted to go back any time soon, and I wouldn't be surprised if they left with the circus and became vagabonds! Royalty, shmoyalty!

As I whimpered my woes to Mom, she just listened patiently, and once I was done sniveling we walked back to camp together and joined the others for some roasted marshmallows.

The train had rumbled on through and stopped in town. It would be here several days, loading and unloading supplies and circus equipment and animals. For the next several days we could hear far-off voices, odd construction and whirring sounds, hammers and a clatter of activity as the circus got underway setting up. There was a large open clearing spreading out from the forest on the west side of the road between our camp and town. If we climbed to the top of one of the boulders nearby, we could barely see the tall necks of the giraffes and the tops of the frame of the circus tent. We often heard the bellow of an elephant, the roar of a lion or the squealing of a pig. Every now and then my sister and I would wander over to watch the progress and look at the animals in their pens. It was very exciting, and I secretly hoped that the circus would begin before my father's return so that we would not have to pick up and leave before being able to see the show and, perhaps, to see Anton once again. I felt I owed him an apology.

Chapter 4

As the days passed in our camp by the river, my mother planted a little garden with some flowers, herbs and summer vegetables. She seemed to like working in the rich soil, her mind somewhere far away, always the tiniest smile on her lips and a faint hum in her throat as the sun streaked her cheeks. She was not the best cook and was not able to obtain the proper ingredients to replicate the recipes she had learned from the cooks at home. I missed those good meals, but she tried her best and learned a few good tricks from some of the women she had befriended in various towns along the way. The boys were always getting into mischief, capturing harmless snakes in the forest to bring back and torment Emi and me with, until harshly reprimanded by Mother; poking at and teasing badgers and porcupines and any other helpless creatures that wandered into their path, chasing bunnies (who found mother's vegetable garden irresistible), inventing new games, throwing rocks, fighting with sticks and wandering too far away across the river and into the forest for my mother's comfort. One day my youngest brother, Jeffrey, came back messy haired, sweaty and wide-eyed with a story of a young boy from town who had been attacked and killed by a bear in the woods; he was sure he and his friend had seen the tracks. From then on my mother forbade him to go anywhere near the woods again or wander out of sight by himself, and insisted that he carry a whistle with him should he run into any trouble. From the look on Jeffrey's face, at the thought of being ripped apart by an angry bear, I doubted he would question her advice.

Phillip was at that awkward stage between childhood and teenager. His body was beginning to change and he was starting to grow a few soft wisps of peach fuzz on his chin for which Jeffrey and Emi were constantly teasing him, and he had begun noticing girls as the enigmatic species we are. He was too shy to talk to them but tried to stand near them. If a girl attempted to say something to him, he'd glance down embarrassedly and find an excuse to leave her presence. He had plenty of other things to occupy his time and mind, and did an excellent job of subjugating his pre-teen urges.

He did not have to be told by our father to "be the man of the house," as whenever my father had left on business from the castle, he always put my brother in charge. Phillip would roll his eyes and say, "but Daaaad..." knowing all the while that the few staff we had would take care of most of our needs. During the months on the road, however, Phillip dutifully fulfilled his role and did more than expected around the camp, fixing and repairing the tents, tending to the horses, trying to make broken things work and generally doing what was needed to help our mother in any way. He was clever and industrious and surprised us with skills and creativity we never knew he had. He found all kinds of ways to make our camp a little more homey, like building a simple fence around my mother's garden with scrap chicken-wire he had found, and making the fire pit look attractive with colored rocks from the river and a little creative stonework. He repaired the wooden steps to the caravan and put up a railing to make it easier and safer for my parents to get in and out, as that is where they slept and kept essential supplies. He built a shade canopy large enough for all of us to sit under, with a wind/rain screen made of discarded muslin. He built a small cage for a bunny my sister had caught and decided to keep as a pet. She named her bunny Sniffles. Sniffles was white and gray with a little brown mixed in, a baby pink nose that was always, well, sniffling, and a cute little white cottontail. Now he had an open-air cage large enough to hop around in with grass and straw to sit and lie on. He seemed quite content to munch on the carrots and plants we fed him from the garden, and to just sit and look around with his little pink nose ever twitching.

He didn't seem at all interested in returning to the wild. There was, however, the occasional frightening predator who tried to get at Sniffles; foxes were the worst, so Phillip hung small bells from his cage that would scare other animals away. This worked as a dual purpose to warn us of a possible invader as well.

This camp was different from the others. Early on, we had occupied an abandoned and broken-down farmhouse, which was small but adequate and kept the cool wind and snow out. But we had to flee when a freak, late-winter lightning storm struck an old tree, setting it ablaze, throwing torches of limbs and fire to the ground and on the roof of the farmhouse and spreading rapidly. It became a fast-moving and violent fire that moved across the plains with such force and violence that the snow didn't have time to melt, but sizzled into hot puddles of water, steam rising like a dense fog blanketing the plain. The crackling, popping and sparks flying were frightening but mesmerizing. It was hard not to watch it unfold, but we barely had enough time to gather our things, harness the frightened horses that were bucking and neighing, and get out of there before the farmhouse was completely consumed.

Our second camp was in an old, dilapidated barn that was drafty, dusty and smelled of moldy hay and horse dung. It had mice and rats scurrying around, bugs, gnats and flies, and bats. The horses didn't seem to mind and happily munched on any edible leavings of hay and grain they could find. We opened the doors of the barn and hayloft, broke one window trying to open it and, with great effort, got a second one unstuck and open. We cleared out fly-attracting garbage and batted dirt, dust and cobwebs from most of the surfaces. We got rid of most of the odors from the old hay, horse and mouse droppings, and gathered clean pine fronds to mattress our bedding and help sweeten the scent in the air. It was still an unpleasant place to stay and we spent as much time outside the barn as possible. We left there when spring arrived accompanied by a heat wave that cooked the barn into a steamy, smelly pot of rot, not conducive to human living. We moved our belongings outside the barn and reverted to living in the tents and caravan again. We put up no argument when Father returned and said we had to break camp and move on.

After that, we landed in the middle of nowhere with a mean, constant wind, very little water burbling up from an underground spring, no nearby town and no natural or manmade shelter. We took turns sleeping in the caravan with our parents, as the fabric of the tents did their best job of fighting the force of the wind, constantly blowing inward, then suddenly ballooning outward, popping violently like an umbrella turned inside out. Surprisingly, they never ripped although we were constantly pounding the stakes in deeper, adding rocks on top of each one and re-securing the ropes. All day and all night, blowing, blowing, blowing. Wind penetrated every possible orifice, whistling and moaning as if it had picked up ghostly travelers along the way. Sleep- deprived, cranky, tired of trying to hold everything down, tame our hair and clothes, and chasing objects blown away, we soon left that camp and moved on again.

A half-day's journey on and we seemed to have found the idyllic spot, with beautiful vistas and gorgeous early summer weather. The nights were clear with bright stars and our two juxtaposed moons: Iridis, the smaller of the two whose faint colors of orange and blue tell the story of the Greek messenger goddess, Iris, colorful cape flowing behind her, and Niobe, the larger, brighter white moon, daughter of King Tantalus. She bragged about having seven daughters and seven sons, scoffing at brother Leto for only having two children. Apollo and Artemis promptly killed her offspring. Niobe, in despair, was turned into stone by the gods. Her glow hangs in the night sky, sadness imagined in the face of her crater-pocked surface. I longed for my telescope. It was a gift to me from my parents for my sixteenth birthday. They knew I had taken an interest in astronomy and with the telescope, although small, I was able to see the universe in ways I'd never imagined. It was a beautiful tool, shiny brass with the finest telescoping optical mirrors set on a sturdy expandable wooden tripod. It was left behind in the castle and I missed it.

Chapter 5

After the train arrived and the circus grew and took shape, the little village swelled into a large town, doubling in size. The saloons were noisy with laughter, music and ruckus. The stores were full of people buying and selling this or that, the small bells above the doors constantly tinkling, signifying active commerce. Our quiet little tavern became the hub of activity with people coming and going to meet, eat and sleep. Artists, poets, students, businessmen and vacationers came to town. Although my mother would have preferred that we stayed closer to our camp and came back earlier in the evenings, she found joy in our excitement and had a difficult time reining us in. Plus, nearly every time we returned from town we brought back food or clothes, a trinket or two or much- needed supplies like tools, nails and rope for repairs, a new hitch for one of the horses, bigger and better water containers, even an old cracked wooden toilet seat that Phillip found in a junk pile behind the general store. He fashioned four short, sturdy wooden legs and attached the seat with a hammer and nails. He repaired the cracks, sanded away the splinters and buffed up the seat until the maple wood shone. He also attached a curved wooden handle from an old orchard bucket that swung down and out of the way while in use, but was very handy for carrying the little loo about. Although we still had to dig holes for our waste and cover it afterwards, to be able to place this little contraption over the hole and actually sit down was far better than squatting to poop in the woods and worrying about your bottom touching sharp twigs, or thorns, a poisonous plant or something worse! My biggest fear was having a creepy-crawly bug or beetle latch onto my bare bottom to give me a bite or sting.

Every once in a while we could talk my mother into coming to town with us to see all the activity and new things brought in by the train. We marveled at the fine lace from France, tasted the smoky tea from Morocco and smelled the pungent incense from India. Soon she was caught up in the fun and we would often find her chatting and giggling with other ladies she had met. It seems like women always have something to talk about.

My sister and I were able to sell our crafts and kept busy making new ones. Now that we had a few coins to spend, we could buy buttons and bows and thread to make aprons, baby bibs, hot pads and writing cards. Any spare change would be brought back to my mother, who would add it to a tin can she kept hidden on a shelf behind other supplies in the wagon.

Besides the crafts my sister made and sold, she found a small market in selling tiny tadpoles she found in a bog near the stream. Children were thrilled to buy the slimy little creatures in various stages of development, from just wiggly, limbless things to ones with back legs and little nubs for the front.

"They're sure to develop into full-grown toads right before your eyes!" she told them. For a penny, you got one tadpole in a small container of dirt covered with a couple of inches of stream water and instructions on care. "Just keep some water on top of them, enough for them to swim around in, give them a little fresh algae for food and keep a porous cover on top so they can breathe and won't jump out. Oh, and you might want to give them a treat now and then." My sister never said exactly what the treats were supposed to be. A cookie crumb? Piece of candy? Some lettuce? "Just a little treat to keep them happy and show your love," she said with an air of knowing. Luckily, we would be long gone before the children discovered that their new pets would die very soon, as they were not accustomed to living outside their natural environment. A valuable and sad lesson my sister learned from that experience. But in the meantime, she became quite popular with her tadpoles and little business, made a lot of new friends, and had a little money she spent on herself for penny candy or new pencils.

Emiline was very particular about her name. She hated it when people pronounced it Emal*ene*. So when introducing herself she always emphasized that it was Emil*ine*. Her brothers were constantly making fun of her, calling her Leny, Leany, Emilemy and Lemon Head (Phillip's favorite). She would cry in anger and run for support to Mother, who would reprimand the boys for making fun of her. We usually just called her Emi, which she didn't seem to mind.

Occasionally she would bring a new friend back to our camp to introduce them to Sniffles and Black, if he was around. Black was a small, sleek black cat she had adopted (or he her) when he wandered into camp, sniffing around the tents and the bunny cage. Emi made the mistake of feeding him, so he found many excuses to hang around. She uncreatively named him Black, although it was clear that he was well kept and fed by someone else. He'd find objects to play with, dark, cool cubbies to explore and sleep in, and things to whack off the shelves in the caravan. He was forever tantalized by Sniffles, trying to reach his little paw through the chicken wire. Sniffles sniffed at the paw but never got close enough for Black's claws to snag. Sniffles seemed to tease Black as much as he tried to torment Sniffles. Black could be seen pouncing on mice and anything that moved in the meadow and grasses, and when tired of getting into mischief or playing, he'd snuggle up to Emi, looking for a scratch behind the ears and purring loudly when she complied. Her friends loved her pets and the way we lived. All of them lived in modest houses in or near town and it seemed such an adventure to camp out under the stars, bathe in the river and cook food over rocks. They often stayed for a little stew or soup just for the experience.

The boys found jobs helping on the train, unloading supplies for the stores or working with the circus doing all kinds of odd jobs. They unloaded, sorted, counted and inventoried supplies. They found an old bike, fixed it up and attached a wooden wagon to it for delivery of goods and supplies. Any kind of odd job they could find, they would take. It kept them busy and full of pocket change. At the end of the day, they were filthy and exhausted.

I mostly helped Mother around camp, did some shopping for food and supplies and, when in town, wandered around watching what other people were up to. Every now and then, I would catch a glimpse of my elusive stranger darting in and out of the general store, running to the livery, driving a horse cart full of supplies through town and generally flitting about, appearing very busy. The street was so crowded now that a glimpse was all I could get, for in the next moment he would have disappeared, swallowed up in the movement, dust and commerce of the town. Once, as I was leaving the dressmaker's with a bag full of loose scraps of material, I nearly ran into him, and would have if I had not looked up at the last instant as he was hurrying down the boardwalk. Our eyes met, he with a hurried, distracted look on his face, and perspiration trickling down his temples and neck, his hair in tangles from dampness and dirt. We exchanged short greetings before he was off again and I was left with a light, hollow sensation in my chest as if I were suspended in air, floating and soaring far above the ground, and I was a little shocked at my reaction. I continued on my way with a smile on my face and wondering if he was thinking about me.

On one occasion as I was headed into town, I saw a curious sight. Between the town and our camp was a cluster of trees near where the forest began to the west. The trees were tall pines, the foliage further above the ground than the conifers on the other side of the river, and thin enough to see a few hundred yards into the forest, in the direction my father would disappear whenever he left. He never took the road. I was always glancing in that direction to see if my father would come riding out through the trees. This one day I noticed a group of four or five men, two on horseback, the others on foot. They were gathered in a semicircle, far enough away to be camouflaged by the trees, sun and shadows. They were barely noticeable. I slowed my pace and listened, as they seemed to be engaged in a secretive, important conversation. One was drawing lines in the dirt as the others looked on, pointing and making comments. I couldn't hear their words; they were too far off and the breeze rustling the trees interfered with their voices. Suddenly I was aware that one of the men on horseback was Anton. He and another man on horseback had on heavy gear and were wearing crude helmets of sorts. Anton was holding a long staff, or maybe a musket, I couldn't tell, but I was certain it was him because of his height and build and the curly locks of blond hair falling out from under the helmet; as soon as he looked up, even at that distance, I was able to see those striking brown eyes. He looked in my direction but I don't think he saw me. I was startled but in the same instant, he and the other rider turned and galloped away. The others turned and walked casually toward town, staying in the trees and not paying attention to the girl on the road. Once at the edge of town they dispersed and disappeared into the crowd.

This was the longest time we had spent in one place, and by now I was aware of much of the town gossip and business among the residents. I was sure they knew all there was to know about us, and we perpetuated the fib that we were just passing through (which we were), on our way to Upshot (which we weren't). So it was a puzzle to me to see those men, and especially Anton in that secretive situation, because very little was hidden from the townsfolk. I felt they were plotting something sinister, and slowly a distrust and wariness crept over me. I began thinking the worst of Anton, as those fellows he was with appeared worn around the edges and not the kind of company one would want for friends. What kind of business was he in? Why did he meet those men in the woods? Were they plotting something of no good? Did Anton "accidentally" meet me just to gain information about my family? Were they part of Boris's team? Against all of my emotions of girlish lust and thoughts; of the dreams I had of walking hand in hand in the clutch of Anton's firm, calloused palm, of being wrapped in his big but gentle arms, his hands placed sensually on the small of my back, his body pressed close to mine, of our first kiss beneath those brown eyes with his hair falling forward, tickling my cheek, the warmth of my body and tingling of my skin (as I had heard other girls talk of such sensations), instead, I thought it prudent to avoid him from now on. My parents would be proud of me for showing such intuition and discretion. And as I browsed around the shops aimlessly, I felt a heaviness swelling up in my chest, and rather than floating gently above the earth, I was, instead, plummeting from the sky to a certain and painful death. They were just silly, dramatic thoughts similar to ones I've had about other boys, and although this felt different, I had to get over him. I would be happy to move on to our next destination; this was just a ratty old do-nothing town anyway.

That evening when we were all back at camp, huddled around the fire with bowls of not-too-bad lamb stew in front of us, my mother, as she always did, asked us to recap the events of our day. Our exploits were different from any we had told when gathered around our rustic dinner table at home. These days, Jeffrey was constantly animated with big stories of happenings that we knew were mostly exaggerated or fantasy. He'd set his meal down on the ground and act out the event with a flourish. This particular evening he regaled us about the exploration of an empty, run-down, half-buried shack outside of town that was said to be the lair of a big hairy monster man, who was known to creep out at night, stalk around town and pop up at windows, frightening little children with his green glowing eyes. If an innocent strayed from the house, they risked an ambush by the monster, who would drag the children back to his lair to devour every last bit of them, teeth, bones and all. The shack was empty when he and his friends found it, but they were sure they saw evidence of the monster in large clawed footprints in the dirt floor, tufted fur clinging to the timber walls, and linear marks on the door. Emi asked if perhaps those were signs of a bear, at which Jeffery suddenly stopped his charades, turned pale, looked at Mom and sat down. The look Mother gave him was a silent but kind warning, eyebrows raised, expressing the possible danger he and his friend could have been in and not from monsters. Her look made it clear that once again, he must be more careful.

Phillip was more reserved but often couldn't hide his enthusiasm for the day, which showed in his wide eyes and colorful speech. He told about the work he found that day at the circus grounds and news of its progress. The big top was up now but they were having trouble securing one of the beams. He told of Miss Bellows, an enormous woman who wore too much makeup and had colorful tattoos on her arms of birds and animals, and one of a snake with its tail languidly crossing her right collarbone while the rest of the slithering body and head plunged downward between her very large breasts, disappearing into who knows where. She apparently caught her husband, who went by the name of Mr. Jumbles, very naked in one of the wagons with Miss Devilin. Mr. Jumbles was not a clown, as his name seemed to imply, but instead the man who took care of the bookkeeping and strongbox, a secretary of sorts. (I suspect they called him Mr. Jumbles because he wasn't very good at his job.) Red-faced with anger and with a sharp carving knife held high ready to strike, she chased him out of the camp and far into the woods, yelling and screaming at him, calling him unrepeatable names as he desperately tried to pull his pants up from around his ankles.

My sister frequently spoke of a new girl or boy she had met who showed her a pet rat, dog, guinea pig or parakeet. Of all of us, she had managed to get invited into the homes of her new friends, and was often asked to stay for a scrumptious lunch or dinner, cookies and lemonade, and even to stay overnight; she was so polite and engaging that the parents loved her. They thought she was a good influence on their children and enjoyed her company.

I didn't have much to say that evening. I told about picking up scrap material for crafts, but didn't mention the men I saw in the woods. My mother listened and smiled or laughed with us; she encouraged our ventures and friendships and reminded us to be polite and watch our manners, stay out of trouble and away from danger (she emphasized this while looking at Jeffrey), to be discreet about who we were but to remember that one day we would have to leave here, so it was best not to become too attached. (This she directed mostly to my sister, who listened with a frown on her face.)

"It may be abrupt, as it has been before. There may not be time to say goodbye, but while we are here, take in all that you see and do and the people you meet so that you'll have wonderful memories and adventures you can tell about for the rest of your lives," she said. I was very quiet the rest of the evening, but decided to start writing again in a journal I had long ago abandoned.

Occasionally, one or the other of us would catch snippets of conversation pertaining to the overthrow of a kingdom far away, with stories of a wretched man who beheaded the king and his family, or that he ran them off and they were later found mauled and eaten by wolves, or that he had thrown them in a dungeon and was using them as slaves. The stories changed constantly from a family of just three, to one of twelve. There was often mention of a baby that was abandoned in the castle to be raised by one of the servants. At first the stories worried and concerned us and we so wanted to correct the gossipers, but Mother warned us that this would only draw attention, suspicion and more questions. By and by, the rumors became more grand and humorous, and we would have a good laugh at our dinnertime meals recounting the stories we had heard.

CHAPTER 6

Finally, the circus was about to open. The posters had gone up, music could be heard in town, buskers juggled and performed to advertise the event, and last- minute preparations were being made. Stands were set up around town with children selling tickets, and there was no shortage of people buying them in ones and bunches and making arrangements to sit with one another. The circus would run for four days, in the evenings and with matinees on Saturday and Sunday. The opening day would be Thursday. This was Monday. I didn't think the town and area could swell any larger with people, but more came from all over the realm with their wagons, horses and carts, children, nannies and dogs. They were packing the inns and barns, camping up and down the river and in the woods. During the event, some of the townsfolk offered rooms, barns and stables and sheds for rent. Even a space on the back lawn to pitch a tent could bring a few cents. It was a nice way to make a tidy little sum of money and meet new people. The noise in town was deafening, with children screaming and laughing excitedly while running about like crazed hyenas, babies crying, grownups speaking loudly and jovially, drunkenness, beggars, dogs barking and fighting. Carts and horses were going this way and that, kicking up lots and lots of dust and adding to the confusion. I enjoyed the energy but it was, at the same time, tiring, too noisy and very hot. I found myself retreating to our little camp for some peace and quiet near the cool river and shade of the willows.

One day I was relaxed on a blanket under a nice shade tree near our camp, taking in the bright sunshine and the warmth of the day. I was fully absorbed in a new book I had picked up at the library called "Amelia's New Adventure." Everyone else was in town and although I could hear the distant noise, it was no more than a muted drone that blended with the gentle rippling of the river and was not at all distracting. I was just getting to the part where Amelia was about to enter a cave on the side of a steep rocky mountain in Aberkasani, a faraway country. She had gone there in search of a lost professor who had been studying the rare native wig- backed Watie Watie, a small northern yellow moth that excreted a fluid said to have properties that could be used to treat cholera. Amelia was just peering into the cave, feeling a cool, ominous breeze on her face and terrified by what she might find (an animal with big claws and big teeth? bats? a crazed humanoid hiding out? or a decaying body perhaps?) when suddenly, I was startled back to the present by the sound of hooves galloping fast up the road southward, away from town. I noticed again, just in a flash, that it was Anton.

He was not dressed as before. He was wearing his usual work clothes, his hair was flying about and he had a very determined look on his face. He didn't even look my way. A few minutes later another horse came cantering down the road from the opposite direction. It was my father, which surprised me. He had never left or arrived by the road before and at first I didn't recognize him. But, although weary, he had a big smile on his face and when he saw me, it got even broader. I was so happy to see him. It had been weeks. I jumped up and ran to greet him as he dismounted his steed while it was still coming to a stop. He grabbed me up and gave me a big bear hug. He was happier than I'd ever seen him on a return from his business. He smelled rough and leathery and he had a beard. He asked where everyone else was, and I told him all about the circus in town and the activity surrounding it, and that the rest of the family was in town at this moment.

He placed his hands on my shoulders, looked me in the eye and said, "We must leave here soon." I was sure he saw the expression on my face turn from pure delight to sadness. He tried to assure me that we were very close to going back home. He said he would explain it all later but right now all he wanted to do was take a dip in the river to refresh, clean up a bit and rest before seeing his wife and the others. I asked him if he had passed a tall boy with long, bushy blond hair on the road, but he only looked at me with a slight glint in his eye and said, "Why, no," then left me standing alone, baffled, while he went to the caravan. I decided to leave him alone as I knew he was exhausted, but whenever he returned from his trips, all I wanted to do was be near him, to talk and cling to him. I wanted some time with him by myself. So with great reluctance, I let him have some privacy and quiet and I went on into town. I was anxious and excited to find my family to tell them about his return, but I wouldn't mention anything about us leaving, as I knew what that meant. No circus!

It was late afternoon by then. The sun was still bright and further down in the sky, but no less blazing and hot. I was already sweating under my hat and my light summer dress was beginning to stick to my thighs, outlining them, and I could feel dampness trickling down my back and between my breasts. There was dust everywhere on the streets billowing up as high as my face, the grit and dirt sticking to my teeth and tongue. There was no good way to stay clean and dry. Everyone, it seemed, had a dusting of brown on their skin and clothes and even the finer-dressed women were fanning themselves as perspiration seeped down their necks. The activity and crowds just seemed to make it that much hotter.

I didn't want to stay long. It took me thirty minutes to find my mother, who was in the back of a flower shop helping four other ladies put together some arrangements for display in the shop and the window. They were chatting and laughing. They welcomed me in and asked me to sit and join them. The room was fresh with softly circulating fans that kept invisible chlorophyll and fragrances swirling in the cooled air. The combined scents of roses, gladiolus, carnations, daisies and all the other blooming and budding flowers were calming, intoxicating. Mother shoved a few vases and ribbons toward me and said I could wrap the ribbons around the neck of the vases and tie them in bows, just so. I was glad to take on the task, as this place was a welcome refuge from the chaos and heat outside. As my perspiration dried, my skin cooled to a refreshing temperature just shy of goose bumps.

The women talked about various subjects to which I was not privy, but my ears did perk up when they talked about Mrs. Jones, whose husband left her when she delivered a baby girl with palsy. The girl was nine now, in a wheelchair and in need of constant care. In addition, she already had two older sons. They were able to work and help out, "…but you can imagine the burden! She's such a brave woman!" She could have put the child in an institution in a faraway city, but refused to do so. She wanted to give that child as much of a normal life and love as possible. She and the boys doted on her and gave her all the attention she needed. Apparently the boys were a couple of the kids that my brothers had gotten to know.

Finally, a break in the conversation occurred when one of the ladies got up and went into another room. Two others gathered up the finished arrangements and took them to the front of the store. Mrs. O'Neil stayed at the table with Mother and me to finish up the rest. That's when, in a quiet voice, as I didn't know how much Mrs. O'Neil knew, I whispered to my mother that Father had returned and was resting at the camp. Her eyes got big and bright and her mouth opened in surprise; she asked why I hadn't said anything sooner and did the boys and Emi know? But before I had a chance to answer, she hurriedly and distractedly finished her last two vases, a big smile on her face, and swept up the vase I was tying a bow on before I had a chance to make sure the bow was "just so." I had to giggle.

Mrs. O'Neil was smiling too and offered to finish up. Mother nearly knocked over the chair when she rose from the table and dashed to the door with me close behind her. When we got outside, she asked me go find the others and bring them home, but to please give her a head start so that she might see her husband for a few minutes before we arrived. Then she took off down the road at a very brisk pace.

I didn't have to stall as it took me at least forty-five minutes to find the others. Phillip was nowhere to be found in town but I located Jeffery just by chance, sitting in the shade of a dirty back alley and playing marbles with some other boys (I think one of them was a Jones boy). When I told him Father was home, he too beamed, dropped all his marbles (which scattered everywhere as the other boys jumped to get them), dusted off his clothes and skipped away in front of me. He said he saw Emi earlier with her friend named Mary. I knew who that was and where she lived; it was just on the edge of town. Sure enough, she was there in Mary's room with books and dolls spread about. Dolls!? I thought she was too old for dolls by now, I'd have to ask her about that later. She said her farewells, thanked Mary's mom for her delicious lunch, and we dashed away.

No one we asked had seen Phillip and we couldn't find him on the way out of town. We checked the train, asked anyone who might see him to let him know we were look-ing for him and that he must come home right away. We checked the circus grounds without luck. Last-minute con-struction and set-up was happening, and everyone was very busy preparing for opening night, but no one there had seen him either. It didn't surprise me that we couldn't find Phillip, as he was always occupied with something, some-where. For all I knew he could have been rounding up a stray ostrich or hammering together a broken wagon wheel for someone. The three of us were anxious to get back and knew Phillip would eventually show up, so we headed to-ward camp, trotting, running and racing each other.

We got back soaked in sweat with sticky hair, covered in dust and dirt, faces red from the heat and exertion. The sun was lower on the horizon, and casting that magical golden hue across the sky and meadow as only a summer sun can do. The stream was sparkling and shining in the sun like millions of tiny shards of colored glass sprinkled across the water. We caught our breath and looked around. Our parents were nowhere to be found, so we headed for the river for a cool splash to our face and arms and a drink of water. Jeffery and Emiline kept asking, accusingly, where our parents were, as if I had hidden them away and would only bring them out after they had asked me enough times. Finally we located them further up the bank, sitting on a blanket, soaking in the sunshine, talking softly, my father's palm resting gently on my mother's cheek.

We ran to them as fast as we could. As soon as Father heard our thumping feet and squeals, he jumped up with barely enough time to steady himself before we plowed into his open arms and nearly knocked him back down again. He gave us kisses and hugs and told us how much he'd missed us, then asked where Phillip was. We told him we hadn't been able to find him, but since it was nearly suppertime he should be home soon. We sat on the blanket, the three of us vying for a space next to him, while Mother looked on with shared happiness. He wouldn't answer our many questions about his latest travels until Phillip returned, as he didn't want to repeat his stories, but he asked us to tell him all about what we'd been up to, about the circus, our new friends and adventures. We excitedly began speaking all at once, pressing our voices into a cacophony, getting louder, leap-frogging each other's stories and trying to be the one to tell the most interesting story. Our parents laughed, but soon gained control and asked us to speak one at a time, starting with Jeffrey.

We had so much to tell him that our thoughts skipped from one thing to the next without finishing the previous thought, as one or the other of us would chime in and fill in a detail or two. On it went, relating everything we could remember from the ongoing set-up of the circus to the work the boys had been doing, the crafts we had sold, the new friends we were making, the rabbit cage Phillip had built. Emi promised to introduce him to Sniffles and Black (if he bothered to make an appearance) when we went back to the camp. We told him about all the new people in town and the supplies brought in by the train, and a myriad of other trivial details of our days. After some time, Mother

suggested we get back to camp so that she could get together some supper, and by then, we were all starving.

Father was introduced to Sniffles and showed honest enthusiasm for the many improvements around camp, even
lingering to marvel at Mother's flower and vegetable garden,
which was doing quite well. Phillip eventually showed up,
sauntering up the road lost in his thoughts, when he looked
up and immediately picked Father out of the group of family members bustling around. He stepped up his pace, but
in a show of teenage indifference, he did not run (although
I could tell he badly wanted to). "Here comes Phillip!" Emi
squealed. Father turned and beamed and went to meet his
eldest son, giving him a big, long hug. Then holding onto
his shoulders, he stepped back and looked him directly in
his eyes. They exchanged a few words that we couldn't hear,
and came walking back to camp with Father's arm wrapped
around Phillip's shoulder and Phillip's around his father's waist.

Mother had intended to pick up a chicken before leaving
town today but in the excitement of seeing her husband,
she forgot. So, she searched the storage lockers and pulled
out some bread, cheese, and dried beans, and harvested
from the garden a head of cabbage, onions and carrots and
some fragrant herbs. Then she proceeded to cut and chop
and mix the ingredients with a flourish and confidence not
seen before. She threw everything in a pot over the fire and
nursed along a chicken stew, without the chicken. Over the
weeks she had gathered some hints and lessons in cooking from the ladies in town. Her plants thrived undisturbed
under the dome of a chicken-wire fence that Phillip had

fashioned for her. Her early crops had been destroyed by the nibblings of various animals in the area (including Sniffles), but her later crops flourished. She was becoming quite proficient at adding tasty herbs to her dishes, changing them from bland to delicious. This evening she added some parsley, dandelion leaves, and some sweet and spicy red peppers and a little salt to the pot.

We settled around the fire with our bowls of chicken-stew-without-the-chicken, bread and cheese, and talked and talked. Father was most pleased. He appeared healthy and very happy and we were all very anxious to hear what he had to say. Finally, sensing our rising impatience, he began to tell us about his past several weeks on the road. He told us that he had been working to build a contingent of loyal followers, many men who had been loyal to my father before the overthrow, and others outside the kingdom who had known about the battle and come to help. There were others who were still in the service of my uncle, but who were acting as spies and couriers for my father and his men. He had devised a scheme to displace my uncle and retake the castle without a bloody battle, and he was insistent that my uncle not be harmed. We interrupted him with dozens of questions, including whether he had been able to access the castle yet.

No, he didn't want Uncle Boris to know anything about our whereabouts or to arouse his suspicions. He assured us that we were safe and that, in due time, he would tell us everything, but for now, "Eat." So we dug in with more fervor and complimented the chef on the delicious meal.

CHAPTER 7

That night I decided to sleep out under the stars, as it was hot and balmy. I pulled my thin mattress and coverlet out of the tent and lay down for the night, breathing in the cool air. The sky was as black as Black. The stars were bright and brilliant, millions in a sky of vastness and wonderment. I could hear faint noises of chirps and squeaks and scurrying of life in the meadow and forest, those critters who wait for the closing of day to wake up and go about their business. I've never been afraid of nature or its sounds; they remind me of the rawness of earth, the place from which we came, our connectedness to our native roots of the earth and the animals, the glorious continuum of time and the mysteries we have yet to explain. I fell asleep with a breeze on my face and the beginnings of a dream about people I didn't know, who were guiding me to a cave.

When I awoke to the early sunlight of the day and the chatter of a hundred birds excited to begin their activities, I found that Jeffrey had curled up next to me, hogging the coverlet. His little fists were holding a corner tight against his chin. He had some drool at the corner of his mouth and was snoring ever so slightly. We all had our different octaves of snoring but Emi was the loudest in our family. She could wake the boys down the hall in a stone castle. I was a deep sleeper and could tolerate it, which was fortunate since we had been sharing close quarters. Occasionally I'd hear my father snoring in the wagon, but it was usually short lived, with a snark and a snort. Probably a result of Mother nudging him just enough to make him stop.

I yawned and stretched and quietly got up, leaving Jeffery in his blissful morning sleep. I took the toilet by the handle, headed for a grove of trees and did my business, washing my hands in the stream after. The day promised to be sunny and bright. Probably hot again. The morning glow was soft and fresh. Dew shone on the grasses of the meadow and millions of tiny sparkly gnats reflected in the early sunlight, busily hovering above short foliage on the banks of the stream.

Suddenly there was a great noise, an explosion that rocked the earth. Dark smoke billowed above the trees to the west in the direction of the circus grounds and turned the early sunshine into a mucky haze of gray. The others, startled by the loud sound, jumped out of the tents and wagon, wearing only their nightclothes. Jeffrey was rattled from his sleep and sat straight up. We looked toward the sound of the explosion, and saw nothing but the smoke. Father dove back into the wagon and was out again in a flash, dressed only in his pants and shoes, his shirt in his hand as he ran toward his horse, mounted it and was gone. The rest of us, our mouths gaping, looked at each other and dove into the tents to dress as fast as we could. It wasn't easy as Emi and I bonked into each other, arms and legs flailing, trying to find our clothes and get them on as fast as the small space would allow. I'm sure Jeffery and Phillip were doing the same. From the wagon Mother was yelling instructions not to leave until we could all go together: "We don't know what happened and I don't want you kids in danger, but hurry, maybe we can help if someone's been hurt."

We were ready almost immediately and anxious to get on the road. Philip rounded up one of the horses and mounted her without a saddle. He grabbed up Emi, tossing her behind him, and took off, passing the rest of us already running down the road.

As we got closer we saw that many other townsfolk were running or galloping toward the site as well. When we got there, we were met with chaos and mayhem, utter confusion with too many people running about and no organization. Men were rushing about with buckets of water, dousing a fire that was burning crazily from one of the wagons parked much too close to the circus tent. Others were yelling for help for the wounded. Some of the women of the circus were crying and being consoled by the ladies of the town. Dogs were crazed and barking, getting in the way, yelping when their tails got stepped on. The confined circus animals were anxious, nervous and dangerously frantic with fright, kicking and gnawing at their cages, howling and crying, baying and snorting, trying to get out, their instincts warning them of danger, wanting to run. Smoke blew about in a palette of grays and blacks, swirling about, creating the surreal appearance of a slow-motion scene in a fog on a large stage. My family split up and went to places we felt we could offer help. I saw my mother attending to a wounded person on the ground, using clean rags to hold over a bleeding wound and comforting the person with soothing words. I heard my father in the distance giving orders. He had taken charge, befitting of a king, and was directing a water brigade, instructing others to move equipment and flammable items away from the fire and to set up barriers next to the tent. Phillip and Jeffery were helping in those tasks. Emi found herself with several other youngsters, who, under the direction of the animal keepers, were freeing some of the animals who were in close danger from spitting fireballs, leading the others away into safety in the forest. Meanwhile many townsfolk hitched their wagons to caravans of the tigers and monkeys, and more panicked and dangerous animals, to drive them away to calmer areas and safety as well.

Some folks had begun to set up a makeshift infirmary and I went to help there. Crude beds and cots were fashioned from mattresses and pallets, and medical supplies that the circus carried, plus a lot more from town, were unloaded in the tent. The injured were brought in for triage, first aid and medical attention. The doctor, dentist and nurses from the local clinics headed the team and directed the volunteers as to what to do and how to care of most injuries. Even Dr. Fangman, the veterinarian, and his nurse assistant were able to help with human and animal injuries.

Although I was shocked at the amount of blood and trauma, and not functioning at my best, I tried to do whatever I could to help, including preparing and wrapping bandages, organizing supplies, fetching water for the basins, rinsing out bloody rags, and basically did whatever I was told to do or could anticipate. Within an hour we had twenty-one injured people crammed in the infirmary. Most were suffering from smoke inhalation, coughing and having serious trouble breathing. Others had minor to moderate burns to their arms and faces. But two had the worst with blistering burns over most of their bodies, their clothes seared to their charred skin, smoke still rising from their bodies. One fellow was moaning in terrible pain, the other was disturbingly silent. The smell was nauseating. Three other people had severe cuts, gashes on their extremities. Mother kept darting in and out of the tent, either bringing in a victim or picking up some supplies for triage in the field.

After a few hours some of us were released to take a break. I had not realized how much time had passed. I felt dirty, sweaty, sick and dizzy. I stepped out and around the tent and immediately vomited. Looking for some cool water and fresh air away from the cacophony and moans of the injured, I stumbled right into Anton. We were both distracted and not looking where we were going, and nearly knocked each other off our feet. Once oriented and steady on my feet, I realized who I'd run into. He was equally as surprised and we exchanged apologies, along with a hearty laugh of stress release. I was rubbing my arm where he hit me with his elbow. He asked me if I was okay and said I looked pale.

"I was looking for some water. I just came from the medical tent and wasn't feeling very well, but I'm better now that I've gotten outside."

"Come on, I'll show you where to get some water. What about your arm there? Did I bump you hard?" he asked, concerned.

"I'll be okay, it's probably just a bruise, and I know where to get help if I need it," I said with a grin as I tried not to rub it.

I asked him where he had been; he looked rather used and tattered himself. He told me he had been removing wood and debris from the explosion and cleaning up near the circus tent. He said the accident was caused by a leak in one of the lines of a gas tank and that when one of the circus workers lit a cigarette too nearby, the fumes sparked and caused the explosion. My mouth and eyes opened wide in shock. He answered before I even had to ask. "The worker is dead, torn apart in the explosion. Bits of him were found lying about. They can't even identify him yet. That will come later when the circus master and owner take assessment of the casualties." Anton had found himself with the dubious duty of locating the man's body parts before the dogs did and placing them in a wooden crate. I think in any other situation he would have prudently spared me the details, but, as with me, he was in a bit of shock and told me how one dog was found gnawing on a bloody arm; he had to wrestle it away from the dog, which did not relinquish it easily. There would be a service for the man later.

We made our way to a fresh potable water tank, took a tin cup hanging on a rack nearby, and drank as if we hadn't had water in days. I splashed some on my face and neck, which instantly refreshed me. We sat on a nearby bench, exhausted but with adrenaline still pumping through our veins. I gazed into the crowd and watched as each and every person took part in aiding and clean-up as best they could. Horses, carts and wagons were coming and going. There was still smoke drifting about, but steadily dissipating as the fire came under control. Anton and I sat there in silence for many minutes, too stunned to talk. Then he asked if my family was there. I told him they were all there and where I last saw them, and that my father had just arrived back to camp yesterday and was the one over there taking charge of organizing. Anton smiled and said he looked like a kind and caring sort of fellow.

By and by, Mrs. Reynolds and her eight-year-old daughter stopped by with a large basket of sandwiches, apples, bananas, cookies and pickles they were handing out. Mr. and Mrs. Reynolds owned the small café in town called The Eat Place. They served large breakfasts, sandwiches and soup for lunch, and stews and meatloaf, chicken, pork and beef for supper. They always had a bowl full of mint candies at the hostess counter to freshen one's breath after a meal. They were well liked and always busy. We each took a sandwich and pickle and I also took an apple and a cookie, and ravenously chewed down each last bite. I was much hungrier than I thought, but it was already early afternoon and I hadn't eaten anything since last night.

Anton and I remained seated and chatted about this and that. He asked about my siblings, their names, ages, and what they liked to do and what their favorite hobbies were. He seemed genuinely interested. I found out that he had two younger brothers. His mother died of pneumonia when he was 15, so his father was left a widower with three boys to raise. His father worked as a blacksmith in town and made decent wages. They lived in a house outside of town to the north. Anton was, as I guessed, 20. His brother Peter was 18 and his youngest brother, Miles, was 14. Peter was away at school studying literature and the arts. Miles was in the local school and worked in the smithy with his father. When I asked what Anton did, he said he had finished his under studies but hadn't gone to college. He said he traveled a lot and did odd jobs. But when I asked him more about his travels he became evasive and didn't want to tell me much more. He said his hobbies were fishing and playing cards, at which he'd apparently become quite good. He often made money playing a friendly game of Blackjack or Poker during his travels, but made it clear that he wasn't a gambler. "I've got better things to do with my time and money."

"I'm glad you said that," and I went on to tell him a little bit about my horrible, drunken, gambling uncle. He listened attentively, then asked me what level of school I was in and what my plans were for the future. He already knew that we had come from out of town but didn't ask from which city or town, and I didn't offer as it dawned on me that I had no ready answer. I told him I had not given much thought to my future yet as I still had another year of under studies. I said I wasn't sure if I would attend the university, or look for work right after graduation. I said I was interested in drawing and painting, and liked to read a lot and write in my journal, but that if I were to choose a career I had thought of nursing. However, chagrined after what I'd been seeing today, I wasn't so sure I was cut out for that career after all. My father had tried to encourage me to pursue my essays more and perhaps think about journalism. I felt like the world and its possibilities were still open to me and that I had time to think about it.

We chatted on like that until I started feeling guilty that I was taking too long on my break. So, refreshed and with renewed energy we headed back to the mayhem. When we parted with goodbyes, he gently touched my arm, which was a little sore, and said, "I hope it's okay."

"It is now," I responded with a coquettish smile, and went back into the medical tent. So much for my resolve to stay away from that man!

By dusk, everything was mostly in order, although most of the animals were kept away for the night, comforted with food and water and gentle voices by their caretakers. The circus master felt it would be better to let them have a few more hours of calm and sleep; tomorrow there would be much to do and a big rush on to get the circus back on its feet. Opening day would be delayed by one day and he thanked everyone for their extraordinary help. A memorial would be held on Thursday for the unlucky victim who died. The others who were too injured to return to work would be replaced, temporarily, with volunteers. Those with the worst injuries were carefully bedded down in a wagon and taken off to Bellmont for a higher level of care.

By the time our family got back to camp, the sky was thickening into darkness and stars were trying to push their twinkle through the canopy of the universe. We were all dirty, sticky and smelly but too exhausted to do anything about it. Mother rummaged through the caravan and pulled out some cheese, bread, apples and dried meat to eat, while Phillip and Father started a fire. Jeffery grabbed an apple and some cheese and went right into his tent. We didn't see him until the next morning. The rest of us sat around the fire, starving, but too tired to eat fast. None of us had much to say and as each of us finished our meal we went to bed. I'd never slept so soundly as I did that night, with intermittent dreams of fires, beautiful mountain vistas, people I'd never seen or met before, animals and abstracts.

CHAPTER 8

The next morning I felt refreshed and very hungry. It was a little cooler with a thin cloud cover over the sky. I immediately stripped off my dirty clothes that I'd never bothered to remove last night, wrapped myself in my cozy full-length robe with a hood. I had made it from some soft, textured terry fabric I'd found in town at Mrs. Abrams' millinery shop, and bartering the fabric and use of a sewing machine in exchange, I helped her catch up on a number of alterations she had gotten behind on when the train and circus came to town. From the fabric, I made four robes, a white one for my mother, a pink one for Emi, a blue one for myself and a green one for Mrs. Abrams, who was most grateful for the help and the gift. I went out to the woods with the toilet, did my business, and headed for the river to clean up. The boys had found a small but deep soaking hole hidden in some trees, not far down the river. The water was a little more tepid than that of the running stream. It was where we did most of our bathing.

I spent a fair amount of time enjoying the luxury of the bath, washing my hair and body and floating gently on top of the water, listening to the eddies and small waves hit against the bank and feeling the water swell and recede against my skin. The birds had awakened and were chirping and cackling, flying from branch to branch or frantically poking their little beaks into the soil near the bank, catching bugs and worms and flying with them back to their nests to feed their baby chicks. By and by, the peace was interrupted by the sounds of the other three running this way. I made haste, got out of the water and wrapped myself in the robe before they neared the bank. They weren't surprised to see me and simply disrobed, and in all their nakedness and no modesty, jumped into the pool.

As I headed back to camp I picked up the heavenly smell of breakfast cooking on the fire. Mother and Father were putting together a lavish feast of eggs, ham, cheese, sweet rolls, fried potatoes, fruit, hot tea, coffee and large glasses of milk. Mother said to gather my dirty clothes and put them with the others on a pile near the caravan. She would take them into town later for a good washing at Carmen and Sophie's. There was a community bath and laundry house in town, a decent- sized wooden and concrete building with three private baths and two shower areas in one section, and a laundry area with four tubs and washboards for clothes in another section. Running water from a large well-fed tank had been fashioned to feed water through tubes into the needed areas. Hot water was heated in a separate tank and could be turned on and off by simple valves. Showers and baths were limited to five minutes and cost six gronies. A tub of wash water cost eight. Inside and outside were lots of laundry lines and clothes clips for hanging up the clean items. It was quite a set-up and earned the owner a sub-stantial income, especially when large groups descended on the town as they had. There was usually a waiting line and a sheet of paper served as a reservation log. However, this time Mother opted to take our clothes to Carmen and Sophie's, the custom laundry business. They took in laun-dry and did it in their own washbasins using a fragrant soap, dried it, and, depending on the item, ironed then folded everything. The clothes always came back smelling fresh and looking crisp. It was more expensive than the city laundry service but Mother didn't want to do it herself this time. She was tired and there was still too much to do at the circus site to be away for hours. She wanted to help, not do laundry! Father agreed.

Anyway, once my sibs had returned, fresh and clean, we sat down and stuffed ourselves with breakfast. We had a lot to talk about, recalling everything we could about yes-terday's disaster. Each of us had contributed in one way or the other and our parents were very proud. We would go back today to see what else we could do to help. Emi said none of the animals were hurt and seemed to be far-ing well amidst the chaos. The larger animals such as the elephants and giraffes were secured off into the forest, and some others like the lions and monkeys were taken closer to town. One elephant, Susie, a favorite old sweetie, was put to work moving lumber and large objects about. She loved the work. She would get "frisky" when directed to do chores and bored when there was nothing to do, demonstrating her restlessness by stomping the ground with her front foot and snorting a lot. She was the same way when performing. She was a good, motivating leader for her partner, Barney, who tended to be more laid back and lazy unless Susie was there to prod and motivate him.

There were a lot of people on the grounds when we got there after our breakfast and it appeared there wasn't much left to do, but Emi and I got to work scrubbing down the signs, benches and caravans, bringing back the brilliant colors of the intricately carved wood and painted murals on the sides. My mother got busy helping to clean up and dismantle the medic tent and moving cots, chairs, trays, and any still usable items back to the clinic in town. Then she helped to take inventory of medical supplies and what would be needed to replace the large medical supply trunk carried with the circus troupe. The big top had suffered some fire damage at one corner and a beam had to be replaced. Some of the benches and the ground inside had burned, but could be repaired before the show. My father and the boys started on that project. The explosion had sent debris flying, much of which landed on top of the tent, singeing holes in the canvas but miraculously not starting any more fires, which assuredly would have burned the whole thing down. A couple of the caravans were lost in the fire and a number of supplies were burned up. Besides the death of the worker and the injuries to others, the damage was, surprisingly, much less than expected, at least according to those in charge. Circuses had learned how to set up the grounds with buffers and perimeters around the performers' quarters, tents, animal enclosures, feed and supply trucks and all the rest, to minimize damage should an event such as this occur. Wagons and carts would be making trips to Iznot and Bellmont and back over the next few days, bringing in new work supplies and lumber as well as hundreds of items to restock the medical supplies used from town: bandages, tubing, syringes and needles, medicines, braces and splints, linen, towels and blankets.

With so many people helping, the time flew by. After four hours we had done all we could and the circus master was dismissing all but just a few of the construction volunteers, bidding us a grateful thank you and, "See you on Friday!" Father invited us to town to dine at the Eat Place and wind down a bit.

The café was very busy but we didn't have to wait long for a table. The Reynolds had added several items to their menu, anticipating an uptick of customers during the circus. We shared a large platter of fried chicken, two big bowls of spiced green beans, buttered noodles, corn, seared greens, rolls and a family-sized salad. It was all fresh, hot and delicious. Mother got hints from Mrs. Reynolds about how she spiced the beans and seared the greens. Everyone in the café was jabbering away, telling stories, some true, some exaggerated, about the last couple of days. We ate heartily and chatted exuberantly ourselves, although by now, it was pretty obvious that we were doing our best to hold back on questions about Father's latest journey, and any news he could tell us about getting back home. He promised he would fill us all in that evening at camp when it was quieter and "not so many ears around." He was just as anxious to hear more about the weeks we had spent without him, and to have some quality time with his wife and family. We finished our meal and split up. Father and the boys went to pick up the laundry, and Emi and I helped Mother with the grocery shopping. We picked up some potatoes, dried beans, some fish, beef, a slab of cured pork, two big fresh aromatic crusty loaves of bread from the baker, some flour, sugar, salt, carrots, cabbage, turnips, squash, apples, oranges, melons, butter and jam. It appeared we were out of just about everything. Mother didn't like it like that. She preferred to have a good stock of goods on hand, "plenty to work with," she said like a seasoned cook.

Chapter 9

A slight breeze had picked up as we got back to camp in the early evening. Black was sitting on top of Sniffles' cage, calmly anticipating our arrival. He lazily jumped off the cage and sauntered up to Emi, weaving in and out of her legs and purring sweetly until he caught the scent of the fish in Mother's basket. He immediately ignored Emi and trotted over to Mother, yowling and purring at the same time, causing him to make a most peculiar, rumbling guttural sound ending with a high pitched "dddurrrr-aat" at the end. As soon as she was able to set her baskets down she threw him a small piece of raw fish, which kept him away until we could unload the groceries and pack everything away in a safe, animal (Black)-proof barrel in the caravan. All odors were gone when Black returned for more tidbits, sniffing the air with the most puzzled look on his face. Soon he lost interest and wandered off to Phillip and Jeffrey's tent to see what kind of mischief he could rustle up. Emi gave Sniffles a carrot and some scrap lettuce greens she had picked up at the store. He went about happily munching on his meal as his little pink nose wriggled rapidly, ears twitching now and then.

Father had gone down to the river to fetch some water while the boys started their chores, dividing up the clean, fresh laundry and setting the piles in the appropriate tents, exercising and feeding the horses, starting a fire, sweeping up the never-ending dust that settled on the tents and entryways, and gathering wood.

Once we finished getting settled, my parents grabbed some blankets and cups and a flask of a liquor drink Father had brought back from his last trip, as well as a couple of pieces of fruit and some hot tea; then we all went to sit near the river. My parents poured their drinks and I cut the fruit as everyone found a lazy position to lounge on the blankets. The sun was near the horizon, beginning to drench the landscape with the rich golden color of the late afternoon in the late summer as seen at no other time of day or season. The breeze was just enough to keep the air from being too hot and stale. It was a most pleasant day.

Finally, Father was ready to tell us about his adventures. He began by saying that he had a most successful trip and that our home was secure, but before giving us details on that, he began by telling us of a most unusual event.

When he left the last time he'd met a man on the road who was selling cheap trinkets and broken pottery. No doubt items he had stolen or pilfered unlawfully. The man was thin, wearing tattered clothing and mismatched shoes. His face was scrubby and his hat was ripped nearly to shreds. He was the kind of fellow you did not want to be around for long, nor engage him in much conversation for fear of him never leaving your side. Father knew full well about these kinds of people. They were worse than gypsies and much more dangerous. They begged, cajoled, teased and intimidated until they got money, food or goods from the traveler; if they didn't get what they wanted they might not hesitate to hurt you by breaking a staff against your leg, or violently pulling one off one's horse or wagon, slamming one to the ground then kicking, just to make sure his point had been made. Sometimes they would get angry or bullying enough to wield a knife and slash your better clothing. They rarely had or used guns, as they were deathly afraid of the law. When approached on the road by a lawman and searched, they did not want to be caught with a gun as they were prohibited from having one. A gun in their possession would cause swift and rough apprehension and jail time in a dank, rat- infested, dirty cell. By the time they got out, their horse would be gone, along with any items they planned to sell or hawk, and they would have to start all over, stealing and pillaging again. They usually slept on riverbanks or under bridges. Travelers called them the "creeps" and young children would hear about their stories from an early age, thus perpetuating their mythical nature. Few had actually seen or run into any of the sort, and although legends had them "creeping" into villages to pilfer or raid homes, there was no one that could actually confirm those stories.

So when my father was approached by this man, he took up his guard and was ready for a verbal, if not, physical confrontation. The man was polite enough, as they usually start out to be, and introduced himself as Max, "short for Maxwell," he said proudly, as if that gave him more status. He tried to engage my father in trivial conversation, but my dad ignored him, albeit his radar heightened and he continued to ride along.

Maxwell did a lot of mumbling and talking to himself and did not seem concerned that Father was not responding, nor did he try to confront Father. In fact they rode side by side like that for quite some time, Maxwell mumbling and my father amused by this odd creep. By and by, he heard Max talking in a low voice about something that caught my father's interest. He was saying something about a far-off castle, "…they was all gone, it was quiet, quiet as a dead man's skull. The man said there'd be food, the chickens was all dead, torn up, been eaten by dogs. A stone with jewels, with magical powers, hidden near the bridge, not true, not true. She was a wearin' a faded pink frock, but the man hit her anyway, he was dead. The cow, thin as the rump of a lame dog, bones pokin' through 'es skin, big men guarding…" The ramblings seemed to be nonsensical but my father couldn't help but listen a little closer. Max was continuing. "If the boy hadn't run off it'd be different. I coulda had it, yes I coulda, but the boy, the boy. The stone, she was a beauty, all sparkly and such. It had powers, it coulda been mine. But the boy."

At this point my father had to interrupt, and politely brought Max out of his ruminations and asked him just what he was talking about. Max raised his head in question, as if he'd forgotten there was someone else on the road with him. His demeanor changed from harmless to suspicious and Father was aware that he might have triggered something in Max that may not be pleasant.

Instead, Max seemed to focus and his expression softened. He looked at my dad and said, "There was a stone, said to have powers, the boy found it. He'd a showed it to his father, but the father d'manded that he hand it over. The boy, feeling that it was somethin' special and not wantin' to give it up, he a turned and ran as fast as a jack rabbit with a bull dog chasin' em. But es daddy was a spitting mad like a rabid rattlesnake went to runnin' after him, yelling he would 'get a whooping twice his size.' The boy ran across the bridge, tripped and fell. His ole daddy caught up with em, grabbed the boy up by the suspenders and began to beat the bejesus outta him. The boy fought back; bitin', screaming and kicking and all the time holdin' on to the stone, til theys both tumbled off the side of the bridge and into the ragin' river fifteen feet below. The daddy gots to swimmin' to the bank but the boy was swept down the river, never to be seen again."

With gentle questioning, my father was able to tease a little more information out of Max, trying to trip up his story and get more details; he was sure Max was just a nutty old man, but Max stayed on track. Apparently he was passing by at the time, headed for the bridge as there had been rumors of the magic stone hidden nearby. It was said that it could only be found when, during a certain hour of the day, the sunlight reflected off a particular nail in a plank near the far end of the bridge, marking the spot under which the stone was hidden.

The problem was that after many, many decades, the bridge had worn out and planks had been replaced with new ones. Those who had searched for the stone would either find multiple shiny reflections of new nails, or old rusted nails that held no reflection. No one knew for sure if the stone was still there or if it even ever existed. Many had tried to find it, spending hours and days on the bridge looking for the reflection, checking each nail, and even pulling up planks, until the bridge was ruined and dangerous and needed to be replaced again. Several men and horses had lost their lives on the bridge, from rotten boards breaking through or fights between creeps and others looking for the same thing. When the bridge was in ruins travelers would have to circumvent the route, detouring twenty-six miles further to find the next crossing place. The legend had been passed down by so many generations that most were sure it was just that, a legend, and very few people these days believed it to be true or spent any time looking for the stone.

On this particular day, as Max was approaching the bridge, he saw the boy running away from it and toward a farmhouse where his father was busy stacking hay. Max slowed and watched the whole interaction. The boy showed his father a shiny object and his father tried to take it away. He saw them arguing, then the boy running, being chased by his very angry father. As the boy and his father fought on the bridge, Max saw something sparkling in the boy's fist and saw it go over the edge with the boy and his father. Max rode fast to the scene, just in time to see the father crawling out of the water onto the bank, dragging his bloody right leg behind him. The boy was swept down the river on his back, banging roughly into rocks and debris, but all the while his fist was still closed tight around the stone. The boy was quickly gone from sight and to, no doubt, a tragic demise. Max's attention was diverted when he heard a woman shrieking and running toward the bridge. Max didn't want to stick around for fear of getting involved or being blamed for the incident, so he galloped across the bridge as fast as he could go, not looking back once. He had hoped to find the body of the boy down the river and retrieve the stone, but the terrain made it impossible to follow the river for more than a mile from the bridge.

Father redirected Max to what he meant by the empty castle, and the men guarding it, that he had referred to earlier. Max hung his head and went to mumbling nonsense again. When Father prodded, Max became angry and began cussing and spitting. He raised his staff as if to attack, but Father didn't flinch and stayed his ground atop his horse. He tried to talk Max down in a gentle tone, but Max's personality had changed. His face had turned red, he began sweating profusely and everything he said was a curse word, a vile sentence or variation thereof. Father finally got tired of this interaction, realizing that Max had nothing more to say and, with a very quick movement, took his rifle, poked it in the haunch of Max's horse and watched as it reared angrily, nearly bucking Max off while fleeing wildly down the road. Father, with a nod, turned and galloped off into the woods.

We wanted to know more about the stone and the legend, and hounded Dad with questions, but he put up a hand and said, "If you want to know the rest, you'll have to wait for me to tell you more about the stone some other time." Mother said it might be a good time to head back to the camp, as the sun was down and the breeze had picked up enough to send a slight chill through the air.

With some grumbling and reluctance, we gathered up the blankets and things and headed back to camp. Phillip and Father tended and stoked the fire while Emi and I helped Mother prepare a pot of light soup. We were all still full from the big late lunch, but she thought we should still eat a little something before going to bed.

Within a short time, we took our seats on a tree stump, flat stones, grassy spots and blankets near the fire, and Mother served up bowls of hot broth with fresh carrots, bite-sized potatoes, onions, and parsnips. She had added a little basil, garlic and crumbled dried hot pepper she had harvested from her garden a month ago, which gave the soup a slight zip. The soup was light, aromatic, warm and just perfect for that kind of night. The fire flickered and snapped in the cool night air and lit the trees and meadow around us, creating moving shadows of trees and imaginary creatures wishing to come out and share our warm fire.

Father continued his story. After leaving the road and Max, he rambled through the woods for a good piece and then stopped at a creek to water his horse, take a short break, and check his compass and directions. He was on his way to Nimly, a small town many miles southwest of our home, our castle. He was to meet some men who had some valuable information that would help Father displace Uncle Boris.

He arrived in Nimly late in the evening and, tired and thirsty, went straight to the local tavern. There were few patrons scattered at the tables and bar, drinking from their mugs, laughing and talking in low voices while a guitarist strummed his instrument and sang a quiet tune on a small stage in the far corner. Father found his acquaintances, ordered a beer and sat down with them.

Pete and Jim told Father that the plan to get rid of my uncle was underway and here it was: All the times that Father had been away on business, while on the road he was setting up a scam to make Uncle Boris lose all of his money and valuables, thus forcing him to relinquish the castle and grounds, by inviting him to play cards and gamble with the local folk. Knowing that Boris was a very good game player, the locals would likely win but a few of the games. The losses consisted mainly of small amounts of cash and goods, but occasionally the townsfolk would lose a good horse, an expensive piece of jewelry, a buggy, or a herd of sheep. This delighted Uncle as he took great pleasure in the ruin of others less brilliant than him. What he didn't know was who these people really were. Since he had come to live in the castle and take over the kingdom, he had never bothered to get to know the people of the towns or their families. His minions collected extra taxes, fees and fines imposed on them for arbitrary reasons such as tying a horse to an "unauthorized" post, or charging people to check a book out of the library, or increasing the fees for shop rentals. The town folks were incensed but had no choice but to go along with the rules, and get more and more angry. That was until my father's plan was hatched.

Some of the men who were taking up challenges to play cards and gamble with Boris were actually highly skilled games men. They were much better than Boris but played the part of jolly old folk just having a night out, hoping to win a little money. Unbeknownst to Boris, whatever was won from him was put in the local bank, saved for future gambling and whatever had been paid for by my father or out of the stash at the bank. Nobody really lost anything.

As the games progressed, word got around, and better and better players came to challenge Boris; however, all of them were employed by my father. They began winning more and more games against Boris, amassing larger and larger amounts of money and goods. Father's team had already won a fair amount of the castle land (our land) and livestock away from Boris. The whole ruse was set up to eventually break him of all holdings, including the kingdom and our castle. But Boris was shrewd and not stupid. If offered too much liquor or the services of too many pretty girls to distract him, he would become suspicious. He was an addicted but serious gambler. He appreciated a good opponent and never cheated, but if he discovered a sleight of hand, a missing card or chip, or questionable signals between players, he wouldn't hesitate to flare into a rage and slash chests, shoot kneecaps, and throw pinching prostitutes out of second-story windows. He could be wild and dangerous if he was crossed or even if he perceived a wrong against him. Father and his followers knew they had to be very careful and move slowly.

Chapter 10

As the months had passed, Father's followers had set up quite a complicated scheme. They were just about ready for the final trounce. Uncle Boris had already lost several acres of our property, as well as the stable and much of our livestock. Apparently Father's friends were working on winning back the carriage house, a barn and all remaining real property. Very soon, they would set up a sting to win back the castle, with the stipulation that Boris vacate and never be seen in the kingdom again. For that, the gamblers were willing to bet all that had already been won. Therefore, if Boris should win the final game, he could remain in the castle and have all the land and wealth back. However, if Father's allies won, unbeknownst to Boris, everything would come back to us, and he would be banned forever. It would be the biggest gamble of all.

The fire had died down to small, stubby flames jumping about on the burnt wood, and blazing red embers that were glowing hot then cool, then red hot, then cool again. An occasional pop and hiss would send a spark shooting up into the night like tiny fireworks. We were all listening to Father's plan with rapt attention, but panic crossed our faces, especially Mother's, when Dad described how we could potentially lose everything. Father, however, didn't seem concerned and in fact, had a slight grin on his face. Mother was staring at him incredulously with her mouth slightly parted. Father suddenly slapped his thighs, startling us, and began to rise.

"Wait, Dad, I have a few questions," I said.

Mother, still looking at him, said, "But honey, how can you..." when Phillip chimed in, "What do you mean we'll lose everything?"

"That's not what I said. I'll answer all your questions but first I must stand and use a tree,"and as he did so, he began a slow languorous stretch.

We got the hint and all stood too, also needing to stretch our legs and take care of a few necessities. Bladders were full and we were thirsty and beginning to get chilled. Both the boys ran off in different directions toward the nearest trees. Emi and I went to the tents for some warmer clothes and blankets. Mother gathered our bowls and utensils and took them back to the caravan. Father rekindled the fire from a healthy stack of firewood Phillip had built on over the weeks. Finally, we had done our necessary business and took our places again around the bigger, brighter and warmer fire. Mother had made some steaming mugs of hot chocolate and brought out a small basket of Mrs. O's "num-num" cookies. (Mother said she helped bake them and got

the recipe so that she may try them on her own sometime.)
We were cozy and content.

"Okay, Blue, I believe you had a question?" Father asked.

"Yes, what games are being played and who are the men running up against Boris?"

"Good question," Father replied. "We started with local gamblers playing simple chess and poker against your uncle. They won a few and lost a few. Then we advanced the skills and games to Concha and Greens. For those we found some fellows from Aberdine who played quite well, in fact, that's when we won back the horses. Next, Boris wanted to challenge someone to craps and NikWik. Many games were played with various skilled players. But, we had a setback when a fellow from another realm showed up to challenge Boris. He was someone out of the blue and didn't know the real purpose of the games. We couldn't not let him play, or Boris would become suspicious. That fellow played many games and played well. He won a number of games in which Boris gambled away some cash and jewels, and we lost our orchards to him."

Mother, who loved our fruit orchards, became angry when she heard this and lashed out, "How could that happen? How could you let Boris strip us of all our belongings? Our land, our possessions, the orchard?"

Father assured her that they were not lost, even to the stranger. After that man was finished with Boris and about to move on, one of Father's friends, a negotiator, with Father's consent proposed to the man a payment for the return of the orchards after explaining the circumstances in which Boris got the land in the first place. Boris's cash and jewels were of no concern, the man could keep that (Mother grunted loudly). The man was understanding and helpful. He had heard of King Hamilton where he came from on the eastern edge of Galloway, and everyone had high regard for him. He could tell Boris was a bully by the way he treated people, and the way he played the games with intimidation and insults. Anyone who willingly displaced his own brother and family, killed innocent people and destroyed a great deal of land, deserved to be put in their place, and as far as he was concerned, rid from this planet!

He settled on a fair payment and offered his help in the future, should we need it. He said he didn't need the orchards anyway since he lived several hundred miles away, but would be happy to pass the word around about what a scoundrel Boris was.

Mother was very relieved to hear this. "So what's next?" she asked.

"The next step is the winner takes all. I am sure our side will win, that's why we must leave here soon, so that we may be in place to reclaim the castle when the time comes," responded Father.

"How can you be so sure we'll win that final match?" Phillip chimed in.

"Because," Father answered, "we have a trick up our sleeves."

"But I thought you said we wouldn't cheat?" said Emiline.

"Oh, we're not going to cheat. But we're moving Boris toward a game that he's not very familiar with or good at.

It's called Quark. It requires a great deal of skill and concentration, as well as mathematical and psychological knowledge. Each round is very quick, but can last hours or days and can be extremely exhausting. It's a newer game, played mostly by very intelligent young university students. It's a game of the younger generation, very strategic. Some people don't consider it a legitimate gambling game, but it has been officially entered into legitimacy by the International Gamers Association. Boris has played it before, but doesn't like it. He can't drink as much during the game as it requires too much concentration, and he's not as fast as the younger ones who play it. The folks who have been playing the previous games against him have bantered talk around about Quark, purposely putting the bug in Boris's ear. He has tried to thwart the idea but word's spread that he's a sissy, a coward. Plus, the bystanders and regulars have been dwindling and are voicing their boredom with the games. They want something more exciting and challenging and you know how Boris craves attention. They compliment him on his vast skills and play up to his ego, making him think he is better than the other players and telling him that his audience would return if they are properly entertained.

"Remember, many of his opponents have been much better than he, but have let him win to make him believe otherwise. So he reluctantly decided to accept the challenge to play Quark for the last. He hired a private coach on the game, but word has it that he is not progressing very well and angers easily when he misses the sub points, especially in the third and seventh round."

"It seems all a little dishonest to me," said Emi.

"Not at all, it's just a little misleading. Do you know how sometimes you purposely let Jeffery win a game of cards, just so he can feel better? Because otherwise, he would get frustrated and be discouraged from playing again?"

"Yeah," she said. Jeffery perked up from drawing in the dirt with a stick and said, "Hey, wait a minute. You don't just let me win, do you, Em?"

"Well sometimes, but it's only after I've let you see how the game goes and how much fun it can be, and each time you get much better. The last time we played Sevens, you won fair and square, and I have to say, I wasn't too pleased."

Jeffrey seemed happy with that answer and settled back with a slight smug grin on his face.

"Yes," Father said. "That's how it's working with your uncle. We're moving him toward Quark for the all or nothing game."

"But how can you be so sure we'll win if the game is so skilled? Who will play Quark against Boris?'" Mother asked.

"We are playing our own game of chance, hon, you have to trust me. We have been working on this and setting it up for a very long time," Father responded, and I thought of all the weeks and days he had been gone on his business. I felt a little sheepish now, knowing that my father had been away doing all he could to procure back our home.

"We have a fellow, a younger man, who has been playing the game for many years. He is the best in the region and perhaps the world. He has won many awards. Few know of him because the game is still not as popular here as the others, but this fellow knows his stuff. He will win, I'm sure of it. He has the advantage of being a stranger from other parts, much like that of the previous gentleman I spoke of, and he exudes innocence and politeness. Something not found in the usual gambler. He doesn't drink, smoke, spit or swear. He's clean and has an air of cocky confidence only found in younger men. No doubt, Boris will take the challenge just to show off and insult this young man."

"What if he fails?" asked Jeffrey with worry on his face. A question we were all afraid to ask.

"He won't, I'm sure of it," said Father. "Okay, it's late, time for bed. I'm tired and I'm sure you are too." There was much grumbling and a spattering of more questions, but Mother said, "Your father is right. We have a few chores to take care of before turning in and tomorrow is a big day, what with the memorial and all."

I had completely forgotten about the circus worker and had planned on making a pretty basket of flowers to set near the memorial. I would see what I could put together in the morning. Suddenly I felt very drowsy and just wanted to crawl into my tent and go to sleep without another thought. But I did my chores and dragged myself to the tent afterward. Emi was already under the blankets, barely breathing a whispered sigh. Just before I fastened the tent fly I looked up at the sky and saw the bright stars, the wisps of clouds passing over the crescent double moons, and thought of how long it had been since I viewed the sky through my telescope. In many ways I have found it to be enlightening, perhaps more humbling to ponder the universe in all its glory through my naked eyes rather than through a glass lens from a library window, occasionally glancing away to consult my astronomy book, then back again, to peek through a two-inch magnifying hole. My thoughts and my gazing into the night sky began to make me dizzy, so I closed the fly and crawled under the covers. Tomorrow, I would catch up in my journal.

I woke in the night to the sound of rain spattering on the tent, a slight chill in the air and a full bladder. Not a good combination. I listened to the rain and tried to fall back to sleep, but my body kept reminding me of something else. Begrudgingly, I gathered up my raincoat and hat, which I'd learned from past experience to keep in the tent, and slipped on my shoes. By now I really had to go bad and rushed to get outside. The rain was soft but steady and wet, so I stepped a few feet away and cozied up to the nearest big boulder, hoping to shield myself while I squatted and let my urine mix with the rain and mud. It must have been quite late, because the moons had already set. The sky was now mostly gray with clouds instead of bright black with stars. I didn't linger and ran back to the tent.

By daybreak, the rain had subsided but had soaked the ground and swelled the river. Rain droplets and dew hung from the leaves of the trees and grasses and darkened the stones. There was a mild mist near the ground and a fresh coolness in the air. Soon, everyone was stirring awake and Father and the boys went to work building a fire to dry and warm us. We'd had a few rains during the summer, mostly in the afternoons for an hour or so, and although it was still

August, this time it felt different. This rain brought the first sense of fall.

The memorial was held in a small clearing in the woods, a few yards from the edge of the big top. The clearing was surrounded by a canopy of beautiful old oak and birch trees. The ground was damp and smelled like fresh pine, wet leaves and decaying wood, a sweet, dark, earthy smell. Mrs. O'Neil had brought in a beautiful wreath arrangement made of daisies, roses, carnations and lilies, interspersed with an array of greens and finished with a big blue bow. I felt less guilty about not making up a flower basket myself. The flowers infused the wet air with a wavering scent of peace and calm. It was hung on a makeshift cross with the name Jim Junkins burned into the wood. About 300 people were in attendance, and Reverend Musky from the congregational church in Iznot performed the service. It was a short and beautiful service. A few of Jim's friends from the circus troupe spoke, and in the end the Reverend rallied everyone to be cheerful and grateful and to attend what would, no doubt, be "The Greatest Show on Earth!"

CHAPTER 11

Opening day was upon us and everyone, my family included, was very excited and anxious to attend. Father was able to buy a ticket at the door even though all three days had been sold out. All the hubbub about the explosion had circulated to other towns and brought more people to Iznot to gawk and talk and see the circus, hoping perhaps to observe some other gruesome catastrophe. Human nature is funny that way.

We were going to the evening show on Friday. Mother insisted we all eat a healthy supper before going, as she didn't want us hungry for candy and sugary drinks. Jeffrey and Emi ate too fast, and not enough according to Mother, but she gave in when Father gave her a look that said, "let it go this time." They ran off early to meet their friends and ride the rides and play the games.

When the big top opened and the crier bellowed to "come one and come all," there was already a crowd of families partaking in the various activities available in the small midway, such as the shooting gallery, bean bag toss, fortune telling, paying to see the bizarre and grotesque tattooed fat woman, the hairy ape man, the Siamese twins, and the double-headed goat. There were vendors for popcorn, candy, meat on sticks, drinks, toys and many others too numerous to name. Jeffrey and Emi were already juggling flavored iced cones, and cotton candy in green for Jeffrey and pink for Emi. Phillip was licking a melting ice cream cone and I saw a pack of peanuts peeking out of the pocket of his pants. Mother had given us each a small amount of change from her tin, to use as we pleased this day, but she sighed loudly when she saw her children spending their coins on sweets after not finishing their suppers.

We made our way to our seats and I looked out over the arena. Except for an ash-darkened area of the tent near the entry and a very faint smell of smoke, you'd never know anything amiss had occurred. The noise from the crowd of voices ebbed and flowed, mixed with laughter, crying babies and music. Soon, the lights dimmed and the show was about to begin. I looked around the arena but didn't see Anton. The big top was packed and it was hard to pick out faces amongst the crowd, but I did get a glimpse of a few people I knew, including the Jacobs. Their young daughter with the palsy was sitting in a wheelchair with her brothers and mother in an area occupied by the elderly and infirm, which was a prime spot for viewing indeed!

The announcer bellowed his welcome through a bullhorn, quieting the restless crowd. The lights dimmed, then spotlights swung about the arena, settling on a decorated tent flap through which the performers would enter.

Almost immediately four elephants emerged holding onto each other's tails. Daisy was in the lead of course, and on top of her sat a pretty girl in a skintight, sparkly, blue and yellow outfit, wearing an elaborate headdress with very large feathers. They circled the arena faster and faster as the girl stood on Daisy and did handstands and somersaults, and flipped dangerously from one elephant to another. Then she guided them to do some tricks on colorful blocks, and they danced (as well as elephants can), honked, stomped and pranced about. Soon a half dozen monkeys with hats, vests or little skirts emerged. They jumped on the elephants and proceeded to make the audience howl with laughter as they stood on their heads upside down, swung each other from pachyderm to pachyderm, knocked each other off in play, rolled under, over and sideways and crawled to the tips of the trunks. They made a tower of themselves on one elephant and in the next moment were teasing the ever-present clowns, pulling off their caps to put on, stealing the ringmaster's horn, and generally creating a lot of mischief and laughter. After that bunch exited, the lions and their trainer emerged. The trainer had them jump through burning hoops, they roared and swatted and balanced on balls, and the trainer bravely put his head in the mouth of one of the lions.

The trapeze artists came out next, dressed in their very colorful, bold costumes. The men were strong and lithe, the women petite and beautiful, and all extremely fit and athletic. They swung from high trapeze bars, building the necessary speed and distance to catch their partners swinging from the other side. They somersaulted in midair, twisted about, hung by their knees upside down while they caught one another; they hushed the audience with their death-defying feats and made us *ohhh* and *ahhh* as they walked the tightrope high up in the air.

Clowns and jugglers with their tricks and magic appeared between the acts. There was fierceness and levity, brightly colored lights and strobes, elaborate costumes, kicking up of dust, the smell of animals and tightly packed humans with their food and drinks. Sweet, sour, musky, dirt, sweat and bitter were the wafting odors. It was everything a circus should be and surely delighted one and all. The show was extra long, and "bonuses" were given for all the audience members for their show of so much help and compassion in the days leading up to opening day. We each received coupons for a free key ring in the shape of a monkey with the name of the circus and the date stamped on it, and a free bag of caramel corn plus a heartfelt invitation to attend the next circus, which would be outside the town of Cobb about 75 miles away.

On the stroll back home, we were exhausted but awake with the buzz of the evening and big grins on our faces. Father carried Emi, who was asleep on his shoulder before we hit the road. Jeffery was more chatty and animated than anyone had the energy for, recalling and acting out the evening's events. Phillip was annoyed at him and kept telling him to "shut up already," to which Father responded with a reprimand. We mostly just wanted to get back and go to bed.

Chapter 12

The next morning was cloudy again but we had no obligations other than our usual daily chores. It was going to be a pleasant day of rest, catching up and enjoying having the whole family together again. Father said we would have to think about breaking camp and getting on the road by the next weekend, which would give us time to say our goodbyes to new-made friends, collect supplies and prepare to get back on the road. Although we were all very excited to get back home, we were also sad about pulling up roots from a place that had become so welcoming, intriguing, fun and interesting the past several months. It would be hard to let Iznot go. Mother particularly seemed most reluctant and pensive over the next several days. She did laundry and shopping, gathering and preparing, but she was quiet. From time to time I saw her standing over her vegetable garden or on her hands and knees, pulling weeds and tending to the soil as if squeezing out the last bits of organic energy she could. She picked the last of the carrots, potatoes, peppers, onions and a few waning herbs, and carefully packed them away. I could tell she was very sad to leave her garden.

Emi teared up and outright cried a lot. Both Mother and Father tried to comfort her, but she couldn't bear the thought of giving up her new friends and beloved pets, especially Sniffles, whom she'd grown quite fond of. Jeffrey and Phillip were more excited to get back on the road. They always looked forward to the next adventure and challenge. Phillip helped Father with the wagon and horses, doing repairs, oiling the wheels, making sure the horses' tack was in good repair, mending the tents and canvases and all such as that, while Jeffrey helped with clean-up and packing. He was a focused kid, so was in his element doing rather tedious chores.

For my part, I helped Mother with the laundry and shopping and anything else she asked me to do, but I also went into town and bought enough fabric, thread, needles and other notions, plus some craft supplies and a couple of games, to keep us busy on the road. Hopefully we could sell some items at our next destination. I also stopped in the library to return some books. I had long since finished "Amelia's New Adventure," which I loved for the mystery and unusual setting, and had read a few books since. I had hoped to have a little change left over to buy a couple of books for the road. My mind wandered to our faraway castle and the small library we had there. It was a cozy space of wood and stone with a tall ceiling, soft lights, a couple of comfy chairs and a rather small cherry-wood desk. The library had a large window with a nice view of our rolling hills, and I found myself more often than not gazing at the sky and landscape, daydreaming of adventures beyond our realm. We had quite a collection of books ranging in topics from history to biography, science, biology; bird, insect and mammal books; maps, geography, mathematics, and of course, astronomy. We also had some fiction and true adventure books, but I'd read all of those. This summer it had been fun exploring this new library and all it had to offer. I must admit I found myself enjoying fiction much more than previously. There was just so much to choose from and so many captivating stories!

Anyway, I had nine books to return and when I got to the library Miss Miss was there; yes, that was her name. In fact her first name was Missy. Miss Missy Miss. I giggled to myself when I thought of her meeting someone named so and so Mister. If they got married she would be Mrs. Missy Mister. She was busy sorting and stacking a day's worth of returned volumes. We always chatted a bit and I dare say she and I had become good friends. She often made recommendations for which I was grateful, as her tastes were similar to mine.

Today when I set the books on the desk and she cheerfully asked what I would like to check out next, I had to explain that we were on our way out of town in a few days and I would not be able to read another book in time. I mentioned that I was going to go to the bookstore to see if I could purchase a used book or two for the road. Her expression of sadness reflected my own. She wasn't much older than me, and I think she liked having someone to chat with and distract her from time to time. She said she would be sorry to see me leave, asked where we were going and whether we would be returning. I answered her the best I could, being a bit evasive and not really giving any details.

"We're heading east for my father's business and I doubt we'll be back as we usually travel to far-off towns. However, I so enjoyed meeting you and talking to you, I will miss that," which I sincerely meant. She asked if I would write to her and I agreed. We visited for a little longer and as I was getting ready to leave, she jumped up and said, "Wait a minute. I can give you a couple of books to take with you. They are books I was going to give to the rummage sale anyway and I think you may enjoy them." Before I could say anything she had turned with a sweep of her crinoline dress and headed toward the back room. I heard her doing some shifting and moving of books. In the meantime I looked around the library and thought of how much I had enjoyed spending time in this little one. I wondered what others were like. Would we be in another town large enough to have a library or a bookstore? And if so, would the books be wildly different? So far, this was the only town in our travels to offer such amenities. Soon, Miss Miss was back with four different books. I stood there with my mouth open in surprise, as they were moderately thick. Substantial enough to keep me occupied for a long time. When I began to protest, she shushed me and said, "I insist, I don't need these anymore. Two are adventure books, one is an interesting history of Africa, and the last is a science fiction book, which not only you but your other siblings might enjoy." I couldn't thank her enough, gave her a big hug, and left with a melancholy smile on my face and a tear in my eye. The books were heavy, and I wasn't able to carry them and the other items I had come into town for. I would have to make another trip.

In the meantime, Emi had reluctantly accepted her fate, and when not helping around camp, spent the days visiting with all of her friends. She had kept herself busy during the summer making little woven ornaments in shapes of animals and people, in anticipation of hanging them on our tree at home at Christmastime. Instead, she gave her ornaments to her friends as a parting gift, and they in turn sent her home with tins of cookies and cakes, new ribbons for her hair, and even a dress that a little girl had grown out of and which Emi had admired. She was reluctant to give up Sniffles and spent much time taking him out of his cage to play with, cuddle and love, and whisper to him. She often had tears in her eyes. Mother suggested that if she didn't want to let him go back out to the meadow, perhaps one of her friends would give him a good home. We were all a little concerned that he may not survive in the wild again, having gotten used to the luxuries of being a well-tended, well-fed and loved bunny. In fact, he'd gotten a little plumper over the last couple of months. He might not be able to run and hop fast enough to avoid becoming a fox's next meal. It was another lesson Emi learned about living creatures that summer. We weren't worried about Black; he came and went as he pleased, and obviously had a home elsewhere where he was well fed and cared for. He just visited us from time to time, I guess for variety and extra attention, and perhaps to tease the rabbit. Cats are funny that way.

Chapter 13

The days eased on with the preparations. At our evening suppers we mostly talked about what else needed to be done before departing. Father said we had to take extra care as he was going to take us back home by the shortest route, eastward through some barren lands, then on through a mountain valley. The route would be rougher, the weather colder, but would get us home weeks sooner than if we'd gone back the way we came. There was a general sense of excitement and anticipation to return to our home, our own real beds, a roof, walls and rooms and familiar objects, the place of my birth, the land and valleys of our kingdom. Mother and Father talked about all the wonderful things we had forgotten about and helped to bolster us up, because we were inclined to dwell on the things we would be missing in leaving Iznot.

The day after my shopping spree, we had two visitors. It was almost midday when Anton came riding up on his steed. We all looked up and I couldn't help but smile widely. He dismounted and greeted my parents with a handshake and a few polite words. I saw Father point and nod to where I was, near the river, washing out some of our rugs and blankets. My siblings followed with their eyes as Anton headed in my direction with a purposeful step, his knapsack over his shoulder. He was so tall and sexy, with a young man's natural swagger. I couldn't help but admire everything about him and realized I was probably blushing. As he approached he had a nice, relaxed smile on his lips, but something about his eyebrows and forehead suggested a slight worry, a concern.

"Blue, I was afraid I wouldn't see you before you left. I'm so glad you're still here."

"How did you know we were leaving?" I asked.

"You know how small towns are, word gets around. It's no secret that you all have been making preparations for a journey. I was gone for a few days and was afraid you might have left already."

"Where did you go?"

"Oh, I just had some business out of town." He said it like my father did, and for a moment the similarity shook me.

We sat down near the bank and talked for a while. I told him the route Father had suggested we take home and how long we might be on the road. I told him I was excited to get back home, and as I prattled on I realized that I was revealing way too much. All anyone was supposed to know was that we were traveling, and to nowhere specific. No one was to know that we actually had a home someplace else. That would arouse suspicion, and too many questions that might lead to our true identities and put our situation in jeopardy. I caught myself short and stopped talking abruptly. Anton gave me a questioning look but I just looked down and away, and said I should get up and finish my work.

As I began to move, Anton took a gentle grasp of my hand and said, "Please don't go yet, I want to spend a little more time with you, and besides, I brought you something for your journey." I settled down again without resistance, still holding his hand, which was warm and moist.

"I wanted to give you something that I hope you can use and may remember me by..." He paused, "but I'll need my hand back to get it out of my knapsack," he said with a grin.

Suddenly embarrassed, I let go of his hand and wiped my palm on my skirt. Another blush. He opened his knapsack, pulled out a package wrapped in brown oil-paper tied with twine and handed it to me. I was giddy and very happy. A present! What fun! My very first from a man other than my father and relatives. I let it sit on my lap while I just looked at it. It was a simple package, slightly bulky, soft, squishy. No ribbons or bows. I slowly opened the package as I glanced up at Anton's smiling face, and there in the paper was the most beautiful sweater I had ever seen. It was thick wool as soft as Sniffles' fur. It was deep blue with small, perfect embroidered flowers of yellow, white and red. It had a big thick cowl neck collar, big sleeves that narrowed at the cuff, and four big buttons made of a shiny luminescent white shell. I held it up in front of me and without words, continued to admire this fine piece of clothing. I'd never had anything like it and certainly nothing as nice.

Anton broke my spell and said, "Put it on, let's see how it fits! I hope you like it. I picked it up on one of my travels. It's handmade cashmere; I picked it up overseas. I thought of you when I saw it. I thought it might look nice on you and keep you warm in the winter months."

By then I had stood and put it on. I was amazed at how warm and comfortable it was, and it fit perfectly. The sleeves were roomy and the collar wrapped around my neck up to my chin. It was the softest thing I had ever known.

"Anton, I love it! It's the most beautiful sweater I've ever seen and it's the best present I've ever gotten! I will wear it and cherish it always."

"Oh, and I have one other thing for you," and before I could protest, he took from his pocket a silver neck chain to which was attached a small brass pendant, something like a rough-edged coin, but when he held it up for me to look at, I had to giggle: it was a cheap little round amulet with the face of a clown embossed in it, with an inscription saying "The Show Must Go On!" He said, "I won it at the circus guessing the number of marbles in a jar. I know it's not much, but I wanted you to have it. I thought it might remind you of the circus and the fun, and maybe less of the tragedy."

I was speechless. It was now clear that he liked me, perhaps as much as I liked him. It made me happy and sad all at the same time. Now I really didn't want to leave. I wanted more time to get to know this man. I wanted to spend more one- on-one time with him without other obligations or people around. I wanted to touch him more, hold hands, hug, and perhaps even kiss. Tears began to fall down my cheeks and when I looked up from my palm with the pendant, I saw concern in Anton's eyes.

"Oh Anton. These are the best gifts ever. I'm going to miss you and I don't want to leave. Even though we haven't spent much time together, you have made this summer very special for me. From the first day I saw you in town with your bucket and brush, your scruffy hair and dirty clothes, you already had my heart. I have thought of you nearly every day since. I'm sorry I acted so strange and aloof."

By then I had taken both his hands and didn't want to let go. As Anton began to say something, Emi came skipping up and rudely interrupted, saying, "Father says you better get back to work now—oh, what a beautiful sweater! Did he give that to you?" she asked, with a quick glance toward Anton while she felt the cashmere.

"Yes, he did," I said with a grand smile on my face. Emi looked in awe first at the sweater, then me, then the sweater again, then at Anton, and said, "I wish I had a boyfriend too."

"He's not a boy..." I began to protest, but stopped as she had turned to skip back rather hurriedly, I'm sure wanting to be the first to tell everyone. I looked at Anton. We both giggled.

"I'd like to be...your boyfriend that is," he said with a proud face, looking directly at me. His eyes were so sincere that it took me off guard. I blushed yet again (I'll have to work on controlling that). "I'd better get back," I responded, embarrassed. "Will I see you again before we leave?"

"I will try, but one way or another I will see you again, I promise." Then, he surprised me by planting a gentle but firm kiss on my cheek, very close to my lips. I walked back with him, hand in hand. At camp, he said a few more words to my family, scruffed up Jeffrey's hair, and shook my father's hand. He then deftly mounted his horse and was gone, headed back to town. Mother and Emi admired my sweater as I proudly showed it off, but for some reason I didn't show them the medallion. It sat nestled under my sweater, cool against the cleavage of my skin.

The second visitor that day was Mr. Jacobson. He rode his horse up to our camp but this time, he was shaven and his mustache and eyebrows were neatly trimmed, he had on clean pants and a clean white shirt, over which was a nice leather vest. We were still bustling around; Mother was cooking something over the fire, Father and the boys were busy with chores. We all looked up when we heard him approach. I was hoping it was Anton again, but when I saw who it was I went back to stuffing pillows with fresh duck down, the feathers invariably escaping and flying softly through the air. Emi was sewing up the ends of those I had finished stuffing, and we were both covered with soft down in our hair, clothes and tickling our noses and skin, causing us to swat at the fluff and spit it from our lips.

Mother and Father stopped what they were doing and turned their attention to Mr. Jacobson. He had a nice smile on his face and greeted each with a handshake. Emi and I had been talking about our preparations, what to do with Sniffles and a myriad of other subjects. She was prattling on about remembering to return a puzzle set to her friend Jane before we left. I was only half-listening to her, as my attention was drawn to Mr. Jacobson.

He was saying, "I know you folks are planning on leaving town soon, so I just wanted to stop by and say a fond farewell. You folks have certainly made an impression on the town." My parents looked at each other with a slightly worried look on their faces, and I could hear them silently wondering what others had heard; what do they know? The sheriff went on to say, "I can offer spare supplies you might need and I can round up a few of the boys in town to help you load, carry or move what's necessary."

"Why that's very kind of you, Sheriff," my father responded, "but it looks like we've got just about all we need for the journey. We just need to tie up some loose ends, then I suspect we'll be out of here in two days."

Emi stopped her monologue in midsentence; she'd obviously been listening as well, and the boys, too, suddenly stopped what they were doing and focused their attention on the conversation. I guess it shocked all of us to hear an actual departure date. Although I knew it was inevitable, I wasn't ready to hear it coming so soon. Emi looked at me, worried, and I said, "Calm down, you knew the time was coming."

Mr. Jacobson went on to say, "I understand you folks are planning on heading east, is there a reason for that? Thought you were heading to Cataract to visit relatives?" His question seemed a little too knowing and prying, but he continued to smile and Father answered without hesitation.

"Well yes, that was the plan but an urgent matter has come up and we have to head back sooner than I expected. I know the eastern route may be a little rough, but I think we'll manage."

"Yes, it can be," said Mr. Jacobson. "I hope you've re-searched your route, and I don't want to frighten you or the family, but just please be careful. Although the roads are mostly good, it is territory not well traveled. There are some dangers to be aware of. Take your weapons and have ammunition ready, you just never know." Mother glanced between the two, obviously quite concerned.

"I think I know what you're referring to," replied Father, "and we'll take every precaution possible. I am grateful for your concern but I think we'll be all right."

"Right, then, I'll be off and let you folks get back to what you were doing. If there's anything I can do for you, don't hesitate to ask."

"'preciate the visit, sheriff, and thanks for letting us stay here."

Mother took his hand and shook it. "Thank you for stopping by, Sheriff. We'll miss this town." He tipped his hat and turned back to his horse. Father walked with him and they talked quietly for a few more moments before the sheriff mounted his horse and was gone. Mother had al-ready turned back to her work, and when Father returned to her side, she lowered her voice and asked him about the dangers the sheriff had referred to. Father assured her that he had been on the same road before, and although it was less traveled he didn't anticipate any problems. He said we might run across a few wild animals like bears or wolves, but "don't worry, we'll be fine."

The boys, who were over by the wagon, looked a little stunned, glanced at each other then went back to their jobs, whispering back and forth. Emi turned back to me and asked, "What was that about?"

"I'm not sure," I responded, and continued to stuff pillows without another word, but all the while thinking about what an odd and rather cryptic conversation that had been.

That evening while sitting around the fire having our supper of meat and vegetables, Mother and Father seemed abnormally chatty about this, that, and nothing at all. Mother went on about wanting to take some cookies to Mrs. O'Neil, and the rest of the chores she would have to do before we left. Father filled in with responses to Mother and talking about finalizing the prep and looking over the map. Finally, Phillip broke in, a bit too loud and forceful, and said, "Will you two stop and tell us what's going on?"

My parents looked up, rather surprised, as if they didn't realize anyone else was within earshot, but Father focused and asked what he wanted to know.

"Where are we going? Are we in danger? How does Mr. Jacobson know so much?"

"Yeah!" we all said in unison. Then Emi asked, "Why do we have to leave so soon?"

Father looked directly at her. "There's nothing here that you didn't already know, Emiline. I told you several days ago that we would have to be leaving by the end of the week. That time is in two days. And you'd better figure out what you're going to do with your rabbit. Tomorrow!" he said rather sternly. He knew how Emi could procrastinate.

"But why do we have to leave so soon?" she said in a bit of a whine.

Father just cocked his head slightly and looked at her sharply as if saying, "don't ask me again."

Mother chimed in and said, "Don't worry, honey, we'll find a home for Sniffles. Let's go to town first thing in the morning and see which one of your friends might want him and take good care of him. Maybe your friend Jane? Doesn't she already have some pets?" Jane had two mourning doves, a turtle and a little mutt dog with brown curly fur, short floppy ears and a medium-long tail. The dog was still young and bounced and ran everywhere. He was very cute and friendly and always wanted to jump on your lap and lick you. They called him Caesar. They had a fence around their yard for him and because of that, Jane would probably be an ideal candidate to take Sniffles, since he could be let out of his cage to run around freely.

We could see that Emi was in a pout. She could be very stubborn and I could see her little mind churning out a strategy to take Sniffles along. "But couldn't we just ta..."

"No!" said Father, "we don't have room for anything extra, let alone a pet. I'm sorry, honey, it's just not an option."

"Okay, now everyone," Father continued, "let's help your mother clean up and get to bed. We have a long day in front of us." Emi sulked on her stoop for another few minutes until Mother gave her a chore to do, when she got up reluctantly and began her task. Bustling began and somehow, the parents had avoided answering Phillip's questions…but none of us thought about that until later.

When the dishes had been washed and put away, and after we took turns trundling the loo and shovel off into the woods, washing our faces and brushing our teeth in a bucket of fresh water from the river, we went to bed. I couldn't sleep and Emi was restless. Soon Phillip whispered through the tent flap, "Blue? You awake? Blue?"

I sat up and parted the flap to let Phillip in. Just as I was closing it, Jeffrey pushed it open and crawled in too. Emi had lit a lantern and we all huddled into a too-small tent, but it was equally warm and cozy and the lamplight sent off a soft golden, flickering glow, causing our oversized, misshapen shadows to dance on the canvas walls. We hadn't been in the tent like this since the beginning, when we first got here and the younger kids were unsure of our new settlement. Once they felt safe, and it became way too stuffy and tight for the four of us, Phillip and Jeffrey moved to their own tent.

"Blue, what do you think is going on?" Phillip began. Jeffrey nodded his head vigorously. "I mean, didn't you think that conversation with the sheriff was a bit strange? Do you think he knows about us? And Mom and Dad seemed so casual about it."

"I know," I said, "I'm not sure." Not wanting to speculate or scare them, I continued, "I don't know how Mr. Jacobson could know who we are. No one else here does and, as far as I know, there haven't been any suspicious questions. No,

I don't think he knows. But, I think he's concerned about us going east for some reason."

"Why?" asked Jeffrey.

"I don't know but as he said, the territory is rough and not well traveled.

Perhaps there's people like Max to be aware of."

"Do you think there are dangerous animals out there?" asked Emi with some worry in her voice.

"What about bears!" Jeffrey said, with his eyes wide and a bit too much enthusiasm.

"No, I don't think there will be bears and I doubt we'll encounter anything worse than what we've already come across in our travels, like the coyotes and badgers, and they never bothered us. Father always carries his gun and I trust him, don't you?" All three nodded their heads, a little ashamed to have doubted him.

The more we talked, the less worried we became, and soon we were giggling and talking about subjects of no particular importance. We must have carried on for quite some time, as Jeffrey and Emiline began yawning and I was in need of relieving my bladder again.

"Okay, everyone, time to get back to bed. We're going to have to finish our prep tomorrow and I for one don't want to be too tired. We'll be very busy, and Emi, you'd better figure out what to do with Sniffles."

"I know!" she said rather angrily, as if to say "I've been told enough."

The boys went back to their tent, I went to do my business, and while squatting in the dark, gazed at the sky with all its brilliant points of light, as if Mother Nature had dropped a curtain of black velvet poked with thousands of tiny needles. The moons were up, casting a soft silver glow on the landscape, and I could just smell the dew beginning to form on the grass. When I got back to the tent, Emi was already turned to her side and snoring ever so softly. I turned out the lantern and settled myself down, listening to the utter silence of the night. Before I knew it, I was asleep.

Chapter 14

The next day was a bustle of activity and everyone was in a particularly good mood, even Emi. The morning had started out slightly overcast and we were worried that if it rained, it would hamper our chores. But as the morning brightened, and the sun burned away the clouds, you could almost hear a perceptible sizzle of steam from the dew and it became a warm and pleasant fall day.

We all had to go into town for one reason or another; Mother, Emiline and I took one of the horses and the wagon heavy with the last load of laundry to wash, and some items found in the caravan and around camp to donate to the local church, as we wouldn't be able to take everything we had accumulated. Father had said several times that he wanted to travel light and didn't want to appear like a wagon full of vagabonds, with pots and pans and blankets and clothes dangling off the sides.

Emi rode in the back of the wagon and held Sniffles on her lap in his makeshift cage, with plans to visit Jane in hopes that she would adopt him. The boys and Father made several trips back and forth to town, gathering horse feed, a few badly needed tools, some firewood, two extra buckets to replace our old, leaky and battered ones, various containers for storage and several other essential items. Since this would be our last night, Father wanted everything ready to go by morning, and promised to treat us to a last night at the inn with baths, a belly full of good food and warm, comfortable beds indoors. That news had helped elevate all of our spirits and motivated us throughout the day.

As the day wore on our chores, although they seemed endless, began to dwindle down. Jane and her mom were happy to take Sniffles and Jane said she had been secretly envious of Emi for having the rabbit. She said she would take good care of him and would give him back whenever Emi wanted. It made Emi feel happy and secure that Sniffles would have a good home. Still, she had tears in her eyes when she turned away from their house. The rest of the day she helped Mother and me, but stole away from time to time to visit almost every one of her friends, to say goodbye and give them the ornaments she had made. Her friends were clearly sorry to see her go.

Mother and I did the laundry and grocery shopping and stopped in to see Mrs. O'Neil at the flower shop. Mrs. O'Neil insisted Mother take a small pot of vibrants with her "to cheer up the wagon." Everywhere we stopped, someone wanted to give us "a little something" for our trip. Cupcakes, a loaf of bread, some links of pork sausage and smoked beef, fresh fruit, a few root vegetables, some crackers and cheese, some new towels and pillow cases, games to play on the road and a few other similar items. By the time we loaded everything up and headed back to camp, Mother was worried about what Father would say about returning from town, not with less, but with more! She smiled as she speculated, knowing that Father was an easy man who would make room for everything. Besides, she justified, most of it was food items and would eventually be eaten up.

When we got back, the camp was nearly cleared and the wagon packed well and efficiently. They had done an astounding job at finding nooks and crannies to hold everything neatly, with easy access to the items we would use most often. Jeffrey had even found a way to attach and carry our toilet under the wagon in such a way that nobody would be able to see it.

Even though we seemed to have a lot more stuff than when we first arrived, there was plenty of room in the caravan for all of us to spread out and be comfortable with spaces for all of us to sleep off the floor on cots and hammocks. And unlike our travels in the spring, when we had piles of junk and useless items that cramped us in, Father had made sure the floor was clear and the windows were free to pull back the pretty curtains and let the sun and air through. Every surface had been cleaned and washed and the windows were sparkling. It smelled fresh! All the lanterns had been repaired and filled with oil so that we would have plenty of light at night. It was actually going to be a pleasant journey. We unloaded and stored the food items and linens, and Mother found a perfect spot for the little pot of vibrants, secured on a shelf near one of the windows so that it would get plenty of sun during the day. It made the wagon look that much homier.

Early that evening, before heading into town, we decided to have one more fire in our little campsite near the river. Although the rocks had been scattered and Phillip's pretty landscaping had been returned to its former natural state (surely Mr. Jacobson would be pleased), the fire pit was still usable. It would be an early evening if we wanted time for supper at the inn and to get ready for bed. Father wanted to make an early start in the morning. So before dusk, we sat down at our last campfire with a comforting cup of hot tea sweetened with honey. The evenings and nights had started to get cooler as fall was creeping its glorious days in, with the subtle changes of golden colors, crisp, bright days and the smells of dry wood and ash. There was a slight cool breeze that blew through my hair but I snuggled deeper into my cashmere sweater and felt a certain warmth and comfort. I could tell Mother and Emi were a bit envious, but not in a bad way. They smiled and only wished they had something nicer than their shawls and scarves, even though those were plenty warm and comfortable. We chatted a bit, but I for one was tired and contemplative. Jeffrey was his usual animated self and talked about this or that subject of no importance, arms flailing to make a point.

Nervous energy, I suspect. Mother talked of the day's chores and events and the "lovely" people of Iznot who showered us with gifts, and Emi noted her success at finding a good home for Sniffles. But mostly we sat quietly, letting the fire warm our faces and knees while it flickered and cracked and popped. The embers burnt bright red-hot, dancing to their own tune, frequently changing hues from dark red to fire gold to black and red again. In those embers and flames I could imagine figures of people, faces and creatures. It had me mesmerized, as fires tend to do. Soon an hour had passed, the fire burned down and the evening was getting cooler, so we gathered our things while Father and the boys doused the fire with river water. The embers sizzled in their death throes, smoke billowing skyward, and he spread the last of the rocks and ashes so as to erase as much of the signs of human intrusion as possible. The wet ash and embers would soon be taken by the earth as rich nutrients for new grasses and plants. Then we headed into town.

It was a fond and distant memory of our first night at the inn. We all took long baths, soaping up well with lots of bubbles in the tubs of steaming hot water scented with potpourri (the boys, I was told, declined that). Then we had a scrumptious meal of brisket of beef, marinated then slow-cooked over a fire in a large pot, sliced thin and covered with something called au jus (a fancy name for sauce). It was surrounded on the plate with potatoes, carrots, onions, peppers, turnips and corn, along with a fragrant loaf of crusty bread and honey butter and a cool, simple chopped green salad on the side. There were only a few other patrons in the inn, clinking their silverware on dishes as they ate and talked in quiet voices. The light in the inn was a soft glow, the tables covered with white linen embroidered at the edges with fancy stitching and a candle set in a crystal vase on each one. We filled our stomachs and made room for some warm apple cobbler with vanilla ice cream on top.

After supper we took a stroll through town one last time. As we passed the now familiar shops and windows, one or the other of us commented with a memory. "That's where I saw my first parakeet and lemming," Emi pointed out as we passed a small pet shop.

"I met Wilber down there. He was funny. I liked him," said Jeffrey, pointing down a dark alley.

"I wonder if Mr. Akbar was able to sell that set of old wheels he'd been trying to get rid of," pondered Phillip while passing Mr. Akbar's Used Junk Shop, where surprisingly, he made a tidy living selling pieces and parts and things he or others had picked up on the road. His shop was fairly crammed with, well, junk and was dusty and dark, but it was fun to poke through for he had every kind of geegaw and gadget you could imagine. Sometimes he'd take in an item like a piece of jewelry, a nice vase or watch and, for a price, hold it on loan for a customer. If the customer was not able to buy it back with interest or if that person never came back by the designated date, Mr. Akbar was free to sell it to the public, at, no doubt, an inflated price. He was a shrewd businessman.

We passed by the flower shop and the tailor's, the smithy, the general store, the bakery and the millinery shop. All closed up for the night. I could hear the rustlings of a stray dog digging in the garbage and the faint voices of people in their homes or yards, wrapping up the day. A few children were still out playing somewhere; I could hear their distant laughter. All the time we were strolling and reminiscing, I kept one eye on a lookout for Anton. I was hoping I would see him one last time somewhere in town, and imagined him pulling me into the darkness of a shadow and planting a wet kiss on my lips, but soon we turned around and headed back to the inn.

As before, the beds were ultra soft and smelled like lilac. The innkeeper had set a fire in the fireplace in each of our rooms, which were welcoming and warm. Emi and I cuddled into bed and she was asleep before I'd even pulled up the covers. I watched the firelight flicker on the cedar walls rising high to the ceiling, making figures and faces as once our campfires had done. The crackling and smell of the burning wood was relaxing and comforting, and although I wanted to stay awake long enough to watch the last ember flicker out, I soon fell into a peaceful sleep.

Chapter 15

We were aroused early by our parents, and it took me a minute to remember where I was and what day it was. Emi and I dressed and put our things together, then went down to join the others for breakfast. Father suggested we eat a lot as we would be on the road for several hours. Lunch would have to be in the wagon or during a short stop. He wanted to make it as far as or further than Pea the first day. It would take us a good six hours to get that far. So even though I wasn't very hungry, I made myself eat some eggs, potatoes, ham and porridge. On the table were biscuits and pastries, fruit, cheese, butter, jam, coffee, milk and juice. I must admit, there is nothing like a delicious morning breakfast, and I stuffed myself. As before, the innkeeper and his wife wouldn't let us leave without an armload of fruit, bread and cheese, and bid us a warm farewell.

When we returned to the caravan, Black was lazily lounging on a blanket in the back. Mother gently picked him up, his claws firmly embedded in the fabric and apparently taking it with him, until Mother detached him and set him on the ground, gave him a loving stroke and a pat on the head, and said, "Now scoot!" But he only meowed, purred and rubbed up against her leg. Emi picked him up and gave him a good nuzzle while I scratched his ears and chin as he purred. Emi set him back down and he made a fine nuisance of himself by getting under our feet, chasing and pawing at dangling cords and material, and climbing in and out of the wagon as we packed up the rest of our things, stored away the food, and scouted the site for any missing items. He kept us annoyingly entertained, but eventually got bored and wandered off with his tail in the air as if in a huff. I guess he felt we were just not paying enough attention to him.

Soon we were on our way, each in a chosen spot in the wagon while Mother and Father sat up front. At first, the kick of the horses and jolt of the wagon were abrupt and rocky, but soon it settled into a soothing, steady, well-paced ride, with very little movement. The boys and Father had done such a wonderful job tightening and oiling the wheels and shaft, and building on strong springs for suspension (traded at Mr. Akbar's for a couple of rusted, heavy buckets and a lock box). The journey would be smooth and quiet save for a few creaks of the wood and the clip clops of the horses' hooves. Emi, Jeffrey and Phillip had broad smiles on their faces and so did I as we headed away from town, back the way we came. The others were looking out our wide windows on the sides, but I looked through the open door at the back of the wagon and watched the dust billow up as the road receded behind us. Through that dust I saw the faint figures of a few men on horses, watching us as we left. One of them, I'm sure, was Mr. Jacobson, but the others I couldn't recognize. I thought it a bit peculiar, as they didn't bother to accompany us out of town but instead sat still until we were far in the distance.

A few miles into our journey and it suddenly hit me that we were really gone. We had left a "home" we had made for ourselves for several months outside of Iznot. We had made friends, participated in activities, seen a circus. The boys had gotten into mischief and Emi endeared herself to a number of friends and their families.

Where were we headed now? Back home, sure, but between now and then we would never have a camp like we did in the beautiful meadow by the river. Mother would not have a garden. There would be no one to play with or talk to outside our family for weeks. Our stops in towns would be brief; Father wanted to make it through the mountains to the east before the snow fell. We would probably not be in a town large enough again to have a library or a bakery and there certainly wouldn't be any Antons! I clutched the clown-embossed trinket dangling from my neck and found tears rolling down my cheeks as I wondered and worried about my future.

Father was indulgent in stopping when we needed to relieve ourselves, but made it clear that all of us were to go at the same time. "No stopping every hour just because one of you didn't take advantage of the last stop," Father admonished. And so we held our bladders as long as possible and tried not to drink too much on the way. However, not

used to the confinement, the first several hours were difficult as my siblings and I became easily restless and fidgety.
We read, played games, bickered and napped, and bickered
some more but soon we just had to get out and stretch our
legs, even if our bladders weren't quite full. Finally, Father
gave in; rather than hear more whining and fighting, he
pulled the horses over to the side of the road where there
was some open space and a small stream.

We all jumped out immediately. Phillip and Emi ran out
to the stream and began splashing each other and throwing
rocks, while Jeffrey immediately took to climbing a sprawl-
ing tree. The area was dry but there were a few trees and
bushes at the end of their summer foliage. It didn't matter
what the area looked like, the day was bright and warm and
we were happy to be out of the caravan. Father worked on
taking care of the horses, loosening their halters and reins
so they could lean down and munch on the grasses, wa-
tered them and brushed them down. Meanwhile, Mother
indulged in a long stretch and a sigh and began putting
together a simple picnic, which she set up under Jeffrey's
tree. We all took advantage of the short amount of freedom
we had by running, jumping, chasing each other, throwing rocks and sticks, and doing whatever it took to exhaust
our pent-up energy. Even Mother and Father came down to
the stream, removed their shoes and socks and let their feet
be massaged by the cool ripples of water as it flowed over
the rocks. We came and went from the picnic site, grabbing bites to eat and running back to what we were doing,
which wasn't much; Emi danced around and sang, Phillip

continued to explore and dabble in the stream, Jeffrey was continually in the tree annoying us with bits of bark he'd throw at us if we wandered too close. My parents lay in the shade of the tree, talking and napping as the sun struck randomly between the branches and waning leaves.

It seemed like only minutes when Father informed us that an hour had passed and we must move on. He wanted to make many more miles before nightfall. We slowly and begrudgingly headed back to the caravan. Jeffrey, however, required a good deal of coaxing and some strict admonishments to get him to get down from the tree. He just kept ignoring my parents until my father reached for a long switch and strode angrily toward him. Father had never hit any of us but his threats were just as good; he could change his expression into one of severe anger and meanness when the occasion arose and the boys constantly tried to push his limits. Jeffrey saw him coming and with wide-eyed shock dropped down from a branch with a thump, hesitated, scowled, kicked up some dirt and threw a rock. Then he sauntered back as slowly as he possibly could, Father right behind him with the switch. We got settled back in and were on our way once again. The second half of the day was much easier, since we had sufficiently worn ourselves out and weren't as crabby as we had been during the first part of our journey. I sat back with one of the books Miss Miss had given me, and was soon absorbed in the story of a little boy and his lost dog. Soon the dusk began to settle in.

We came upon a tiny little town, appropriately called Pea. It was nearly deserted but there was one grocery, a tavern, a church, a school and a postal office, and just a few small houses scattered about. The town did not look very inviting but we were hungry and tired. Father told us to wait in the caravan while he "checked it out" and disappeared through the bat-wing doors of the tavern. A few minutes later he came out and spoke with Mother. There seemed to be some hesitation to stay there, but ultimately, he came to the back and said, "We're going to go in for a bite to eat, but that's all. There are some folks in there who may appear rude and drunken, but I think they're okay, I want you kids to stay close and don't say anything. We'll just eat and leave."

"So we won't be staying the night here?" I asked.

"No, honey. After we eat, we'll be on our way and find another place to stop for the night."

So we piled out, tried to straighten our clothes and hair a bit, and went into the tavern as if we were all held together by a tightly knotted invisible rope. Jeffrey clung to Mother's skirts and Emi got closer to me when we stepped through the door. The room reeked of tobacco smoke and the odor of musk, perspiration, wet leather and dead meat. The air was dense with a yellow-brown smoky haze and the lighting was poor and dim. There were only men in the tavern. Four or five sat on bar stools and another dozen or so were scattered at tables. All of them were drinking and most were smoking. On one of the tables were playing cards divided among the men and a pile of coins in the middle of the table. Their conversations abruptly stopped when we entered and they all turned toward us. Everybody quieted. They were rough-looking fellows with unkempt hair and clothes, and missing and decayed teeth. Almost all were wearing greasy old hats and road-worn jackets, dirty pants and boots. There was only one man at the card table who looked better dressed than the others. He had on clean clothes, a nice black leather hat covering a head of shiny black hair, a trimmed black beard and mustache, clean pants and boots. Although he looked the nicest, he seemed to sneer suspiciously at us from under his hat while chewing on a toothpick. There was an old mangy dog lying nearby that had seen better days. He had a dirty bandana around his neck, mats in his fur, several scars, and a blind eye.

The only friendly face, and that was stretching the term, was the bartender who said, "Well, don't just stand there, come on in. These boys won't bite ya," and with that, one of the men at the bar scowled and growled like an angry dog, which caused all of us to jump and everyone else in the room to erupt with laughter. "Now, Marv, don't scare the nice people," said the bartender, smiling at our expense. "These folks is travelers, let's show them some friendliness."

It was a most uncomfortable scene. I heard Mother whisper to Father, "Maybe we should go," but Dad took her gently around the waist and guided her to a table furthest away from the rest, while we shuffled close behind. The room of men kept their eyes on us until we had scooted our chairs out, sat down, then scooted them back in quite noisily. Only then did they resume their loud conversations, drinking and gambling. We looked at each other around the table, each with frightened eyes and trying not to move or bring any more attention to ourselves. Father was the only one who seemed relaxed and sure of himself, which eventually made us all feel a little more at ease.

Soon, the cook came through the swinging kitchen door with a basket of bread and butter. He was a large, fat man with a dingy, very dirty apron on. It had a lot of grease splatters and I could almost pick out the items he had cooked: spaghetti sauce, gravy, something yellow, and orange, perhaps vegetables? He had a layer of perspiration on his forehead, his face with a day's worth of whiskers and blushed from heat. Mother and I glanced at each other, I'm sure with the same thoughts: "Oh my goodness, will we be eating the remains of all that's on his apron? Has he even washed his hands? Are we going to be sick?" He plopped a basket of bread down on the table and was gone without a word. Surprisingly, the bread was warm and steamy with the fragrance of freshly baked whole rye, and the butter appeared to be fresh-churned and sweet. Father took the first piece and the rest of us followed. It was delicious and I realized then how hungry I was. Very soon, the cook and the bartender arrived with hot bowls filled with tender beef, potatoes, carrots, baby peas, onions and leeks in a savory broth. The aroma was marvelous and the taste scrumptious. We had glasses of milk for each of us, a growler of beer in a frosty glass for Father and a glass of cool white wine for Mother. It was almost as if we had ordered off a menu in a fancy restaurant. We even had a luscious, warm bread pudding for dessert. The meal was outstanding!

As we were finishing dessert, Father whispered some-thing to Mother, then got up and headed toward the table of gamblers. We all had our eyes on him as he shook the hand of the man in black and pulled up a chair. The three of us looked at Mother in astonishment and asked her, "What's going on? Does he know that man?" She just shrugged with the same expression of puzzlement on her face that we had. In about twenty minutes, their conversation apparently at an end, Father again shook the man's hand and returned to our table. He pulled out the chair for Mother and with a smile said, "Let's go." He and Mother spoke as we returned to the wagon but he wasn't inclined to answer any of our questions. He said we would stay the night there in the wagon, on the edge of Pea, and head out first thing in the morning.

We all seemed to sleep soundly with full bellies and a quiet night. Soon the sun was beginning to shine through the windows and the birds began their chirping. It was very early but Father had already been up seeing to the horses and getting them hitched up again. Mother rounded up some cheese, bread, fruit and milk for us and informed us that we would eat our breakfast on the road. So after taking care of morning necessities in the cool early light, we were on our way once again.

Chapter 16

For the next several days we settled into a routine of travel as we had at the beginning of our banishment. Early morning risings were the norm, a stop or two for a quick break, eating on the road. Sometimes we pitched the tents, made a campfire and slept outside; sometimes we slept in the wagon. And on occasion, Father drove us all the way through the night. During those days, we didn't come near any other town.

The landscape was changing and it was becoming noticeably cooler. We were beginning to layer on clothing and I gladly donned my new warm sweater, snuggling the collar up close to my chin. I found it to be so warm that once in awhile I'd remove it and let Emi put it on. Sometimes, it was hard to get it back, but a stern look and threat of death by maiming would most often prompt her to relinquish it. The boys fought and bickered a lot, and Emi would take sides and make things worse but most days, Mother would join us in the back (I'm sure to calm the restless natives) and begin reading to and teaching us our studies. She had bought some new pencils and paper for us and would patiently instruct us in math, reading, history, geography and science. I helped the others as much as I could, partly as an excuse to keep from my own studies. I felt a bit superior in that regard, but Mother caught on to my motives and assigned me upper-level calculations, and made me write essays from the books I was reading or write a report from one of my textbooks. At least it kept us occupied and I learned a lot. When not studying, we played games or read, and often I found myself just staring out the window, daydreaming and watching the world go by. We were seeing more small hills and valleys, and when we stopped or I took the front passenger seat while Mother stayed in back, I could see large, snow-topped mountains in the distance.

"Father, where are we going?" I asked.

"Home, I hope," he replied.

"You don't seem too sure."

"Oh I'm sure we'll get back, I just hope Boris hasn't destroyed it."

"Do you think he would?" I asked, a bit worried.

"Not if our plan goes well. But Boris is unpredictable and if he gets wind of what we're doing, he could be capable of anything."

"Who was that man back in Pea?" I blurted out.

"Oh, he's just someone I had previously met on the road," he explained.

"That town gave me an uneasy feeling." And we talked a little more about Pea but especially about the characters in the bar, the cook and the meal. We exaggerated and elaborated and had a good laugh.

"I miss Iznot," I said with a sigh.

"Yes, that was a nice town and maybe someday we can take a trip back to visit."

"Maybe on the train!" I said with enthusiasm.

"Perhaps."

I admired my father, and when I looked at his profile as we rode along I was captivated by his good looks. He was tall with a strong build and very handsome. He always seemed to carry a little smile on the corner of his lips. His dark hair and eyes made him appear mysterious, and he had a strong chin with a dimple in the middle of it. I could see why Mother fell for him and why women cooed when he was near. He was a mostly happy, self-assured man. He had an easy way about him and was kind and fair, which was why he was so well liked in the kingdom. But when something was irritating him or he got angry, he became a force to be reckoned with. His voice can be booming and intimidating and his eyes can take on the appearance of hot fire irons. At those times he seems to grow in height and structure, his back and shoulders broaden and the muscles in his neck distend. The few times he had to scold or discipline us were the times that he transformed from a loving, sweet man into a raging devil. He was not one to use violence and certainly not on his wife or children, but his change in voice and demeanor was enough to bring us back in line. When he and Boris had their many heated arguments, both of them could spit lightning, but Father could rage in a way that was rarely seen and very frightening.

"What are those mountains up ahead?" I asked.

"Those are the Minocks. They sit on the western edge of the kingdom of Chancy."

"That's close to us, isn't it?" I asked excitedly.

"Well, I guess you could call it close. It's still several hundred miles between the Minocks and the edge of our kingdom. We still have a long way to go, honey, and I want to get through the mountains before the snow flies."

"They're very pretty," I said as I gazed at the green mountains topped with high ridges, and valleys of snow reflecting varying colors of gray as the clouds passed over.

"How long before we get there?" I continued.

"Maybe a day or two, and then if we're lucky, we can make it through the valleys in three days. It might be a little rough, but once we're through, the journey should be easy," Father replied.

I pulled my sweater up closer and rested my head on his shoulder as we lumbered along. Father made me feel safe.

By and by the mountains got closer. I was mesmerized by their size and beauty. They were mammoth, with lush green forests of pines, ferns and hardwoods rising from the earth until transitioning to dry, rocky cliffs and crags above. There were multiple waterfalls to behold, and even from a distance they looked large. Rivulets, streams and rivers flowing from the mountains into the valleys and plains from whence we came began to take on a new meaning;

they were born from these mountains and had flowed hundreds of miles to nourish the lands to the west.

Chapter 17

We arrived at the base of one of the smaller hills before it grew to a height of many thousands of feet. It was about noon on a Thursday. Father pulled us up near a river in a warm, protected valley surrounded by forest and huge boulders the size of elephants, away from the wind. He said we would spend a couple of days there while readying the wagon for winter weather. He instructed each of us on what we must do to weatherproof the wagon: close up the windows and attach the wooden shutters, put up the back door, check for cracks and leaks and plug them with paraffin and tar. Prepare the horses with extra blankets and water, store food to assure against anything freezing, get out all of our stored winter clothes and blankets, and there was much more to do. He wanted us to begin right away, and then informed us that he would be leaving that evening to scout the country and route and to pick up needed supplies. It had been so long since he had gone on one of his trips that his news took us by surprise.

Both parents assured us that he would only be gone two or three days, and reminded us that we had gotten along without him many times before. This time felt different for me. Maybe it was just that I had gotten so used to having him around for such a long stretch, or maybe it was because on this leg of the journey I felt more connected to him. In Iznot, there had been more time to do things as a family. Even though Father was gone frequently and for longer periods of time, there were many evenings spent eating by our little campfire, taking walks along the road, swimming in the river, telling stories, visiting with friends in town. I realized that back in the kingdom our family, though close, was not as connected, and didn't spend as much time together. There were always distractions. We spent most of our days in school, doing chores or with friends, Dad worked at running the kingdom and helping on the land, Mom with her volunteering and household needs. It seemed a lot more hectic and now, I found I wasn't really missing it.

So we set about doing as many of the heavy chores as we could while Father was there to help. The boys helped to hoist the shutters and doors up, move the heavier equipment, organized the tack, and hauled and cut enough wood to last us. Emi and I helped Mom bring buckets of water from the river for storage, then started on the rest of it. The fact was that even though we'd been gone from Iznot just a few weeks, the caravan had gotten rather messy. We found it easier to remove everything from the wagon, set it out on the grass and go through it all piece by piece. We unpacked warmer clothes, washed and hung out to dry our summer clothes, along with the lighter linen we'd been using, to allow them to air and freshen before packing them away with sachets of cedar and lavender. We cleaned and reorganized all our pots and pans and cookware. We cleaned out the food storage barrels and tins and threw out any old food we deemed inedible. Father had always warned us to bury raw refuse or throw it very far away from our camps so as not to attract animals. Often, he would take the refuse and trash with him on his business trips, and dispose of it several miles away. We didn't have much raw refuse this time, so were able to bury it in the vicinity but several yards away.

Emi, who was washing out some clothes at the river, returned saying that she thought she had heard some squeaking and rustling in the woods. She said it sounded bigger than a mouse but smaller than a mountain lion, and mountain lions don't squeak. With that news we made sure to seal any small cracks in the floor, sides, windows and canvas of the wagon. One time, early on, we had returned to the caravan to find mice had invaded every nook and cranny. There were chew marks on the barrels, bread bags had been eaten through, there were crumbs and mouse droppings everywhere, our bedding had holes in it, and it was just a big mess. So, we made an extra effort to look for possible entries for little critters and plugged them up.

By late afternoon we had gotten just about all the heavy chores done and Father was ready to be on his way. He saddled up Charlie and Mother tucked a canteen of water, some sandwiches, cheese and bread and our last two apples into his knapsack. He promised to be back as soon as possible and said he would bring fresh fruit and produce if he could. He kissed us all goodbye and hugged and kissed his wife quite passionately, making us blush and turn away. Jeffrey said "yuck." Then Father was off.

There was still more to do but the day had been long and tiring. Mother said we could leave the rest of the chores for tomorrow, said it would give us something to do to occupy the day. We finished up in the wagon, and although the days were still mildly warm the nights had become chilly, so we set up the beds with our heavier blankets. We decided to leave some of our clothes hanging as they weren't quite dry yet and instead, with Mother's blessing, the four of us took off to explore the area more. She admonished us to stick together and be back in about an hour. By then, the sun would have begun setting and she wanted us back before dark. The boys had already set up a nice campfire and we would eat when we got back. I believe she wanted some quiet time to herself, perhaps to rest and read or take a nap.

The area we were in was stunning. There were so many things to do and see that it was hard to stick together; Phillip wanted to explore the river edge with its dense shrubbery, rocks, animal trails, bones and sand bars. Emi found an empty bird nest with a cracked spotted blue eggshell in it, some interesting rocks and twigs and a tiny whitened skull—maybe a vole? Jeffrey mostly ran circles around us, slapped us with sticks and annoyed us; he climbed trees and found some mounds with holes in them to poke sticks into, trying to rile up the homeowners.

I loved looking at the surroundings of mountains, the high changing clouds crossing the deep blue sky, the dried grassy landscape of yellow and orange, the distant water-falls. The sounds of the forest were different from what I was used to. There were numerous birds chirping but I didn't recognize any them. I heard the squeaky noises Emi referred to, as well as rustlings that I couldn't see or iden-tify and decided they were mice. In the distance I thought I heard a large animal bellow, maybe an elk or moose. There was moss of different colors on the rocks: blue, red, yellow, green. Some was fuzzy and soft, others like the blue ones grew fast to the rock, looking as if the rock were painted, and were prickly. Willowy knee-high ferns grew at the base of the pines, and there were stands of mammoth trees with white trunks as large around as a mill wheel, with foliage reaching far into the sky, dwarfing all the other trees and casting dark shadows where they stood. The forest was beautiful yet foreboding.

Although it wasn't quite dusk, I heard my mother's for-midable whistle. It was her signal for us to return if we weren't paying attention to the sun or time. Somehow she managed to create a very loud whistle that carried far sim-ply by putting her thumb and third fingers between her lips and blowing. I had never been able to perfect it. My whis-tles usually came out with flat notes and spit, but the boys were getting better at it.

My mother rarely had to use that technique to summon us back. The hair on my spine tingled. It took a little time to gather up my sister and brothers but soon we were headed back to our camp. On the way, both Jeffrey and Phillip mentioned the squeaky noises and rustlings that we had all heard by now, and we speculated as to the nature of the animal. Emi said she thought she saw some eyes watching us in the bushes, which promptly fed the imagination of the boys. They said it was monsters and spooks and they loomed over Emi with their arms up high and fingers spread, taking wide steps like they imagined monsters would take. Emi squealed with enjoyment, but I could tell when she looked up at me that she was a little scared, not of the boys, but by what she had seen. "Just mice," I said nonchalantly.

When we got back, Mother was tending the pot on the fire, but there was something else. Normally she would hang wet clothes on a string running between trees or posts. But as we approached, I saw that she had hung a number of items all around the wagon and on the branches of a few nearby trees. The scene was rather humorous looking, as there was my mother in her long work skirt and knit sweater, an apron wrapped around her waist and a bandana on her head from which wafted several strands of loose hair. She was stirring a steaming pot over an open fire and in the background was the caravan covered with Phillip's underpants, Emi's nightgown, two of my skirts were draped over bushes, Father's pants dangling on the doorway, some of Jeffrey's socks. Each piece of at least two-dozen items was gently flapping with the slightest of breezes. My first thought was that we were coming upon a forest witch, stirring a brew made of lizard tails, slimy slugs, caterpillars, the eyes of a newt and gold dust. I imagined the clothes hanging about to have belonged to victims who had suc-cumbed to her deadly potion.

We raced the last couple hundred yards, out of breath, right up to Mother. Her smile was sweet when she looked up.

"We heard your whistle," I said.

"Good, it always seems to work," she replied. "I thought we should eat early and turn in before dark."

"Why, is something wrong?" asked Jeffrey.

"No, no honey, but there may be animals that we're not familiar with around here so I think it best to play it safe."

"Is that why you have our clothes hanging about?" I asked, a bit worried.

Emi chimed in with urgency, "We heard squeaking nois-es and saw *eeeeyes*,"

she emphasized with her own wide open.

There was a hint of a gesture my mother made, one of concern, her right eye barely twitching, almost squinting, but such a wisp of a moment that I could have imagined it. Phillip and Jeffrey joined in with their assessment of what we experienced.

"Certainly there was more to your discovery adven-ture than that! What else did you do?" she asked, changing the subject. Soon we were telling her about the river, the woods, boulders, dried-up, paper-thin summer flowers, the mosses and the many varieties of mushrooms. Emi showed her what she had collected and Mother fingered each one with genuine interest.

We went about preparing and eating supper, taking care of dishes, cleaning up and going about our nighttime needs without the subject of animals again, and none of us questioned the forethought of mother's laundry decision.

By the time we were shut in the wagon and settled in for late conversation, game playing and reading, it was turning quite dark. The evening noises had begun with frantic scurrying, distant barks, twitters, cheeps, scratching noises, and birds singing their sweet, soft melodies preparing for a night of flirting. Then the evening transitioned to the natural noises of forest creatures waking for their time of hunting and eating. As the night darkened the noises transcended to utter calmness, with just the faintest whizzing of mosquitoes blended into the natural night melody of soft breezes rustling through the trees. Sleep was deep. I woke only once, thinking I was hearing those squeaky noises and faint scratching and scrabbling, but my partial consciousness blended it all into a dream and I fell immediately back to sleep.

Chapter 18

It was early morning when I began hearing a lot of commotion. Our horse Spirit was neighing loudly and thumping about. Everybody but me had left the wagon. There was yelling and screaming, "Get out! Get out! Go away, shoo!"

I pushed open the window and was immediately confronted by a strange creature staring back at me with a solid black face and body and little beady eyes. Within seconds of my thoughts trying to process what was going on, it had jumped into the wagon and was running about, throwing blankets and covers about, trying to open vessels and tins. I was stunned to stillness and pinned against the wall, watching the slithery figure go about destroying our wagon. I let out a scream, picked up a nearby belt and began swinging at it. It became more agitated, looked at me and hissed, showing a set of ominous fangs, and scurried around, just missing my lashes. The wagon was jostling and rocking, creaking and cracking as I tried to hit the animal and chase it out. Finally, it darted back through the window and I slammed the shutter shut as fast and hard as I could.

I hurried out of the wagon to see a scene of chaos: the boys and Mother were frantically chasing the creatures away from the wagon, but they had already pulled down and ripped a number of pieces of clothing, gotten under the wagon and dislodged several pots and pans, and boxes of tools and supplies. There was stuff all over everywhere. Spirit was kicking up dust and dirt, frightened and braying, struggling to free herself from the rope that was becoming tangled in the tree trunk as the nasty creatures hopped and ran about, squeaking and making a ruckus and seemingly taunting the horse. I picked up rocks and sticks and tried to fight them off, but there must have been dozens of the animals and they were very quick and nimble. These creatures stood about three feet high with sinewy arms and legs, a slinky black midsection, spindly toes and fingers. The heads were shaped like a large raisin or a civet cat, if you've ever seen one. They were hairless, all black and shiny as if coated with axle grease. They could run on all fours or upright.

All of a sudden we heard a piercing scream and turned to see Emi running towards us, crying and screaming, holding her right hand in her left with blood splattered all over her nightgown and streaming down her hands and arms. The sight was shocking. We stopped our war barrage and ran to her as quickly as we could. Her screams had scattered the slinky animals away for the time and allowed Mother to capture Emi in her arms, both collapsing to the ground.

Emi was in a panic, crying big tears, obviously in pain. Everything seemed to be bloody; she was holding so tight onto her right hand that Mother had to pry apart her left fingers to get a look at what was going on. Phillip and Jeffery, sweaty and in disarray, looked on, while I sat beside Mother and tried to help calm Emi. Finally, Mother was able to see that Emi's index finger was bleeding profusely, and before inspecting it any further she pulled off the sash from her robe and wrapped Emi's hand, then instructed the boys to go fetch some water and rags. They both looked wide-eyed at each other and I could tell they were thinking *Not down at the river! We'll be devoured by the creatures.* But Phillip immediately took charge and told Jeffrey to rip up the clothing that had already been damaged, and he would get the water from the barrel in the wagon.

In the meantime, Mother was soothing Emi with soft words and asking if she was hurt anywhere else. Emi, shaking, scrunched against Mother's chest, shook her head no between sobs. The boys were back in a flash and Mother began sponging away, first the blood on her face and neck, then her arms and methodically working towards her hands, trying to calm her the whole time. The rest of us kept a vigilant eye on our surroundings, but only saw the black things scurrying in the bushes and looking out with their menacing eyes. None of them tried to approach. Spirit had calmed down some and except for some squeaking and rustling in the woods, it was otherwise quiet.

It took some time and Mother tried to be as calm and gentle as possible, but she was finally able to soak off the sticky, bloody cloth from Emi's hand and get a look at the damage. Mother was brave, but the rest of us took in a breath of shock as it was revealed that Emi's index finger had been bitten off down to the middle knuckle. The boys turned away and Jeffrey pushed himself up against Phillip, who put his arms around him. Both had tears in their eyes, as did I. The sight of Emi's bloody hand and her mangled finger was too much for me and I almost vomited, but instead diverted myself and asked Mother what to do.

"Blue, go fetch the medicine box and clear off space and make extra room for her in the wagon. Boys, start a fire and begin heating some water, free the horse and let her go, then gather up what laundry you can. See what's salvageable. The rest, tear into rags for wound cleaning and dressings." I could tell that some of the instructions to the boys were to keep them busy and out of the wagon for a while.

I jumped into the wagon and went to work. I found the medicine box right away; it was tucked tightly in a space with easy access and hadn't been disrupted by the chaos. I jumped out of the wagon and ran it over to Mother, then ran back inside. Although it was risky, I opened the window shutters and door and as quickly as I could, began picking up and straightening up the mess that had been made. Mother's vibrants were spilled out on the floor and potting dirt was everywhere. I scooped up what I could and shoved the little limp plant back in the pot. I picked up overturned utensil drawers and a crate of potatoes, straightened a couple of shelves, and replaced books and games that had been scattered. Then I cleared out a large area on the floor and laid down several layers of bedding, covering them with a soft muslin sheet and piles of blankets. I pulled out a couple of sprigs of dried rosemary from Mother's stash of herbs and tucked them under a pillow.

In the meantime, Phillip had wisely informed Jeffrey that they were going to start many small fires near the wagon in hopes of warding off the animals. Jeffrey had freed the horse after untangling her rein and slipping off her harness. With a swift kick and snort, she took off running into the woods. She would manage better loose than tied up, and we could only hope she would eventually return for some oats. Mother had begun ministering to Emi's hand as best as she could. It was quite painful and Emi shrieked and cried out frequently, breaking my heart and making me cry.

I told Mother that her bed was ready, and she scooped Emiline up in her arms and carried her to the wagon. Phillip, anticipating as he does, had set a clean bowl of warm water next to Emi's bed and had attached the steps to the back door. He was waiting like a guard as Mother approached with Emi in her arms. We helped them up and Jeffrey followed behind with the medicine kit. After trying to sneak a peek at Emi, Mother instructed them to go back out to continue what they were doing.

Mother laid Emi gently on the bedding and we began getting her nightclothes off. The blood had soaked through and in some places had become plastered to her skin. Each time we moved her or tried to loosen her sticky clothing she'd whimper and cry out. Soon she was freed of her clothes and cleaned up by a steamy warm sponge bath. We dressed her in a fresh nightgown, then tucked her into bed. Mother opened the medicine kit, took out a small corked jar of purple liquid and gave her a spoonful, telling her it would help the pain go away and help her sleep. It didn't take long before she drifted into a deep slumber. Mother and I let out equally heavy sighs, which made us smile. It was an odd moment of camaraderie. I took the dirty, bloody bowl of water out, dumped it, then retrieved another heated pail of water from the fire and set it down next to Mother. I went about getting the rest of the blood out of Emi's hair as Mother unwrapped the hastily tied bandage on Emi's hand. As we worked, I asked, "What were those creatures?"

"I'm not sure but I think they're called Inky Dinks. I heard the term mentioned in Iznot, then again in the saloon in Pea. I really don't know anything about them and I think if Father had known about them he would have said so, or moved us elsewhere."

"They're creepy and scary," I commented. She just nodded her head as she was concentrating. Emi's index finger was fairly macerated. It wasn't a clean cut. The bone was mostly gone but there were a couple of tiny shards poking out of the end of the wound where the tissue was raw and ragged. The rest of her hand and fingers had some minor scratches but otherwise seemed to be okay. Mother had a time trying to clean her finger as it bled every time she touched it. She reached for some small shears from the kit and I took a deep breath, not knowing what her intentions were. As I watched reluctantly, she gently and deftly trimmed the tissue and bone until it looked neater and had clean edges. I was rather surprised at myself for watching but was fascinated by the whole process. If I thought too much about it I had to turn away and choke down my nausea. Mother broke my selfish revulsion and asked me to hand her the iodine from the kit. She dabbed a good deal of it on the wound, intermittently squeezing down tight with the cloth to tamp the bleeding. Soon she was able to wrap the finger in some clean gauze and a bulky dressing. I brushed Emi's hair and wrapped it in a towel for warmth.

"How long will she sleep?" I asked.

"Probably a few hours, but she'll be in pain when she wakes. Do you see that jar of clear liquid in there?" She nodded toward the medicine kit. I got it out and handed it to her. "This?"

"Yes. It's some pain medicine that should help later on,'" Mother replied.

"Where did you get all this?" I asked, realizing that the kit was stuffed with all kinds of medical supplies and concoctions.

"Miss Cambridge, the nurse in attendance after the explosion. She put this kit together for me. She insisted I take it, saying that it was very necessary to carry medical supplies when traveling. I'm so grateful to her now."

"How do you think Emi will be?'" I asked.

"She's young, and it's only her finger which she'll eventually learn to do without, so I think she'll be fine," Mother said, looking at Emi lovingly and sadly at once, her eyes moist, a tear nearly ready to fall. No mother wishes harm upon any child, especially her own.

By now, the boys had poked their heads in to check on us.

"How do you think it happened?" I queried mother.

Jeffrey chimed in and said, "I think she got bit by one of those things when she went into the woods to pee."

They began asking Mother the same questions I had and she repeated her answers to them.

"What should we do now?" asked Phillip.

"Have you seen any more of them while you were out there?" Mother asked, looking at them both.

Phillip answered, "I don't think so, but I could hear the squeaking and see a little rustling in the bushes."

"Yeah," Jeffrey affirmed. "Will they come back?"

"I don't know but we should be prepared." '

"How?" we all asked at once.

Mother suggested we keep several fires going. She had suspected something was amiss yesterday and that's why she hung the laundry out, in hopes that the movement would scare off any animals. Since it didn't seem to work, and since these were animals none of us were familiar with, we really didn't know what to do. We speculated on their patterns; out in the day, but were they gone at night? None of us heard anything until early in the morning. Were they omnivores, carnivores or herbivores? Why did one attack Emi? Did she provoke it? We wouldn't know that until she awoke and could tell us.

Phillip suggested making a fence of sorts around the wagon and hanging items that would jangle, jingle, clank and make noise. That way we could at least be alerted if they came close. Mother thought that was a good idea. But first, she said, we must eat, and leave Emi to sleep.

So Mother and I gathered together a late breakfast of cheese, bread, milk and some apples, and we sat down on the ground close to the wagon wheels and on the steps. I was ravenous and probably ate too fast while keeping an eye on our surroundings, looking for any suspicious movement.

After we ate, we began the process of setting up a perimeter. Phillip and Jeffrey hammered sturdy stakes of dead wood into the ground and strung rope between the posts, while Mother and I gathered together pots, pans, cups, a couple of mirrors, some tools, wire pieces, metal from the horses' tack and anything else we could securely fasten to the rope, making sure that, if breached, each object would clank and make noise.

By the time we were done and the several perimeter fires had been stoked, it was midday and we were exhausted. The day was slightly cool but the sun was bright and I had worked up a sweat. I badly wanted to take a dip in the creek, and I knew we would have to collect a lot more wood before nightfall to keep the fires going. So I suggested we all go to the creek together, clean up, get more water and collect wood on the way back. I received a look from the boys that said I was utterly nuts. After a brief discussion of pros and cons, Mother said the only way she would allow us to go is if one of us took our whistle and blew it constantly so that she could hear us, and we all must stick very closely together. She didn't like us going off for even a short distance by ourselves, but couldn't leave Emi alone and knew that we needed water and wood. She found a little metal whistle in storage and gave it to Jeffrey. Phillip and I collected large pails for water and we set off arm in arm to the creek, Jeffrey tooting the whistle in a constant obnoxious rhythm.

The trek, although tense, was uneventful and we took turns cleaning up in the stream and blowing the whistle. Phillip filled the pails and Jeffrey and I gathered large armfuls of wood, then we headed back without seeing any movement or hearing any unusual noises.

Chapter 19

When we returned, Mother was standing on the steps
with her mouth open and I realized she was looking
at something behind us. I turned quickly and saw a dozen
or so of the Inky Dinks crouched low, coming out of the
bushes behind us, very slowly and non-threatening, more
curious like, but I pushed the boys forward anyway to make
them step faster. Phillip nearly tripped and jostled his pail,
spilling a little water. Jeffrey dropped a few pieces of wood.
They both said "Hey!" in anger but realized I had done it in
a bit of panic. They turned and saw the Inky Dinks. Jeffrey
stopped whistling and dropped all the wood as he ran into
the wagon.

Phillip and I set the pails down next to the wagon and
joined Mother on the step. Mother was still watching the
creatures and instructed Phillip to get the shotgun, "Now!"
The animals had stopped a few feet away and were watching us intently like a troop of wary monkeys. The fires were
burning and the dangling items on the fence were gently
swaying in the breeze, glinting in the sunlight, making the

slightest wind chime noises from time to time. Phillip returned in a flash with the gun and Mother held it fast and ready to use if necessary. Phillip suggested she fire a shot to scare them away, but she was inclined to see what they would do first. She didn't want to rile or agitate them.

So we watched, and watched, and watched. They in turn watched us patiently, and watched, and watched. We were in a standoff. I found myself smiling at the humor of it. It all seemed so ludicrous and I could only imagine what it might have looked like to a bystander. We didn't know anything about the Inkys. Were they intelligent or stupid? Did they act on instinct or learned behavior? Who would make the first move? What was their intent? Jeffrey was inside looking out the window, and suddenly we heard him tweet the whistle. What was he thinking? Probably just as bored as we all were, but the rest of us turned and shushed him to be quiet. At the same time, the Inks tilted their oddly shaped heads as if listening without fear, with instead, it appeared, some interest. Jeffrey whistled again from the safety of the wagon, and Mother stormed in from the steps and angrily snatched the whistle away. "What are you doing?" I could hear her as her voice rose.

"They seem to like it," he responded. "I think they were following the sound. Look, they're calm," he said while pointing out the window. Indeed, the animals seemed to be quite calm in a curious kind of way. Mother put the whistle to her mouth and began softly whistling. The Inks began slowly slinking toward the wagon. When Mother stopped whistling, they stopped and did nothing until she started again. Emi was still fast asleep, snoring under the blankets, deeply oblivious to all that was going on. We crowded around the window as Mother continued whistling, more gently now and even with a bit of a tune, if one can say a single note instrument can make a tune. Nonetheless, the Inks seemed interested, if not under some kind of control, and approached just to the edge of our makeshift perimeter. There they stayed. Mother stopped whistling and we watched. The Inks just mingled there, occasionally grabbing up some grass to eat or gnawing on a stick, glancing at us now and then. A couple even wandered off as if bored. Mother whispered that that was a good sign, maybe they were herbivores, but it didn't rule out that they could be omnivores. They seemed content to just linger on the periphery so we decided to each take a watch, playing the whistle from time to time just to stave off our own boredom.

But the excitement of it all had made our bladders more active. Mother was the first to venture out and slowly, carefully descended the steps and squatted near the wagon, all the while keeping her eyes on the Inks, while Phillip was ready with the shotgun perched on the window sill should they suddenly become aggressive. Jeffrey gave a toot on the whistle from time to time. They lounged more comfortably than we did! A couple of the younger ones played with each other near their mother. By and by, after a long while we found we could go in and out of the wagon without fear as long as we hummed, sang or whistled. If too much time went by with a quiet lull, they would begin to squeak and get agitated. So all of our activities that day were done with us making music or noise in one form or another. How would we keep this up all night?

Emi remained asleep until late in the afternoon, when we heard her beginning to moan and become restless. Mother was at her side in an instant. Mother gently lifted Emi's head into her lap and calmly stroked her hair. Emi woke in a lazy, drugged stupor, hot and sweaty with her hair stuck to the side of her face, creases in her cheek, and dry, chapped lips. She groggily complained of being thirsty and hungry and needed to relieve herself, but as soon as she said that she came to a start, her eyes bugged out and she asked with urgency and fright, "Are they still there? Are they gone? Mom, Mom!" And she began convulsing in tears.

"Sshhh, sshhh, darling," soothed Mother. "They are still there, but they are quiet and won't hurt you, I promise. We've found a way to keep them away." I slipped her a cup of water that she slurped down in one long gulp. "Now tell me, what happened this morning?" Mother continued.

Emi sniffed and blew her nose and said, "I just went out to the forest to go to the bathroom. I had to take the shovel, and while I was out there I kept hearing these scratchy, squeaky noises like we heard yesterday. I looked around but didn't see anything and went about my business. When I was through covering the hole, out of the corner of my eye, I saw this black slinky thing. At first I thought it was a monkey. It didn't look mean. In fact it looked curious, so I put my hand out and tried to talk to it. I wanted to pet it. It finally approached me, but when it got close, it suddenly lurched forward and bit my hand! Mom, I was so scared, and then I saw blood, and I didn't know what to do and I ran back here and..." She began sobbing again.

"Sshhhh, it's okay, it's okay. Let's see if you can get up and I'll help you go to the bathroom," said Mother softly.

"No, no!" she exclaimed in a panic. "I can't go out there, don't make me, I can't go out. I'll just hold it in, but I can't go out again, Mom, I'm scared and my hand hurts."

"Okay, okay, I won't make you go out, we'll figure out something."

And with that, Phillip was already out the door and down the steps. We heard him bumping around under the wagon. Jeffrey whistled a few times and in a half second Phillip was back in with an old rusty bucket and the faithful toilet seat. He set it up in a corner, and strung a sheet from wall to wall, securing it with a couple of nails. Then he stood back proudly, took a royal bow and waved his arm in a grand fashion toward the "bathroom" and said, "Your majesty, your throne awaits." We all laughed, including Emi. He had managed to accomplish a fine feat to take care of his sister and to inject a little humor into a tense situation. We helped Emi up to the toilet while the boys waited outside.

"Hey mom," we heard Jeffrey call from near the wagon. "They're gone!"

Mother and I poked our heads out and sure enough, the critters were gone. Happy! Happy! But we knew it might just be temporary. We helped Emi finish up and changed her into some fresh night clothes and warm socks, then I wrapped my sweater around her shoulders and coaxed her to come sit on the steps to get a bit of the warm sunshine before the end of the day. In the meantime, Mother went to work gathering some items to make an early supper. I asked Phillip to build a fire for cooking and stoke the others. Jeffrey took a challenging sprint to gather up the wood he had dropped earlier, and the boys went to work on the fires as well as securing any of the hanging items that might have come loose from the rope fence. I sat with Emi for a bit, my arm around her, casually glancing at her wrapped-up hand, and smiled as she lifted her face to soak in the sunlight. I could tell the fresh air was already doing a world of good. Soon, I went in to help Mother with the preparations. The boys ventured out to the stream with Emi's dirty clothes and a bucket for water, whistling all the way. We could hear them from our camp while we put a pot on the fire.

"Where's Spirit?" Emi suddenly asked as she looked around at where she'd been tethered.

"The Inky Dinks were agitating her too much and she was getting all tangled up, so we had to untie her and let her go. She hasn't come back yet. She was pretty spooked,'" I answered.

"She'll return," Mother assured us.

We ate supper and turned in early, the fires still burning and crackling. Emi's hand was throbbing something awful, so Mother gave her another spoonful of elixir to ease the pain and help her sleep. We closed up the wagon and I settled down to read my book while Mother and the boys played a game of cards under the lantern light. We didn't hear anything outside but a slight breeze tinkling the items on the fence.

I must have fallen asleep although I don't recall when. My book was smashed between the covers and a few pages were bent when I was awakened just at dawn by the same screechy, scratchy sounds and commotion as yesterday. I knew right away what it was and jumped up to grab the whistle from the window ledge. I began blowing it more forcefully than I intended in our closed space and it startled everyone else awake immediately. I shoved open the window while blowing and saw the Inky Dinks scattering hither and thither, then they disappeared into the woods. Mother in her nightgown and the boys in their long johns were crowding the window to look. Sure enough the critters had done a bit of destruction to a couple of the fires that had gone out through the night, and it looked like they were trying to tear things off of the fence. The damage was nothing compared to yesterday's havoc.

"Good!" Mother said decidedly with her hands on her hips. "It looks like we've found a way to keep them out."

The wagon was very stuffy. The boys went about opening the other window and door and Jeffery jumped out to go behind the wagon. Phillip and I followed soon after, cautiously keeping a lookout, our bladders just about to burst. I took a big stretch in the early daylight and went back in the wagon. Mother was sitting next to Emi, who hadn't awakened yet. Mother looked worried and was gently removing the bandage around Emi's hand.

Emi's face was flushed and perspiring. I took in a breath when I saw her. Her lips were pale and she had deep, dark circles around her eyes. She didn't look well. "Mom, what's wrong with her?" I asked.

"I'm not sure but I think she may have an infection. I'm going to have a look at her wounds. Stay near, as I may need your help cleaning and changing her dressing. Ask the boys to heat some water."

They had stayed outside and had already begun, under Phillip's direction, to clean up the mess left by the animals. Phillip had started the main cooking fire and was already heating water for tea. I told him Emi didn't look well and to heat more water for wound cleaning.

Mother had removed the bandage and set it on a piece of paper when I went back in. The bandage was wet with some thick greenish-yellowish ooze and blood on it, and had a putrid smell. I covered my mouth and turned away, ready to get out of there, but Mother stopped me and directed me to cover my nose and mouth with a piece of cloth and, "come help." It took all I had to choke back the vomit. Emi's hand was red and swollen. What was left of her finger was purple with a layer of pus at the end of the wound. The whole thing looked and smelled disgusting.

Mother yelled out the door, "Phillip, bring some water in here quick!"

Jeffrey ran up to the door, but as soon as the odor hit his face he turned around. Phillip came in with a container of water, and he too was shocked by the smell and the appearance of Emi and her hand. As he set the water down, with his arm across his nose and mouth, he asked in a muffled and worried tone, "Is she going to be all right?"

Mother didn't say anything but went about dabbing and cleaning the wound; I held Emi's arm elevated as instructed. "There are no red streaks yet, but we're going to have to get your sister to a doctor right away." Thus the obvious dilemma: Since Spirit hadn't returned there was no mode of transportation. We didn't know where we were or where to go, and we had the Inky Dinks to consider, plus we didn't know when Father would return. In fact, it dawned on me that we were stranded and utterly on our own, alone. I saw the deep creases on Mother's worried forehead as she concentrated on Emi's wound, and knew she was thinking the same. Emi weakly moaned every now and then but it was clear she was feverish and wasn't going to wake easily. Phillip returned with a cool, wet cloth to apply to her forehead and disappeared again.

"Won't Father be home soon?" I asked.

"We can only hope so," answered Mother without much conviction.

I tried hard to come up with a solution, but we were out in the middle of nowhere and it was way too far to try to walk back to Pea.

Mother finished cleaning the wound and doused Emi's hand in iodine, then began wrapping it in clean bandages. She asked me to tear a length of material long enough to wrap under her elbow and around her arm and fasten it to a chair nearby to keep it elevated. It seemed to work fairly well. Then she said she was going to mix up some medicine to give Emi to help the infection, and set about pulling several little bottles out of the medicine box as well as a small cup-like container and a mortar and pestle. She began mixing and crushing herbs and combining them with a little drop of this and that. She was in such deep concentration that she didn't notice when I stood up and exited the wagon. Before I left, I turned and had to smile at the sight of Mother in the guise of a medicine woman, her hair put back with a bandana, a towel on her lap, concocting a healing brew of who knew what, and half expected her to begin chanting and burning incense. I marveled at her adeptness and knowledge.

I threw the scarf off my face as soon as I exited and took a deep breath, but that didn't help the dizziness and nausea, and I bent over and retched, unable to throw anything up but a little acrid bile. It occurred to me that we hadn't eaten anything since last night. The boys were standing back watching me, worried. Phillip came over and put a damp cloth on my sweaty forehead. After taking some deep breaths I began feeling better. There was a cool morning breeze, which helped, and I could hear the birds singing. No sounds of the Inks for which I was very grateful. I did not want to go back into the wagon but knew I should try to be responsible and get together something to eat. I knew if I had something in my stomach it would settle it and, no doubt, the boys were starving. So I gathered my wits, wrapped the scarf back around my nose and mouth, took a deep breath and held it, and ran back into the wagon as fast as I could, tripping on my nightgown. I grabbed whatever foodstuff I could find as quickly as I could, not even glancing at the patient and her attendant.

When I came back out, I had an armload of some apples, a partial loaf of bread, a little cheese, a piece of ham, an onion and a potato. I surely didn't feel like eating any of it. I put the ham, onion and potato into a pot over the fire, figuring it could simmer to make a soup or broth for later. Then we found a spot near the fire and began eating the cheese, bread and apples. I started slow, not knowing how well the food would sit in my stomach, but soon found I was quite hungry. We ate in silence and listened to the woods. Once finished I told the boys that Emi was very ill and that we were going to have to figure out a way to get her to a town with a doctor. I told them to go into the woods and see if they could locate Spirit. "Take some grain and an apple with you to help entice her back."

"But we can't go out there alone!" Jeffrey said in his worried little voice.

"You'll need the whistle," I said and gave it to Jeffrey.

"I don't want my finger bitten off!"

"Look, we have to do something. Mother is attending to Emi and I know she won't leave her side. I don't need the whistle. I can sing, sort of, and Mother certainly can. Take the rifle," I said as I looked at Phillip. "Don't go far or be long. Spirit may be right nearby but afraid to come in. I'll clank a spoon on a pan frequently, and if you begin to get out of hearing range, turn around and come right back. And keep whistling so that I know you are still in range."

"What if we get lost?" Jeffrey asked, still quite worried and unsure of this plan.

"We won't get lost!" said Phillip rather angrily. "Let's go." And with that he grabbed

Jeffrey by the collar and shoved him forward.

He gathered a rope for Spirit, and the gun. I gave Jeffrey an apple and some grain to store in his pockets and told them both to be careful. "Don't worry if you can't find her soon, we'll figure something else out," and at that I gave them both a hug and they were off. Jeffrey was lagging a little behind until Phillip gave him another good shove. Before they disappeared into the woods, I saw Jeffrey pick up a big stick and start whacking the trees and bushes, and whistling loudly.

I returned to the wagon and told Mother what the boys were doing. She was distracted, dabbing Emi's flushed face with cool water, but nodded with acknowledgment. I went back out and tried to clean up some of the mess and debris that had accumulated over the past day, all the while clanking a pot to make noise for the boys. After about thirty minutes, the whistle became fainter and I began to worry that the boys were wandering too far, so I ventured to the edge of the woods and began clanging steadier and louder to draw them back in. Soon I could hear the whistling getting louder and within minutes the boys were back, safe, but without Spirit. They looked dejected but happy to be back, sprinting the last few yards then plopping down, out of breath. I offered them some fresh water, which they accepted greedily. They asked about Emi. I didn't have anything new to tell them. They said they had not seen any of the Inky Dinks and no sign of Spirit.

Each of them poked their heads in the wagon and consulted Mother about Emi's health. She said nothing and just shook her head. I could tell she was exhausted so I offered to take over while she rested, changed and ate. With much reluctance she finally gave in and I took her place next to Emi. Mother stood up stiffly, arched her back and stepped out of the wagon. Phillip told Jeffrey to grab some bread and more cheese, while Phillip gathered some blankets and a pillow and ran out of the wagon. He wanted to set up a resting place for Mother under the cool shade of the wagon. With the cleaning of Emi's hand and the flow of the breeze through the windows and door, the foul odor was no longer noticeable. I tried to give Emi little sips of water through her unconscious lips, readjusted her hanging sling and fluffed her pillow. Then I took a bit of a sponge bath myself with some of the clean water from the bucket, and changed into some fresh clothes.

I got out my book and made myself a comfy place next to Emi and began reading. It was quiet outside except for the slight tinkling of the items on the rope, the breeze blowing gently through the trees and the birds singing their daytime songs. I must have fallen asleep for the next thing I knew, someone was blowing the whistle, and there were footsteps and Phillip yelling, "Get out of here!" The Inks were back.

Chapter 20

It was midafternoon now. I checked on Emi. No change, but she looked comfortable. Her breathing was steady although a little labored. I looked out the door and sure enough, the slinky, ugly, annoying critters were scurrying about in the bushes nearby and squeaking loudly. Mother was coming out from under the wagon in a bit of a daze, still in her nightclothes; she must have slept deeply—good for her. Phillip was running around stoking the fires. Jeffrey was whistling frantically as he jangled the rope, creating quite a cacophony. I was angry and sad. How long were we going to have to put up with this? Shouldn't Father be back by now? How could he just abandon us like this? How would he feel if he came back to find his family mauled and eaten to death by Inky Dinks?! I bet that would make him think twice about leaving! I knew I was overreacting but I was frustrated and angry nonetheless.

Just about that time we heard the hooves of horses coming up the road from the direction of Pea. In about a minute there were four men on horseback galloping toward our camp in a rush. As soon as they saw us they stopped abruptly.

"You folks having any trouble?" one of them asked. He was dressed all in brown, rough and scuffed leather from the hat on his head to the boots he wore. We all looked at Mother, who said in haste, "Yes! How did you know? I'm so glad you're here! My husband is gone, he should be back soon but we've got these Inky Dinks, at least that's what I think they are. They've been invading our camp and one bit my daughter, who is seriously ill! Can you help?" Mother pleaded.

"Where is your daughter, ma'am?" the leather man asked as he dismounted.

"Emi, she's in the wagon, her finger is infected. She's very ill. She's in here," she said as she directed him to the wagon.

The other three were already off their horses, rifles in hand but with a controlled calmness. I realized that one of them was the dark-haired man from the tavern in Pea Father had spoken to. He assessed our camp, nodded as if satisfied with our arrangement, and asked, "How many have you seen?" The boys looked at me.

"I don't know, maybe two dozen or so. They hide out in the bushes and scurry around."

"And they squeak a lot," said Jeffrey.

"They don't like singing," I said.

"Or whistling," said Phillip.

"We've had to sing and whistle and make noise day and night now for two days," I said, slightly exaggerating.

"Yes. They are pests," said the dark-haired man, "and can be dangerous when provoked or frightened, it doesn't take much."

"What can we do about it? Our horse ran off and Father hasn't returned."

He assured us that he and his partners would help. They offered to move us through the mountain valley to the other side. There were no Inky Dinks over there and by then, Father should be back. At that moment, leather man stepped out of the wagon with Emi in his arms. She was limp and pale and looked even worse in the daylight. Mother was close behind.

"I have to get this little girl to a doctor right away," he said.

"I'm going too," Mother defiantly announced.

Before we knew it, the men had fashioned a makeshift carrier on top of one of their horses, to cradle Emi with a place for Mother to sit behind her. Mother told us the men would help us and that she would be back as soon as possible. She kissed each of us and before we could think about it or say any more, they were off in a cloud of dust, galloping so fast I thought Mother and Emi were going to tumble off.

The dark-haired man noticed our fright and confusion, and tried to calm our fears by assuring us that we would be safe and free of danger once we got through the valley.

"Look, I know your father. You can trust us." This was enough to appease us for the time being. He instructed us to take down the rope and noisemakers and prepare to leave right away. The other men helped to stamp out the fires and secure the wagon, inspected the wheels and tethered their horses to the wagon. I worked inside the wagon to straighten up, putting away the pots and pans and mirrors and other objects that had been dangling on the rope fence as the boys brought them in to me. Phillip brought me the pot of soup, hot and steamy, so I covered it with a tin lid and set the pot inside a larger bucket, stuffed wood around it to keep it from moving and hoped the soup wouldn't slosh out. I dumped the toilet bucket Emi had used only once to pee in, but decided to keep the "bathroom" intact for possible future use, and I neatly organized and put away the medicine kit Mother had been using. We were all scrambling about to make the task quick. We wanted to get out of there so fast that none of us asked any more questions until the wagon was rolling down the road in the quickly fading light of the day.

Two of the men sat in the jump seat while the other rode alongside. The three of us sat quietly in the back, trying to make sense of what was going on. My heart was beating fast. I peeked out the window and as I saw the road recede, I also saw the Inky Dinks frantically scrabbling around the remnants of our camp. *Good riddance!* I thought. The mountains were looming in front of us. Before it got dark, I pulled out some dried meat and bread to eat and gave the boys the last of the dairy milk, while I drank some water. The pot of soup would have to wait. We remained quiet while eating but soon the silence was broken.

"What's going on, Blue?" Phillip asked.

"Where did Mom and Emi go? Is Emi going to be ok?" Jeffrey asked.

"How will Father and Mother find us again? Who are those men? Should we trust them?" continued Phillip.

"I don't know any more than you do at this point, but Mother seemed to trust them, she wouldn't have left otherwise," I answered. "I'm sure everything will be all right and we'll be safe. It's better than staying in that place," I said with scorn.

The boys nodded in agreement.

Our conversation continued with pondering and speculations, and I did my best to calm the boys and make them feel at ease, although underneath, I was scared to death. "Do you want to play a game?" I asked, trying to distract them.

We got out some cards and played a few hands of nit-nit until Jeffrey began yawning. It was late by then so I helped them settle into their bedding, and gave them each a motherly kiss good night on their foreheads.

Sleeping in the wagon was always very easy for me. I liked the rhythm of the horse's hooves on the road, the gentle rocking of the wagon and the smell of the road wafting through our cabin. I slept deeper and more soundly than I had in days and awoke very groggy and disoriented. Dawn was lighting the sky; it was cool. We had stopped moving. Both boys were snoring. And it was very quiet. I pulled the blankets up to my chin, snuggled back down and fell asleep again.

I'm not sure how much longer we slept, but it was apparent that none of us had awakened until the dark-haired man unlatched the back door and asked if we were ready to get up. The three of us struggled to get our bearings and wiped the sleep from our eyes. The boys left the wagon in their long underwear first. I decided to urinate in the bucket in the caravan loo, as I was reminded that we were in the company of three strange men. I got dressed in some warm wool pants and shirt and, over that, my "Anton" sweater, as I called it. I fingered the pendant on my chest and stepped out of the wagon.

Chapter 21

The sun was brilliantly bright and we were dwarfed by huge, imposing, snow-topped mountains looming all around us. The road had given away to a grass- covered wagon trail. On either side were green grasses and an abundance of colorful late fall wildflowers. We were in an alpine mountain valley, and it was gorgeous. It looked like summer again, but the chill in the air suggested otherwise. The dark-haired man had been watching me and was amused at my wonderment. He had the air of a person proudly showing off a canvas he'd acquired of all the glory of Mother Nature.

"I never properly introduced myself," he said as he put out a hand to shake. "My name is Ohm.'"

"I'm Blue," I answered back as I took his hand.

"I'm sorry to hear that," he said with a mischievous smirk on his face. It was a joke I'd heard many times in my life so I just smiled back.

"Him, over there by the fire that's Bobby, and Wilt is the short guy with the thinning hair and the paunch," he said while pointing at each of the men. The boys had found a spot to sit near the fire and were eating something while engaged in conversation with the men.

"Are you hungry?" Ohm asked as he guided me to the fire. He made introductions to the others while Bobby served up a hot, steaming plate of eggs, bacon and biscuits with jam. What a treat! We hadn't had a breakfast like that since eating at the inn in Iznot! Jeffrey was crouched on his haunches, Phillip on a rock and both in their dingy, thread-bare long underwear. They were quite a sight with their tousled hair, but happy as could be. I took up a spot on a log that had been rolled near the fire. The fire was large and warm, crackling and spitting sparks into the air.

Jeffrey informed me that we were in the Repleat moun-tain valley and that Bobby said it would only take a few more hours to get to the end, at which point we would set up camp and wait for our parents. Ohm told us that the fourth man, James, had probably taken Mother and Emi to Escavaro to the south, where there was a good clinic and knowledgeable doctors. It was a big town, of about one hundred thousand people. He was sure Emi would get the best of care there.

"How will Father know where to find us?" I asked anxiously.

"Oh, he'll find us. He's a very resourceful man."

"How do you know him?"

"We go back a long way. I knew him before he met your mother. Then I left for a few years to work overseas. Your dad and I reconnected again not long ago. He would come through Pea from time to time while on business in the region. He knows a lot of people and recruited a number of men to work on his ranch."

"Ranch?" said Jeffrey in a surprised and questioning tone. I saw Phillip whack his brother's thigh. "Ouch!" said Jeffrey, annoyed. Ohm just gave them a nonchalant glance.

The boys had picked up on the inconsistency as did I, and as much as I wanted to probe more into the story of our "ranch," I kept my mouth shut. Ohm went on to tell us that Father did some trading of various goods and from time to time spoke of his wife and family.

"I feel like I've known you for a long time, since you were just children," he continued. "Now I see you're all grown up. Your parents must be proud of you." Before I could ask anything more he said, "Eat up, we'll be on the road again soon. Let us know if there's anything you need and we'll see if we can fetch a servant to get it for you," he said with a wink and a grin. The boys laughed. Again, a bit of humor at which the three of us giggled, but I couldn't help wondering if Ohm knew more about us than he was saying. I remained a bit suspicious.

As the men left the campfire and went about doing things around the wagon and camp, Jeffrey said, "They seem real nice" as he munched down another strip of bacon.

"Yeah, I like them," added Phillip.

We finished our breakfast at a leisurely pace, savoring each and every bite, feeling a bit special that someone else was waiting on us and taking care of the chores, while we enjoyed this beautiful valley and crisp morning without the fear of the Inky Dinks lurking about. When we finished I told the boys to get dressed and help in whatever way they could. I took up the dishes and washed them the best I could with the dwindling amount of water in our barrel. There was no stream or river nearby. Soon we were on our way again.

Jeffrey and Phillip were invited to sit up front with Wilt, who was quite chatty and regaled the boys with stories of adventures on the road. Ohm had galloped on ahead and Bobby, who had said but a few words the entire time, rode alongside. That left me, gratefully, alone in the wagon. I opened the windows and the back door but found it too cool, so I closed a shutter on each window and cracked the glass open just enough to let some fresh air in. I played house for an hour or so, straightening things up and organizing nonessential items. Mother's vibrants had taken a beating with the Inks. It had lost all its flowers and the low foliage had begun to get scrawny and yellow. I fluffed up the dirt, gave it some water, and set it where it would get a little more sunshine but be protected from the breeze, hoping it might come back to life.

Enjoying the time without the others and being able to think to myself seemed like a luxury of the past. My mind wandered from concern for Emi and Mother, to wondering where Father was, to more questions I had about Ohm and his relationship to Father. Then I thought about Iznot and Anton and finally fell to wondering what condition we would find our home in, or if it was still there. Every now and then, I found myself gazing out of one window or the other, just daydreaming or transfixed by the mountains and the beauty of the valley. The mountains were extraordinarily huge, creating their own weather system of clouds and gloom circling around the tops of the snow-covered peaks, while the valley below was bathed in sunlight, greenery and color. I had never seen anything like it. It was mesmerizing and made me think of the ancients who worshiped the gods up above and pondered the powers of creation. How they too must have marveled at the majesty of nature, just as I was doing now. And what about the very first travelers through this valley? What could they have been thinking? Did they know where they were going or were they simply forging a new route? Finally, I decided to use my time fruitfully and first caught up in my journal, then read a little in my astronomy book. I had just started a chapter on the formation of the planet Whomp when I last took up the book on our way out of Iznot. Now, I found it even more engaging and fascinating. I felt inwardly happy and peaceful and was able to open my mind to the wonders of the universe.

After awhile, I found myself getting restless and bored and very badly needing to use the toilet. I was happy for Phillip's little bathroom set-up and stepped behind the curtain to relieve myself. Just as I was in the middle of a trickle, the wagon came to a halt with a slight jolt, causing me to lurch forward, nearly spilling the bucket and dribbling a little pee right down my leg. Yuck I thought as I steadied myself to clean up and pull up my pants. Just as I stepped from behind the curtain, Bobby appeared at the back door saying, "We've got a little problem here," and turned and left without further explanation.

I stepped out of the wagon to see that we had come to a stream crossing, but the bridge had been wiped out. Only a few boards were stuck on either bank. Everyone was at the bank, assessing the situation. The stream was thigh deep and moving fast. My heart sank, as my first thought was that we would have to turn back. I didn't see any way around it. The men and the boys were discussing, pointing, contemplating and deciding on what to do. It was clear that the boys were just as involved in this leg of the journey as the men and were feeling self-important. I felt a bit like an outsider, just a girl who should stick to cleaning and cooking. After all, isn't that what women do? Then I spotted a rather large fallen tree a ways off and had an idea.

"What about the tree? ...Hey. Hey," a little louder. Nobody was listening, "HEY! What about the tree?" I said louder and more firmly. With that, they all turned and looked at me, a little puzzled and annoyed as I pointed to the tree.

Thirty seconds passed. Then Wilt said rather condescendingly, "Well, it's much too big to move, although it would get us over by foot. We couldn't get the wagon over, though."

"Hmmm," pondered Bobby.

"No," I said. "I was thinking maybe you could take the bark for a bridge, it's quite large and appears quite thick. Maybe you could lay it out flat-like across the river." It was as if the words were spoken by an alien. They all looked at me, dumbfounded, then Bobby said, "Yep, might work," and headed straight for the tree. Jeffrey and Phillip stood still, just looking at me with gaping mouths as if they'd never heard me speak an intelligent word before, but were soon running to catch up to the men at the tree. I followed, figuring I might have more clever advice to add. At least I could supervise.

After talking and assessing the situation, they went back for some tools and a horse. I just watched, rather proud of myself, and munched on an apple I found in a pocket of my jacket. They went about sawing very large vertical and horizontal cuts through the bark, then with a crow bar, sheer strength and the help of the boys, they managed to loosen the bark in one huge piece with a giant loud CRRAACK that echoed through the forest. It was so thick and difficult to extract that they almost gave up, but soon it released and came loose in one big hunk the size of a side of an elephant. They hitched a rope to one end of the bark and the other to Wilt's horse, and dragged it back to the stream near the wagon.

The men and my brothers were sweating profusely. This job required a lot of back-breaking work. I wanted to pitch in and help but didn't really know what I could do, so instead, I grabbed a couple of buckets and filled them with stream water to replenish our water barrel. Then I went inside and made some sandwiches.

I watched them through the window, grunting as they repositioned the behemoth and began to guide the horse across the stream with it. Bobby was navigating the current and rocks, while the boys and Wilt guided the wood from the bank. It looked to be plenty thick, wide and heavy enough to hold the wagon. The task was arduous and difficult, as the hunk of bark kept hanging up on the rocks and debris or wanting to catch the current and float downstream like a shallow boat. Bobby slipped and fell in the water with a big splash but was able to get up himself up, soaking wet and looking like wilted seaweed. The boys guffawed and I laughed too while in the comfort of the wagon.

Soon, the horse and Bobby had made it to the opposite bank and he secured his end of the bridge to a large boulder about three feet over the stream, while Wilt and the boys worked to secure the near end to the thick tree trunk. It now had a slight slope from one side to the other, but looked to be gradual. When they were sure it was tight and stable, Wilt walked over it, then back, then over halfway, and jumped up and down a few times. The bridge didn't move. Then he guided Bobby's horse over it. The horse took a reluctant first step onto the wood, then walked over to the other bank without hesitation. Lastly, Wilt, Bobby and the horses walked single file back over it. Two horses and two men on the bridge at the same time and there was no sagging or drifting. It didn't rock back and forth or wobble. It looked like the bridge was steady and safe and would support the wagon.

The men and my brothers came back to the wagon dirty and sweaty, and as Bobby stepped through the door he said, "Great idea, Blue, I think that old dead tree was just waiting to become a bridge!" I blushed at the unexpected compliment, and offered up the sandwiches and fresh cold water to drink, for which they were very grateful.

After lunch and a short break, at which time Bobby changed out of his damp clothes into dry ones and the others cleaned up, they hitched Wilt's horse to the wagon. I straightened up inside, closed any open vessels and secured everything down as best I could, then I got out. Wilt guided the horse and wagon to the bank while the rest of us stood by. Wilt took the horse a few steps onto the bridge until the front wagon wheels made a secure purchase. The men slowly but steadily maneuvered the horse and the wagon across the bridge. Only once was there a near disaster, when the back right wheel came close to rolling off the edge but was steadied and reset, just in the nick of time. Otherwise, it went fairly smoothly. Bobby came back to help me and the boys across, taking a firm but gentle hold on my arm, which was truly unnecessary as the bridge was so stable, but he left his horse behind. Rope was a valuable commodity and they weren't about to leave it there, so Bobby and Wilt went back over again to retrieve the rope and Bobby's horse from the other side. They cut the end of the rope that was around the tree and then wrenched the hefty bark away from the rocks and bank, and let it go with the stream. Once it was free it took the current and swiftly took a turn to the center of the water, then abruptly and violently slammed against the opposite bank, getting stuck on the edge by wood and sticks. The end where we were standing was still attached to the rope, the rope to the boulder.

Bobby and Wilt mounted Bobby's horse and carefully stepped across the stream to the bank, dismounted, and Bobby climbed aboard the bark. Because the rope was so taut on the rock, Bobby had to cut it from there. He knew that the tension on the rope would cause the rope to snap back with enough force as to inflict very serious injury on someone. As soon as the rope was off it did exactly that, snapped away and landed on the bank while the bark wobbled and moved a little more, but soon caught the river debris again and was stuck. Bobby was on all fours and didn't get dumped. He righted himself and stepped though a couple of feet of shallow water back to solid ground. He was very lucky the wood hadn't broken loose and carried him down the stream. Ohm, in the meantime, loosened the rope from the boulder, rolled it up and packed it onto his horse. It was a shame that the bridge couldn't be left for the next traveler, but the plan from start to finish was brilliant, and I felt privileged to have been a big part of it. Soon we were on our way again, the boys and I walking now, enjoying the fresh cool air and exercise.

It was a pleasant day, mostly sunny with a few clouds and a gentle cool breeze. You could feel winter's nip in the air. The boys spent their energy running about, finding rocks, sticks, pinecones and other assortments of nature's detritus to destroy or play with. They chased each other, and me, and had friendly air-boxing matches. I picked some unusual wildflowers of purple, pink, yellow and red, and thought of Father, Mother and Emi. I hoped Emi was getting good care and that we would all be reunited soon.

Bobby had said we weren't far from the end of the valley, and once we got through, we'd set up camp again and wait for Father to return. By the end of the day, we'd walked and played ourselves to blissful exhaustion, and climbed back into the wagon for a rest while the journey continued. I set the wildflowers in a small jar with some fresh water and placed them on a counter near the poor, shriveled vibrants. I was hoping the influence of the fresh flowers might revive Mother's plant by osmosis. "Come on, you're not dead yet! Look how nice we are! Come back and show us all your beauty! You can be as healthy and colorful as we are!" The boys were settled into reading and soon I joined them.

It wasn't long before we were slowing down and when I looked out the window, I saw that the mountain valley had receded behind us and a vast and wondrous sight met my eyes. I roused the boys to come look and we jumped out of the wagon as soon as it had stopped. The vista in front of us was as breathtaking as the mountain valley, but much different. You could see for miles and miles across rolling plains of dry yellow grasses, waving in the breeze and creating a canvas of ever-changing patterns under the late day sun and clouds. There were patches of light snow here and there on the otherwise dry landscape, and a vista of trees, large boulders and small buttes dotted the countryside, as well as shallow ravines snaking through the plains. It was very reminiscent of our own homeland. I could tell the boys were thinking the same; their eyes widened and they didn't bother to conceal large grins. Wilt and Bobby had begun untethering the horses, which took playful jumps away from the wagon into a shady spot under a tree and began munching on the grasses. With the direction of Bobby, the boys went about setting up camp and making a fire. I heard Jeffrey ask Bobby if there were any Inks here and he was reassured that there were not, that we would be safe here and Father should have no trouble finding us.

I pulled out the pot of ham soup, which had remained cool in the well-packed pail, and diced up some old sprouted potatoes. I worried that we would not have enough food to last another day. All that was left was a little dried beef, a few sad- looking root vegetables, a small chunk of cheese and some dried-up bread. We still had half a barrel of water, but no milk. The herbs Mother had used were gone by now, but I found some wild parsley, and added that and some salt and pepper to the soup.

Bobby and Wilt seemed impressed and the boys were satisfied, and I was happy with the day-old meal too. The men talked about subjects that didn't interest us, like the price of beef and what 'ole Woodruff had been up to lately. The boys and I ate mostly in silence as the dark of night descended upon us. Phillip kept the fire stoked, and the warmth enfolded me. I brought my Anton sweater up around my chin, feeling the soft fuzz of the baby wool, and fingered the amulet hanging from my neck. The evening was quite pleasant, the night turning very black. The moons were both tiny fingernails hanging in the sky and the stars were bright and vast. It was not often that the moon phases were in sync. I put some water on the fire for tea and coffee, and Wilt began a story.

"There was once a dragon that lived on top of a mountain in a dark cave full of crystals..." As Bobby stoked the fire from time to time and we took sips of our belly-warming liquids, Wilt exaggerated and animated his story, one that he had obviously told before, maybe even to young folks like us. He had a voice that could change for the different characters and he seemed to take pleasure in his small talent. The story concluded with a happy ending late in the night. The three of us lazily left the fire circle, took care of our nighttime duties, and quickly fell asleep to sweet dreams.

Chapter 22

We must have slept very hard, because when we awoke to the smell of coffee brewing and ham and sweet rolls cooking, it was already midmorning. I could hear the men chatting and laughing but another voice penetrated my subconscious— Father! Phillip and Jeffrey were aroused at the same time. We bounded out of the wagon just as Father was striding toward it. He had a huge smile on his face and took all three of us up in a big bear hug. We were so happy to see him, and I instantly felt relief and a sense of safety.

We bombarded him with numerous questions: Where have you been? How did you find us? Did you have to cross the deep stream? Do you know about Emi? Have you seen Mom? Do you know where they are? Did you hear about the Inky Dinks? Did you see Leatherman? (I found out later his name was James.) As we clung to him like monkeys, he herded us over to the fire, where Bobby was serving up plates full of steaming food. As we ate ravenously, Father explained everything.

He told us that he had just come from Escavaro. "Emi is doing much better, although the doctors had to amputate her finger in order to save her hand; the infection had already begun to spread. They want to keep her in the hospital for a few more days to make sure she is stable and well enough to travel. Mother is with her and doing well, but very worried about you kids. They will stay in Escavaro for now. I'll send for them when we're closer to home. In the meantime, I picked up plenty of supplies to last us, so we should have enough to eat. Here, have some fresh milk. It was milked from old Betsy just this morning." He poured us some of the white elixir; we gulped it down, and then had seconds.

"Everything is in place for our return home. We'll stay here one more night, then head on. It will take us only a few hours to reach our realm. I must be there for the final game that will be played the day after tomorrow. Your uncle has been losing quite a bit in the games, and we have most of our property and goods back. He took the challenge for the final game of Quark. When he loses, we'll get the castle back and anything else left on the table. He has become very contentious and angry and has been drinking more, which isn't helping his game. According to my sources he's signed an agreement, should he lose, to leave peacefully once the games are over. Of course, he still doesn't know who's behind all this and I know he'll be loath to lose to a man barely in his twenties! Which could make him dangerous."

"How can you be so sure he'll lose, Father?" I asked.

"Don't worry, he will. He has been getting coached in Quark and has gotten very good, but the man he is playing has been playing the game since he was three. Nobody can beat him, not even your uncle."

"Who's the man?" asked Phillip.

"A fellow who lives very far away and whom my men recruited for the job. He has quite a reputation where he comes from, although he keeps his skills mostly to himself. The rumor is that he even plays around the world and usually wins big. He's smart and patient. I have a lot of confidence in him."

"Wow," I said, "he sounds pretty remarkable."

Father smiled.

"What's his name?" queried Jeffrey.

"Um, I'm not real sure," answered Father, "they call him Skeet or Maverick or Shark or such."

"But you've met him, right?" I asked.

"Oh yes, it's just that he doesn't like to let others know his real name so that he can remain discreet." Father was still smiling and for some reason I felt he knew this fellow's real name, but wasn't telling us. Anyway, it didn't matter, my stomach had butterflies from the excitement I felt about going home. We finished breakfast as Father answered many more of our questions.

"I always knew where you were. No, I didn't know about the Inky Dinks, and I'm very sorry you had to go through that. They are nasty little critters. You were all very brave. Since I came from the south, I didn't have to cross that stream. Yes, I saw James. He is a loyal friend and kept me up on your travels and gave me regular updates on Emi and your mom. He is presently near the castle, helping to set up the last of the plans. Yes, Mother and Emi are doing well. They have each other and the city is large so it has everything they need. Your mother has made a couple of friends. She refuses to leave Emi's side at the hospital except when Emi is asleep. Then she might take a walk, window shop, eat, or nap. Bobby, here, will leave this afternoon and go back to Escavaro to report to Victoria on where we are and how you are doing."

"Can I go with him?" I anxiously asked, and the boys wanted to go too.

"I don't think so, Blue, It would only complicate things and Bobby won't have the room for you, I'm sorry."

I thought it was such a brilliant idea. I could go help Mother and Emi and free up space in the wagon. When he said no, I was extremely downfallen, but managed, I thought, to hide my disappointment. I got up and began collecting the dishes.

"We'll stay here most of the day, then head out again this evening. By morning we should be near enough that you should recognize some familiar landscape.

Then, as they say, it should be smooth sailing!" He said this as he raised his arms in the air in a grand, punctuated gesture with a big smile on his scruffy face. It was just then that I noticed that he hadn't shaved or had a haircut in many days; however, he looked tanned, muscular, healthy and happy. I couldn't help but smile.

He continued, "So the day will be yours to enjoy as you please. I noticed a small creek over there you can explore if you'd like."

Soon, everyone was up and bustling about. The boys helped with a few chores and I loaded the dishes in a large basket to take to the creek in the direction Father had pointed. I heard the boys laughing and bounding their way up to me. We were all in good spirits, except that I still wished I could go with Bobby to see Emi and Mother. Oh well, it would be only a couple more days. When we got to the bank, I noticed that it was a fine little creek indeed. There were ripples and eddies and small but deep water holes in various spots along the way. There were even little sandbars enclosed by soft shrubs. The water was cool and refreshing. The boys were not modest and stripped down to their naked bottoms and jumped in.

After washing the dishes and setting them out to dry, I couldn't resist doing the same, so I unclothed down to my underwear and jumped in too. We romped in the cool, refreshing water, splashing and playing, swimming and bathing all at the same time. As the boys continued to play, I climbed onto a sandbar in the middle of the stream where I could lie down, hidden by the foliage, and let the air dry my goose-bumped skin. I fell into a dream-like state of quietness and peace. My senses were alert and bright to the feeling of the hairs on my neck, chest and arms getting prickled by the air, listening to the rippling and gurgling of the water and rustle of the weeds, to the birds chirping and tiptoeing through the branches of trees, and the sounds of the boys laughing and splashing a short distance away. I was so relaxed that perhaps a nap snuck up on me, because I was suddenly shocked when the boys shouted, "Boo!" It made me jump and bolt to my elbows as the boys guffawed. I was mad for about ten seconds, and then started laughing too. Phillip said he had an idea; he thought we should make something for Emi that Bobby could take to her in the hospital, to let her know we were thinking about her. I thought it was brilliant and we began tossing around ideas. Since we couldn't agree on one particular item, we decided to each make an individual gift instead. So the boys dried off with their clothes as I waded across a shallow spot, trying not to get too wet again. We dressed and gathered up the cookware and headed back to the wagon.

The men were working on the wagon, inspecting the damage by the Inks and of the river crossing, and doing what was necessary to fix any problems. The boys put on fresh clothes and we went about gathering items for the gifts they could make. We had scraps of material, string, paper, needles, thread, buttons, lace, pencils, and of course, lots of natural items to choose from around the camp. I decided to make Emi some gloves out of some soft material and pieces of leather we had in our craft box. Once I got my supplies together I sat down in the shade of a nearby tree and began my project. Jeffrey went off and was collecting pine cones, pine needles, leaves, sticks and other such items, while Phillip was somewhere off on his own.

An hour or so went by and I heard Father's voice, looking for us. He saw me under the tree, walked up with a quizzical look on his face and asked what I was doing. I told him about Phillip's idea and that I was making some gloves for Emi. I held them up to show him. I had pieced together some of the leather for the palms with some thick pink felt for the top. Inside, I had sewn some plain wool fabric, hoping they would be nice and warm. I was just finishing sewing some lace around the cuffs. They looked really nice and I thought I might make some for myself and Mom in the days to come. The boys were approaching with their projects as Father was admiring my handiwork. He had his fingers on his chin and kept cocking his head back and forth; he said my gloves were quite nice but, trying not to alarm me or hurt my feelings, carefully pointed out that I might have made a mistake; the right glove was missing a finger, but as soon as he said it he began laughing out loud. When the boys came up to look, Phillip too began laughing but Jeffrey wasn't getting it. Father pointed out that I had made the right glove without the index finger, the one that Emi no longer had! He thought it was very funny and that Emi would love them.

"You don't think she'll be offended?" I asked.

"No, no. I think she'll see the humor in them and the usefulness. I think they're very nice."

Then he asked to see what the boys had made. Jeffrey held up a scrap of wood that had all kinds of objects attached to it. He said it was a picture of our journey from start to finish, made mostly with forest material. He had used sap for glue, he used a thick pencil to draw outlines of the wagon, rivers, landscapes; the circus tent was made using some white and red material for the tent, and he cleverly carved, painted and drew little animals from bark. The Inky Dinks were made of squished ants, and he made some rather odd-looking horses out of pebbles, grasses and mosses. He found a round seed that he designated as the town of Pea. Then he had filled the landscape with bark, pine needles, straw, string, dried-up flowers and leaves. He even had made tiny stick figures of each of us in various places on the board. It was a scrambled, yet pleasing picture. Jeffrey is not usually the thoughtful or creative one, but he managed to show some skills and a work of love with this.

With much enthusiasm we asked to see what Phillip had made. He had been standing quietly with his arms behind his back, but now he brought them forth and showed us a beautiful little doll about five inches tall from head to foot. The head and body were made by stuffing cotton and moss into some muslin pieces, then tying them together with strands of twine around the neck, legs and arms. He had made the hair out of pieces of Bobby's horse's tail, which is black, attaching it meticulously to the doll's head by needle and thread. He trimmed it into a neat shoulder-length cut. The cute little face was made with tiny buttons for the eyes and nose, and he sewed a little line for her lips and used a dab of wild red raspberry juice for color; then he had sewn in some eyebrows. Her eyes were a little lopsided but her expression was very sweet. He had clothed her in a flowery little dress made of some material he had found in the craft box. The doll was very soft, sturdy and easy to hold in one hand. I could see Emi loving it.

Father was very pleased with our projects. "Very thoughtful indeed. These are very nice gifts. She misses all of you and I'm sure getting these will make her very happy. Now gather up your things, it's getting late and Bobby will be heading out soon. We'll eat something, then get on the road ourselves."

A fire was roaring in the fire pit near the wagon; the warmth made me realize that I'd gotten a little chilled sitting under the tree and that it was later in the afternoon than I realized. I took the gloves inside, put on my sweater and went immediately to the fire, warming my hands and feet. Wilt and Bobby had started cooking some food, while Ohm fiddled, as he most frequently did, with various tools and equipment, usually fixing or repairing something. On the fire was a pot of heavenly scented chicken stew with vegetables, fresh pan biscuits browning in a cast iron skillet, and what looked to be an apple cobbler just beginning to bubble in another pan. These men were quite resourceful and knew how to eat well! The boys got dressed in warmer clothing and joined me at the fire. When the food was ready, we poured some cups of milk for ourselves while the men drank mugs of beer. The meal was marvelous and quite filling. I even asked them for the recipes for the biscuits and cobbler.

Soon the dishes were washed and put away and I retreated to the wagon to wrap up the gloves. Father knocked on the doorway, asking if he could come in, and without waiting for an answer made his entrance. "Blue, I've been thinking, I'm gonna let you go to Escavaro with Bobby after all. Bobby says it's not a problem at all for him and he would like the company. Besides, I think you deserve some time away from the boys and this road trip. You can visit Mother and Emi and see what the big city has to offer."

"Oh Father," I said as I jumped up to hug him. "That's the best news I've ever had! Thank you! What should I take? What should I wear? When are we leaving?" I asked excitedly.

"You can take that old knapsack I have, with a few clothes. I'd wear your long underwear and riding pants to get there. Wear some layers on top to keep you warm. Maybe your sweater would be good." As he was talking, I was already gathering up some items. "Don't take too much, as there isn't a lot of room to pack it on Bobby's horse."

"What about our gifts to Emi?" I asked.

"Don't worry, we'll find room for those," he said as he stepped out of the wagon. I was so excited I could barely think straight, and bustled about until I thought I had everything together. I wrapped Emi's gloves in some tissue paper and string and bounded out of the wagon. The boys had securely wrapped up their gifts in oil-paper and twine, and were helping Father and Bobby pack up the horse and supplies.

The boys seemed only slightly disappointed that they couldn't go too, but teased me about getting rid of another smelly sister and how much more room they'd have in the wagon, and now they can do whatever they want, 'cause they would be with the men. "Yeah, we can fart too!" Jeffrey exclaimed. Phillip batted him in the arm.

Bobby mounted the horse and Father gave me a big hug before helping me up behind him. They rigged a leather strap around my waist, attached to the saddle to keep me secure. "I don't want you falling off if you fall asleep," Bobby said in jest, and patted my thigh.

Father surreptitiously slipped me a small leather pouch heavy with some coin. "Get yourself something nice when you get there," he said with a smile and a wink. We said our goodbyes and trotted off. It felt so good to be free! To be headed to a big city! To see Emi and Mother, whom I've missed.

I felt a little awkward at first, straddling behind and riding off with this man I didn't really know, but Bobby began to make me feel very comfortable by chatting and conversing. He wanted to know all about me: my interests, what I liked to read and study, and about some of the adventures on my travels. We talked a lot about books, as he was an avid reader, mostly of history. I told him how I've learned to cook and use herbs and spices, which led to a long conversation about food and recipes, which Bobby had a major interest in. He said all the women in his family were good cooks and he couldn't help growing up appreciating the finer details of taste and of meal preparation. His favorite dish to make was spaghetti and meatballs, passed on from his Italian grandmother "who always used a hint of fennel in her meatballs." We'd stop now and then to stretch our legs and let the horse rest, then be on our way again. He said it would take about six or seven hours to get to Escavaro. I asked him a little about the city. He told me how large it was, and there was a castle on the hill that belonged to King Robert III and his family. He said the city had everything you could imagine: dress and clothing stores, butchers, a library, candy stores, stores for food and vegetables, shoes, gifts, linen, glassware, hats and lots more. It sounded wonderful and I was especially excited to see what the library had to offer. So, on we went, talking and laughing; Bobby was witty and had a good sense of humor. I found out he was 24 years old and a rancher by trade, but that he often did courier work to be able to travel and make some extra money.

Eventually the day turned to dusk. We stopped for a short time to make a small fire and eat some dried beef, crackers, cheese and hot tea. As we sat there, I began to realize that Bobby was a very handsome man with a twinkle in his eye and a permanent smile on his face. He was very comfortable with himself and confident. I could tell he knew what he was doing and could take care of himself... and me, if anything should happen.

I was deep in my thoughts when he said, "I hope you know how well respected your father and family are."

I looked up, a little puzzled.

"King Hamilton is well known in many parts. He has lots of allies and friends. The plan he has put into place to regain your kingdom is solid and there is no doubt that in a few days, you will all be back home safe and sound again."

I was shocked! "How do you know all that?" I asked. "Nobody's supposed to know. We were sworn to secrecy, to keep our identities unknown," I said with a little indignation.

"I'm sorry, I guess I didn't know that," he demurred, as he refilled my cup of tea and pulled a small canteen out of his knapsack.

"So, what else do you know?" I asked curiously.

"I know pretty much all about your travels, there have been many people watching out for your family. We have been working with your father all along. It is very important to a very large region that your father regains power and that your uncle be banished. He's a very ugly man and would not do this world any good."

"What makes my father so important?" I asked.

"When he first came to power after your grandfather died, he made a point to meet and get to know other kings and important officials in all of the provinces. By doing that, and breaking the age-old code of isolation, he was able to forge communications that went well beyond a hello and friendly slap on the back. Instead, he was able to open up trade routes, create jobs and put more people to work. Small farms and ranches were able to grow, and towns and cities began to thrive, and it was all due to your father."

"How could I not know all this?"

"Well, part of your father's charm is his fairness and humility. This all started long before you were born, even when your grandfather was still alive. To you, he's just a dad who runs his kingdom, not a braggart like your uncle. Not many children learn the importance of their parents until they are much older. Information travels fast and your father's reputation became well known. I learned about him a few years back when he came to Begali, where I'm from. I was doing some odd jobs for the magistrate when your father showed up. That's when I met him. I guess we kinda hit it off and we've been friends since."

I pondered that for a moment, then asked, "Does my mother know about all those people helping us out?"

"That, I don't know, but I suspect she must've. By the way, you look a lot like her, very pretty."

I didn't expect that and I only hoped that there was enough flickering firelight to hide my blush. Then he offered me a sip from his canteen. "Would you like some?" he asked, holding forth the container.

"Oh no, thanks, I don't drink alcohol, unless it's a bit of wine from our cellar on a special occasion, and that's been forever."

"Suit yourself, but it's just going to get colder tonight and this will help warm you."

"Maybe, just a little bit," I said, feeling a little more grown up, on my own, and hadn't I been making my own decisions? *What will a couple of sips hurt?* I thought as I emptied the last of my tea and held my cup out. He poured just a little, and I took a cautious sip of the strong elixir and scrunched up my face in response. Bobby giggled and said, "Not like your wine. This is whiskey. It takes a little getting used to. Don't drink it if you don't want."

But I tried a tiny sip more. It was very strong and bitter. Another little sip and I could feel it warming my throat and stomach. Bobby began cleaning up as I lingered by the fire. Whiskey wasn't so bad after all. I finished it and got up to help him. I felt a little flushed and a little giddy in a good way, and I was glad to have been offered the drink. I was feeling pretty lazy but mimicked Bobby's moves, and soon we had mounted the horse. Bobby had thrown a heavy blanket over my back and shoulders, one long enough to cover my thighs. It was very cozy and smelled of hay, firewood, and cinnamon. We chatted a little more as we started down the road, but I was getting sleepy. He must have sensed that because our conversation fell silent.

Suddenly I was awakened by mumbled voices and laughing, and a distant clanging. I sheepishly realized I had fallen asleep against Bobby's back with my arms wrapped around him. When I lifted my head up, I saw a small drizzle of drool that I'd left on the back of his coat and quickly wiped it off with the blanket, hoping Bobby wouldn't wonder what I was doing. I hoped it wouldn't leave a stain. We were clippity-clopping through a city. A big one! Escavaro! Although it must have been quite late, there were people on the roads, the saloons were busy with music and laughter, the shop windows were dazzling with reflections from the amber glowing lanterns that lined the cobblestone streets and boardwalks. Bobby brought us to a halt in front of a hotel, dismounted, and threw the reins over a hitching post.

"Come on down now, sleepyhead. My instructions were to bring you here. This is where Victoria is staying," he said as he nodded his head toward me and extended his arm, his fingers signaling me along.

Finally, I was oriented. "Mother!" I exclaimed as I nearly fell off the horse in my excitement to get down.

"Whoa, whoa, careful there. You don't want to fall and break your neck and end up in the hospital with your sister, do you?" he said with a grin. "Follow me, your mother is waiting."

We stepped into an open, airy lobby with high ceilings, a floral carpet that ran wall to wall, white wainscot and pretty wallpaper. The furniture appeared soft and comfortable, and there was a scent of hyacinths in the air.

As I gazed around, I peered into a sitting room off to the side, and noticed the hair on the top of the head of a person sleeping in an overstuffed chair with her back to me. I approached quietly and sure enough, it was Mother.

"Mom," I said in a whisper so as not to startle her. She drowsily opened her eyes and raised her head. As soon as she saw me she jumped up and wrapped me in her arms. "Oh Blue, I'm so happy to see you! It seems like ages!" and she proceeded to ask me questions in such rapid fire that I wasn't able to answer a one. Finally she said, "You must be exhausted, let's go upstairs and get you settled in."

As we passed through the lobby, Bobby was just finishing the registering process for his own room. He beamed at our smiles and Mother thanked him for getting me there safe. I too thanked him and he said he hoped to see us tomorrow. When we got to our room, I was suddenly overtaken with exhaustion and saddle soreness and plopped down on the bed.

"Here, you must be famished. I saved a sandwich and some fruit for you," Mother said, as she handed me the items and a glass of water. I didn't know how hungry I was until I started eating.

"How did you know I was coming? Father almost didn't let me."

"We talked about it before he returned to you. I had a hunch he would relent. But it depended on how Bobby felt about having a passenger along. I want to hear all about your recent days and the boys, how are they doing? How was the ride over?" And so we talked while I ate, both of us sitting on the edge of the bed. I told her everything I could remember, and she filled me in on Emi and her health. She said she was doing very well and would be released from the hospital in another day or two. I could see her tomorrow. I told her about the presents we made for her and she told me a little about the city. "Oh Blue, you're gonna love it! There's so much to see and do, and just down the hill is the ocean! It's beautiful! I want you to experience it all," she said.

I cleaned up and changed into a nightgown, climbed into bed next to my mother, and fell immediately into a deep, peaceful, dream-filled sleep.

Chapter 23

It was late morning when I awoke. Mother was already up and dressed. She greeted me with a cheery "Good morning," followed with "You may sleep in as long as you like. I'm going down to talk to Bobby for a bit and have some coffee. Take your time. We'll get some breakfast when you come down and go see Emi later." And with that, she was off.

It felt heavenly to lounge under the crisp sheets and covers of a real bed. My sore legs and tush reminded me of how many hours I'd spent on horseback. The sun was streaming through the windows and I could hear the faint bustle of the city below. I lay there daydreaming and just thinking. It was luxury! I must have dozed off for a few minutes longer, but when I awoke the second time I was fully awake and ready to get on with the day. I was so anxious to see Emi, and the city! And the ocean!

Our room had a separate room for bathing with a sink, toilet and tub. So I stripped down and took advantage of a much-needed bubble bath. This hotel was truly fancy. It had indoor plumbing and little bottles of bubble bath, hair wash, soap, powder and lotion for guests to use. I wondered about the cost of such a room. Soon I was clean, dry and freshened up. I knew I smelled better and was a little embarrassed to think of how long it had been since I'd had a proper bath. My hair was in wet clean tangles, my feet damp and without the pervasive dust between my toes. As I gazed in the mirror above the sink, I was surprised to see someone I barely recognized. My skin was tanned by the sun, my freckles were a softer shade of brown, and my hair was longer and wavier, with sun-brightened highlights. My body was more curved and my breasts larger. Had we really been gone long enough for these changes to happen?

I kept staring at my image as I combed my hair and turned side to side. I liked what I saw. I felt feminine, older. I tried different ways to fix my hair and settled on a low ponytail, fastened with a band at the nape of my neck, a few tendrils escaping around my face. I strode naked into the bedroom and began to get dressed. I put on a clean albeit drab shirt and a corduroy skirt, pulled on my only shoes—boots—and headed out the door.

Mother and Bobby were sitting at a cloth-covered table in a small dining area. The room was filled with natural light, lovely carpets and furnishings and lace curtains. I took a seat and was greeted with smiles from both of them. "Hi honey, how did you sleep?" she said, as she fingered some strands of my fresh hair in a loving sort of way.

"My, don't you look rested and well and quite pretty this morning," said Bobby. I blushed and thanked him for the compliment.

"Here are your art projects. I suspect you want to give them to Emi when you see her." He held up his knapsack, then set it down beside my chair. I ordered some tea and a light breakfast of fruit and a muffin from the waitress. I ate slowly as Mother and Bobby finished their conversation, which had to do with business of our land and management. I didn't really follow it. My mind was elsewhere, anxious to get out and see Emi and the city.

Soon, we were finished and stood up. Bobby shook Mother's hand and kissed the back of it. "It was so nice seeing you again, Victoria. I'll be seeing you again soon." Then he turned to me and said, "I enjoyed your company on the ride here. It made it less lonely and much more enjoyable. Perhaps we could meet for lunch or tea before you head home?"

"Perhaps," I said shyly and looked at Mother, who was simply smiling.

He then took my hand and kissed the back of it as well. Such a gentleman!

We all walked out together, and he held the door open for us and tipped his hat as he headed down the boardwalk. "He's a nice man," I said to Mother.

"Yes, he is, and I can tell he likes you. Let's go! I've got a big day planned for you. First stop, the hospital!" I threw the knapsack strap over my shoulder and ran to catch up with her.

The city was vibrant, full of life and color. The towns-people dressed in very fine clothes, the men in top hats, shiny shoes, pinstriped suits, bow ties, waistcoats. They had trimmed beards and mustaches, and most carried canes. I also noticed several men wearing denim, with holsters and guns at their hips. Most of the women were dressed in beautiful full dresses of lace, embroidery, buttons, and pearls. They had on sparkly earrings and necklaces, and hats of all kinds, and some carried parasols. The younger citizens tended to be dressed in a hodgepodge of clothing, still, somehow classy. The boardwalks were clean and litter free and the streets were laid with cobblestone. There were people on horseback, some guiding wagons, dogs herding sheep down the middle of the road. Workers, cleaners, trash collectors and many other service types were going about their day. Every window we passed was a shop or business of some kind: apothecary, hat shops, tailors, bakery, cloth-ing stores, shoe stores, restaurants, pubs and bars, a magic shop, a small museum, a butcher's, flower shop, a law office. It was overwhelming and very exciting. I wanted to stop and look in them all, but Mother was walking ahead with a purpose and I did all I could to keep up.

We passed by a nice park with a small playground for children, a fountain and gazebo, and just on the other side was the hospital. It was much bigger than I expected. Three stories, a large entrance surrounded by a grassy area, some park benches and flowerpots full of color and greenery. Inside the door was a reception area that Mother bypassed and went straight to the lift. I'd never been in a real hospital before and I didn't know what to expect. The hallways were bright with clean white tiles, arched windows and high ceilings. Nurses in uniform and doctors in white coats were bustling about, deep in thought of their daily plans. We rode the lift to the second floor and stepped out to a nursing station. The nurses at the desk exchanged pleasantries with Mother, and Nurse Ruth (it said on her name tag) told us that Emi was in good spirits and had slept well. She said Dr. Sanders would be in a little later.

We headed down to Room 202. Mother knocked softly and walked in. I was close behind but little apprehensive.

Emi was sitting up in bed with a stuffed toy next to her. As soon as she saw us she beamed brightly. I ran and wrapped her in my arms. "I'm so happy to see you! How do you feel? When can you come home?" I asked all at once.

Mother had taken a seat beside her on the other side of the bed and gave her a kiss on the forehead.

"I feel much better, but see my hand?" she said, as she held up her bandaged hand with her index finger obviously missing. It took me back a bit, but I tried not to let her notice. "It seems to look good from what I can tell. It's no longer swollen. Does it hurt?" I responded.

"Just a little bit, but it's better every day. The nurse cleans my hand and changes the dressing twice a day, and Dr. Sanders said I should be able to leave here, maybe tomorrow."

"That's great, Emi. We've all missed you. Oh, I almost forgot. Your brothers and I made you some gifts," I said as I pulled the projects out of the knapsack, handing her one at a time. "Here, this one's from Jeffrey. He wanted to show you our journey. He put it together with objects he found around our last camp spot. See, here's the carnival and some animals made from seeds and feathers, he drew the road connecting everything, but look, here's Iznot and the circus and Pea is that one seed. He smushed some ants into tree sap to make them shiny like the Inky Dinks, but didn't want to show much of them, that's why they look more like blobs." I looked at Emi's face as she held up the picture and looked at all it depicted. She was smiling her biggest. "I love it!" she exclaimed.

Then I pulled out the doll Phillip had made. She was amazed and fascinated. "He made this?"

"Yes, see how he made her hair from the tail hair of a horse, and then he trimmed it? He even made this dress for her."

"I'm going to call her Isabelle. I'll love her forever!"

I noticed Mother was rapt with smiles and interest, and wanted to look more closely at the gifts once Emi had passed them to her. I was reluctant to give her mine. I should have made her a toy or something else. Now I was afraid she would be hurt. I slowly removed it from the knapsack and while doing so explained, "Emi, these are what I made for you. The weather was turning cold in the mountains and I thought you could use a pair of gloves for your journey home, but I'm afraid I may have misjudged. I hope you're not offended."

I gave her the tissue package and watched as she opened it. She held the gloves up, a left one and a right one, inspecting each with care. A frown of puzzlement, then a slow smile crept across her face, a giggle then a hearty laugh. "This one is missing a finger!" she exclaimed as she held the right one up for Mother to see. Mother opened her mouth in a bit of shock, and then began laughing too. I was so relieved and giggled along with them. She tried them on. The left fit perfectly. She wasn't able to fit the right one on all the way over the bandage, but we could see that it was also going to be a perfect fit once her hand was free of the dressings.

"They are so warm and pretty, Blue. I love them! Thanks."

Mother said, "You did a real nice job, Blue. They look very warm and comfortable, and thank you for bringing a little humor into a dark situation."

We chatted over the projects a little longer and then I picked up the stuffed animal, a rabbit, sitting next to Emi. "Who's this?" I asked.

"That's Sniffles! Anton brought 'im to me!"

Mother interjected, "She insists Anton visited her one night and left her the rabbit. I tried to tell her that Anton was far away and that maybe it was a nurse or one of the nuns that visits children in the hospital, but she won't hear of it."

"It was him! I know it was. He whispered to me to get well and put the bunny under my arms. I was sleepy but tried to open my eyes so I could see him. When I did, he was just pulling the door shut behind him. But I know it was him! I could tell by his voice."

We stayed for a while longer, walked her around the hallways, brushed her hair, talked to the nurses and doctor while they changed her dressing and inspected the wound and stitches. The wound was clean, with just a slight hint of redness at the seam of stitches. I could tell it was still a little tender as they removed the dressing, cleaned the wound and re-bandaged it, but Emi seemed to accept it with just a squint.

"She is doing very well," said the doctor. "We should be able to let her go home maybe as soon as tomorrow. She'll have to follow strict instructions and you too, Victoria, you'll have to watch this closely. She should probably rest now. You may come later on to visit again." He was a tall, slim man with sandy hair (Dr. Sanders, of course) wearing a white hospital coat and a fine bow tie. His name tag confirmed that he was Dr. Sanders.

Mother thanked him and we gave Emi a hug. Our visit indeed tired her out; she fell asleep as we were going through the door.

"I'm so glad she is doing well. I was really worried about her," I said as we made it down the hall.

"Yes, she's a brave little girl, and seems to be taking her new challenge in stride. They have been working with her to teach her how to hold utensils and write without that finger, and she is doing remarkably well," said Mother.

We talked about Emi until we left the hospital. Then Mother turned to me and said, "Okay, now it's time to take you out on the town! First to the hair salon for a nice wash and trim, then we'll get you some new clothes. After that, I'll show you the city, it's so beautiful!" she said enthusiastically.

"Does it have a library?" I asked smiling, as I hurried along.

"Oh, you bet. A very big one too. Come on, let's be on our way."

First stop, the hair salon, which was on 4th Street tucked between a hardware shop and a bakery. The smell of fresh bread and pastries was intoxicating and I couldn't help stopping to gaze at the delicacies through the window. "Later, come on now," Mother said with a smile.

We stepped into the salon, where there were three swivel chairs just for the clients, two of them occupied by women in various stages of coifing, draped in pink and white gowns covering their clothes and arms. Across the room were a couple of nice upholstered chairs for visitors, along with a silver tea service on a coffee table and magazines to flip through. There was a lot of friendly chatter and the sound of scissors snipping, brushes brushing, and soft music in the background.

The proprietor took long strides across the shop to meet us. "Hello, Victoria! This must be the daughter you've been talking about! What a pretty young lady," she said as she gently took a strand of my hair in her fingers.

"This is Blue, my oldest. Honey, this is Mrs. Merkle, she owns the shop."

We said our hellos. "Your mother has been such a delight to get to know, very smart woman I must say. My, your hair is beautiful! What would you like done? Let's get you over to this chair and have a chat. How old are you again? You must have had a long journey. Have you seen our city yet? You must visit the museum, and the ocean! And we have a lovely park with lots of flowers."

I looked at Mother for guidance, as this woman was one stream of thought and question after another, but no way to answer. Mother just nodded, suggesting "just go with it." I followed Mrs. Merkle to the chair and let her drape me. As she continued to chat on she pulled back my hair, lifted it, scrunched it in her hands, felt the thickness and texture then said, "First, your hair is rather dry, so a good wash and conditioner would do wonders. It's so nice and thick but I think you would do well with a style that would uplift it and create body, and trim it to frame your face, bring out the curls and your natural highlights. We should cut a few inches from the length, but not much, maybe give you some wispy bangs too." She looked at me and Mother. "What do you think? Maybe you'd prefer a bob? Some of the young girls are doing that now. Fashionable at the universities, but personally, I think it makes them look too much like boys."

Mother chimed in, "No, I'm betting Blue would like to keep it a little longer, am I right, Blue?"

Ah, my chance! "Yes, I think trimming a little and shaping is good. I don't want a fringe, as I like to pull it back from time to time. Simple, I think," I said with less conviction than I'd planned.

"Very well!" said Mrs. Merkle. "Let's get started." She guided me to a shampoo sink and for the next hour, I was literally in her hands. She gave me a good sudsy scrub while massaging my scalp, then dabbed on a thick conditioner, rinsing thoroughly after each step. She led me back to the salon chair and began deftly cutting away; lifting here, pinning this piece back while trimming there. I was fascinated with her every move and skillful use of scissors and comb. I thought about how surgeons must use their instruments just as precisely. I answered her questions as she would let me, but mostly listened to her talk about many different subjects. Mother had taken a seat in the lounge area and was peacefully reading a magazine and sipping on some tea, glancing up from time to time to watch the progress. When finished, I was very happy. My hair was shiny, wavy, and smooth and smelled faintly of honeysuckle. She had cut it to about mid-neck length and had shaped it in such a way as to be quite flattering. My highlights shone and my skin and eyes seemed to pop. When Mother saw me she said, "Oh, my. Honey, you look stunning!"

More small talk ensued, I paid Mrs. Merkle with some of the money Father had given me, and we were on our way.

"Next stop," Mother said, "to get you some new clothes."

My hair felt buoyant, light and sexy as we made our way down the road between people, baby strollers, horses and wagons. Mother pulled me into a shop before I had a chance to read the sign on the door. It was a store exclusively for undergarments! I didn't know there was such a specialized store. Mother had always bought them for me before. I had never shopped for any myself. At first I was shy and embarrassed, but Mother stepped right up to the counter and casually introduced us to the saleswoman. Her name was

Miss Handkerchief. At least that's what I thought I heard. It was really Miss Hankesschoff. Obviously German. A very pretty woman in her thirties I would say, with her blonde hair pulled up into a braid around her head, smooth skin and blue eyes, lighter than mine. She had an enviable figure and wore a very flattering dress. I was intimidated but she immediately put me at ease when she guided me over to some displays of underwear and bras. She picked out a few things she thought might fit and sent me to try them on in the dressing room, while Mother browsed the shop.

Miss Hankesschoff would pop in now and then to check on my progress, catching me near naked and embarrassed, but she was so skilled and knowledgeable that soon I was more relaxed, and although my modesty nearly overwhelmed me, I was nonetheless having fun. When I removed my old bra I realized that it was so worn out and sheer that by now it looked almost like fine lingerie. The new bras I tried with the help of my "personal attendant" fit snugly and comfortably and gave my breasts a flattering contour. I picked out four. Each had some kind of feminine adornment, a pink bow, some lace, a little pastel ribbon. I did the same with underwear and a new slip, finding equally beautiful pieces. I left with a new set on—I couldn't bear putting my old, dingy, sagging and torn things back on. They went straight into the trash! The rest of the finery was wrapped in tissue paper and placed in a pretty bag with a small rope handle.

Next, the clothing store. I didn't know shopping could be so much fun! I bounced through the doorway of "Jessie's

Fine Clothing for Women," my confidence now high. The shop was busy with several women browsing racks of dresses, skirts, blouses, parasols, hats, gloves and such. I had never seen so much all at once in one place, and just for women! A saleslady, who didn't introduce herself and seemed a bit stuffy, directed Mother and me to an area of clothing for my size. Mother started looking through the rack like an expert. She'd hold something up and ask if I liked it. "What about this? I think this would look good on you, here's a blouse with a nice color for you," then on to the next item. I was browsing myself and amazed at the choices and taken aback by the prices, but found several items that struck my fancy.

Next thing I knew, I was being directed to a dressing room with an armful of clothes to try, Mother right behind me. The room was small but big enough for the both of us to move and turn around in. There was a little upholstered chair where Mother took a seat, and a large mirror for viewing. Mother handed me one piece after another as I tried them on. *This one doesn't fit right but I like this dress, don't you? Here, try this blouse with that skirt. Oh yes, nice! Yes, I like it too.* And on it went, mother and daughter, giggling, commenting, remarking until after an hour I had found just what I wanted. I walked out with a pretty dress on, fitted at the waist with a sassy sash, small pearl buttons gathering down the front, a flattering neckline and bodice that showed off my new, uplifted figure. In my bag bulging to the top were a full, soft skirt made of cotton and silk that came to my knees and flounced as I walked, two more dresses, a pair of flattering pants, four blouses, a belt and a new purse. My money was dwindling fast but Mother smiled and said I deserved a new set of clothes. I had gone too long without.

"Oh, but what to do about my horribly worn, scuffed-up shoes?"

"Not to worry," said Mother. "It will be our last stop, then we'll have some lunch and I'll show you some of the town." So, off we went again, me with my precious packages and Mother leading the way.

The experience was exhilarating and I breathed in every sight and sound, smell and feel of the city. The shoe shop was a little less exciting, but fruitful. I left wearing a new pair of comfortable ankle-length, brown leather shoes that were cut with a little flare and some cross stitching, just what I needed to complete my new outfit. I also got another pair of more practical shoes to travel and to run around in. When we stepped out into the sunlight, Mother took my shoulders, looked me up and down and said, "Blue, you have grown into a lovely young woman. I am so proud of you," and wrapped me in her arms for a big hug. "Come on now, I'm hungry, what about you?"

"I'm starving," and off we went.

"We're going to meet Bobby at a favorite café. They serve delicious soups and sandwiches as well as stews, and other items."

On the way, I asked Mother about what she knew of Bobby. She told me that she had met him and Wilt some time back. She hadn't met Ohm until Pea, but said Father had talked about him over the years. She didn't know James at all and he was rather quiet, but he got her and Emi to the hospital very fast and with care. She said they were business associates of Father's and were helping in the plot to regain our castle. "There sure seems to be a lot of people involved in that," I said. She just smiled. She said these men had been of great help and she trusted them all.

We didn't have far to go to the café, but in those few blocks we passed all kinds of interesting storefronts festooned with flower boxes and sculptures in front: those selling knick-knacks, kitchen items, furniture, clothing of course, pottery, baby things and much more. I so wanted to stop and go in them all. Mother allowed me a peek in the windows, but knew if we lingered too long, we'd be late for lunch.

Chapter 24

We arrived at Café Monica at 3rd and Xeshlel Streets. It was busy, but Bobby was already there and had reserved a table. Fancy place, with white linen tablecloths and napkins, lots of shiny hard wood and wainscoting. There was a separate pub area and the whole place was full with business people and residents dressed in proper clothes. I felt out of place until I looked down at my new dress and shoes, and my hair was clean and cut, and I felt very good about myself. I strutted in behind Mother and was met at the table by a debonair-looking Bobby. He had cleaned up nicely and looked rather handsome. He stood and pulled chairs out for first my mother, then for me.

"My, Blue, you look simply lovely. I like the way you've done your hair." I blushed and said, "Thanks, you don't look so bad yourself."

"And Victoria, you always look like a queen." Mother just smiled and took a seat.

The menu was full of mouthwatering items to choose from, but I decided on a bowl of tomato, spinach and basil soup and a sliced turkey sandwich with lettuce, tomato, avocado (what a treat!), and some kind of olive compote spread on the turkey, served on fresh-baked and toasted sourdough bread. It was served with a side of fresh-cut fruit. Mother had a bowl of chicken and hominy in a light, aromatic broth with a little cheese and parsley sprinkled on top, served with a side of steamy cornbread. Bobby had the steak special, which was served with au jus and a side of steamed brussels sprouts. The meals tasted otherworldly and exotic. I saw other dishes of steamed clams, baked chicken, roasted lamb, grilled shrimp and other equally enticing dishes and sides being served all around us. I tried not to be rude, but couldn't help craning my head to see what wonderful dishes were passing by for fellow diners. We talked about this and that, Mother and Bobby excitedly telling me about the city and the ocean, and Bobby asked me if I had seen the palace yet. "What palace?" I asked, rather surprised.

"There's a beautiful palace on the hill to the south, but you can't see it very well from here, what with the tall buildings. It belongs to Count Armand Escavaro and his wife Andrea. It has been in their family since the early 1100s. They are the ones who established this town, which has evolved into a grand and rich city."

"How did they make their money?" I asked as I took another bite of my savory sandwich.

"The family started out in steel welding and apparently produced weapons for the war of the Domonots in the twelfth century. That brought them the bulk of their wealth. Then, with shrewd investing, shipping and foreign land buying, the money just multiplied. This is the wealthiest region in the whole realm. If your mother would allow, I'd love to show you around a bit and tell you more after lunch." He said this while looking coyly at my mother.

"I think that would be fine, Blue. I'd like you to experience more and it will give me time to wrap up some loose ends and get over to the hospital again."

"I want to spend more time with Emi too," I said, sounding poutier than I meant to.

"Oh, you can. Why don't you have Bobby bring you back to the hospital at say,

around four?" I was torn but so very excited to see more of this wonderful city, and I knew I only had one day, so I agreed.

"It's settled then," said Bobby, as he took another bite of his juicy, tender steak.

After lunch, we stepped out into the warmth and sun on the boardwalk. There were a few wispy and fleeting clouds and just the slightest occasional breeze.

Mother took my shopping bags and headed toward the hotel, while Bobby guided me in the opposite direction.

The city was electric and bustling. So much to look at and shops to explore! We stopped in the culinary store and looked at all the shiny pots and pans, beautiful porcelain dinnerware and fancy silverware. There were all kinds of various utensils and objects for cracking an egg, peeling potatoes, scoops with holes in them, mixers, steamers and other modern supplies for cooking that I never would have imagined. We perused cookbooks and talked about food.

We went on down the road, passing multiple clothing shops and mercantile stores, a millinery store displaying very fine hats for men in the window, another bakery, more cafés. We passed by the opera theater and playhouse and then, the library! I was so excited and insisted on going in. It was a huge building with three levels. Stacks and stacks of books from floor to ceiling. There were open tables with work lights with people and students dutifully studying at them, and private little cubbies with comfy chairs and lamps. The floors were carpeted and as with all libraries, there was a hushed silence and muted whispers. I began looking at the various rows and categories of offerings and could have been lost in there for a week, but Bobby gently touched my arm and said, "This is a glorious library, but I've got another place to show you that I think you'll be equally as interested in."

"Another library?" I asked.

"Not exactly; come on, if we have time we can stop here again later." I reluctantly followed his lead, craning my head at as many titles as I could glimpse.

We walked another block and he guided me into "Penderback's Used Books and More." Another type of establishment I'd never heard of. The proprietor bought and sold used books at a lower price than new books. The store had a musty smell to it and a pall of dust seemed to hang in the air. The lighting was poor and it was small and cramped, with rows and rows of books. Not only were there books packed in the shelves, there were stacks on the floor and on top of the shelves. Most of them were pretty tattered and worn. Nothing like the pristine library we'd just been in, and I was a little disappointed. Bobby saw an older plump man toward the back of the store, standing on a small three-tiered wooden step stool, feather-dusting one of the shelves, which just seemed to spread more dust throughout the store.

"Hiya, John!" Bobby shouted as he headed toward the back. I followed.

"Looks like a never-ending job ya got there," said Bobby with a smile.

"Yep, but I never get tired of caring for these old gems. Oh look!" said John as he stepped off the stool with Bobby's hand on his elbow. "Come here, I just got this in the other day, and thought of you." He led us through a maze of books until he reached his counter. A customer had barely enough room to complete a transaction, what with the books and junk piled on it.

He leaned down behind the counter and came back up, blowing the dust off a book and gently brushing it with his hand. "Here ya go. It's a signed first edition print of 'The History of Man' by Edgar Powell. A mighty fine copy considering it's nearly a hunnert years old."

"Where did you get this!" asked Bobby, trying to hide his excitement

"A friend of mine who helps me find rare books came in with it. Said he found it while traveling in Italy. Figured I'd be interested. He was right. I paid him a fine dullur for that one."

"Wow, must be worth a small fortune," said Bobby as he carefully leafed through the pages. This whole time I was standing next to Bobby, just as fascinated by the old tome as he was, and as if he'd noticed me for the first time he turned to me.

"Oh, sorry, John. How rude of me. This is my friend Blue. I'm showing her around town. She's quite a reader herself. Blue, this is John Penderback. He's owned this store for thirty-five years."

"Good to meet you, sir," I said as I extended my hand to shake.

"Well, you certainly are a pretty one," he replied as he took my hand in his. "Wish I was younger. I'd swoop you right up for my own self!"

I blushed.

"So what kinds of readin' do you like, young lady?" He hadn't let go of my hand yet. He was dressed in rumpled brown trousers held up by a pair of suspenders over a faded blue and green-striped shirt, the tail of which was nearly untucked from his pants. He was portly, with a shock of messy gray hair and a short gray beard. He wore spectacles on his nose and peered over them while addressing us. He had a kindly face.

"I mostly like true adventure stories and good fiction."

"Well, I've got some goodies for you then," he said excitedly and trotted off through the rows again, excusing himself as he squeezed by a couple of customers thumbing through books of interest. He came upon an area of books labeled "Fiction" above the shelf and stopped.

"Here ya go. The adventure novels are in the next row over. Should keep ya busy lookin' for a while. Here's a goody I recommend. It's the true story of a fella who sailed the Indian Ocean but capsized and was adrift for a hunnert and twenty- one days before he landed on a deserted island. Quite exciting, this one," John said as he tapped on the cover and handed it over to me.

I started paging through it. There were so many interesting titles and subjects that I sat down on a little stool and pulled out one book after another. There was something about this stuffy place that was, despite its appearance, cozy and settling. Not at all like the library but equally as interesting. There was something beautiful and fascinating about the oldness of the store. I loved the smell of the old leather and paper jackets, the sound of the crisp pages as I flipped through them. I became lost in them and hadn't even noticed that Bobby and John had gone back to the counter, talking.

It must have been thirty minutes before Bobby found me, now sitting cross- legged on the floor near the fiction section, with several novels stacked by my knee.

"Ready to go, Blue? I've got lots more to show you." He shocked me out of my reverie.

"These books and choices are amazing! He has quite a collection."

"Yep, best bookstore this side of the world. Did you find any you'd like to get? I'm sure he'd give you a good deal. He likes to bargain."

"Well, yes, too many," I said as I glanced down at the stack I'd accumulated. "But I really don't have any money left after buying all these new clothes."

"Of all of those, which do you like the best?" Bobby asked "Bring them to the front and we'll see what John wants for them. You may be surprised at his prices."

So I picked out my top three choices. One was the one John had pointed out to me, another was a story of the first woman explorer to the western plains of Eurasia, and the third was a fiction about a brother and sister who lost their family in a terrible fire and sought to find distant relatives in a faraway city.

I took the books to the front where Bobby and John were still talking and joking. "Well, let's see what ya got there, Blue." I handed the books to John.

"Oh yes, these are all excellent choices."

"But I don't think I can afford them," I lamented.

"Well, let's see. This one, 'The Sailor's Story,' I'd sell for two quandries and a drew, and this here 'Shout to the Heavens' would normally go for six drew but I'd give it to you for four, and let's see, 'Finding Home' I could letcha have for a penny."

I'm sure he saw my face of disappointment, as I knew I didn't have enough money and certainly shouldn't be spending it on books. Then I heard Father's voice saying "get something nice for yourself and have fun."

John turned each book over and hummed and hawed. "Tell ya what, little lady, I'd take a pence and a half for all of 'em." I looked at Bobby, who had a bright and hopeful look on his face. He nodded slightly, indicating that it was a good deal.

"Okay," I said, pulled the money from my new purse and set it on the counter. John went about wrapping the books in brown paper, took the coins and handed me the package with a big smile.

"Thank you very much, sir. You have a very nice store."

"Why thank you!" He shook my hand. "She's a keeper," he whispered loudly and gave a wink to Bobby, who smiled and led me out of the store.

Bobby carried the package for me and continued to showed me all around town, the beautiful parks with fountains and green lawns, quaint neighborhoods with pretty little houses, all well kept, small lakes with trails around them. We stopped in what he exclaimed was "the best bakery in the world," where he bought us each a sugary puffed pastry that was so light and delicious it melted in my mouth. We laughed at each other's powdered-sugar-covered mouths and cheeks. Then we headed down to the ocean.

From town, you couldn't see it at all, but as we walked down a cobblestone road, I began to feel a slight breeze and smell the fresh air of ocean water; then I heard the waves, and there it was! It was beautiful and vast, with crashing waves doing their best to jump over a stone barrier holding it back from the promenade. The water was pure and clear and smelled of salt and fish. Bobby guided me to the left and we walked down the tree-shaded promenade until it met the sandy beach. It was lined with flower boxes, artful statues and benches. The path opened occasionally to tiny parks with green grass, picnic tables and play areas for children. At the beach we took off our shoes and strolled through the warm sand, massaging my tired feet and toes. A gentle wave occasionally made its way up the beach to kiss my feet and ankles, washing away the sand and leaving tiny seashells in its place. The warm air and breeze, the sound of the waves and squealing of small children playing in the water were intoxicating.

We came to sit down on a piece of driftwood, gazing out, dreaming, thinking. I could see a ship way off in the distance that appeared to sit on the very edge of a rippling piece of blue tissue paper, its hull pasted to the whiteness of the sky. To the south I could see a shipping area with boats and docks and occasionally I could hear the faint bellow of a horn. We sat in silence for the longest time. I loved the breeze soothing my face, flirting with my skirt and tickling my hair. The strength and power of the ocean were as humbling as the mountains I had recently passed through. I thought about the boys and Father, and wondered how their journey was going and hoped that it was uneventful and easy. I thought about Emi and the strength she had shown through her ordeal. I thought about my determined and resourceful mother, a woman I admired for her beauty, intelligence, her sweetness and her kind heart.

The time was coming very soon that we would be home again. Our adventure almost over, it will have been nearly year. So much had happened along the way. There were so many stories to tell. We had met so many interesting people. I had met Anton. My stomach gave a little lurch when

I thought about him. I wondered where he was now, what he was up to. Was he traveling again? I hadn't needed to wear the sweater since coming to Escavaro and I had left the necklace in the hotel room. Was that subconscious? Perhaps knowing that I might see Bobby today?

Just then, I was brought out of my deep thoughts by a light touch on the top of my hand. Bobby was placing a seashell on it. It was a small, twisted shell with the most intricate design and colored like a rainbow, shimmering in the dappled light. I brought it up to my eyes, balancing it carefully, still on the back of my hand. It was so perfect. Each curve of the shell made for a purpose, and the colors splashed like well-placed paint on a tiny canvas. Bobby was looking at me with expectation and I smiled widely.

"Blue, this may be inappropriate, but I wanted to say that I've really enjoyed the last couple of days getting to know you. You're not only beautiful, but very smart. You have such an easy nature. You're easy to talk to and it's not awkward to be silent at times with you."

By now, I had lowered my hand and was clutching the shell in my palm on my lap. I was blushing and relishing in his attention. I didn't expect this at all from Bobby and I was a little uncertain of my feelings. He seemed like such a self-made man. Someone who didn't need anyone else in his life, but as he spoke, he looked down at my hands, lightly brushing my fingers with his, then looked up to my face, gazing into my eyes. He was sincere and honest. He continued, "I'll be accompanying you home with Victoria and Emiline. I don't know if I'll see you after that, but Blue, the truth is that I'm really fond of you and I'd like to find a way to see you again sometime."

I gave him a second, not wanting to interrupt if he had more to say, but he just took a deep breath and seemed to relax. I was stunned and flattered and the truth was that I too, had enjoyed our time together and didn't want it to end. Surprising myself, I leaned forward and place a quick gentle kiss on his lips. It was sweet and thrilling. I had never done anything that bold before, but it felt like a natural thing to do. He smiled, then took my hand and stood.

"Come on," he said, "I have to get you back. Your mother is probably wondering if I kidnapped you." He helped me up from the log and steadied me as I brushed sand off my legs and skirt. On the way back I found another unique shell for Emi and tucked both shells in my pocket. We walked back, hand in hand, both of us grinning.

The city now seemed too noisy and busy. The sea had enveloped all the city noise and had been soothing and calming. The contrast was alarming. We made our way back to the hospital so that I could visit with Emi again.

"Here are your books" (which I'd nearly forgotten about). "Thank you for your company and allowing me to spend the day with you." He kissed the back of my hand.

"It is you I must thank," I said. "I never would have done or seen as much if it weren't for you. You are an excellent travel guide!" I said with exaggeration and flair, so that we both laughed. Then I kissed him on his cheek and turned to enter the hospital.

"Tell your mother I'll meet with her later to finalize plans for tomorrow."

"Will do," I responded, barely turning my head and giving a little wave.

The truth was that I was exhausted from the day and just needed some time to myself. A nice nap and a cup of tea would be a wonderful thing. But I was anxious to see Emi and Mother. I walked swiftly through the corridors, avoiding nurses, attendants, trays and gurneys, then bounded up the stairs to the second floor and into Emi's room. I was a little out of breath, my face was flushed and my hair, I'm sure, had lost its coiffure and was a mess as Mother looked at me, rather surprised. She was seated in a bedside chair with a book on her lap. "Goodness, where have you been?" It occurred to me that I might be looking like I'd been frolicking in a haystack and was suddenly a bit embarrassed.

"Oh, Bobby took me all around town and down to the water. Mom, have you seen it? It's beautiful! I got some shells. See?" I said as I pulled them out of my pocket. "Bobby gave me this one, and this one is for Emi. But first we stopped at a bakery and had a delicious little pastry after lunch, then, we went to a used bookstore, have you ever heard of such a thing? I got three books at a bargain. Bobby knew the owner. And we walked all over town, he showed me the parks and playgrounds for kids, and he showed me lots of other shops and we stopped in the library. He told me how the town got its wealth, from steel, and we went to a museum and..." On I went, realizing that I really had done a great deal in those afternoon hours. Mother listened with a smile as I went on excitedly. Then with my last breath I asked, "Where's Emi?" as I noticed she wasn't in her bed.

"Oh, she's down the hall visiting some of the other children. The nurse went to get her. They should be back any time. But you know Emi, she can make friends with a stump! She's probably met every child on the floor and is saying her goodbyes." We laughed.

Mother and I talked on, comparing notes about the city, what I'd seen that she hadn't and vice versa, until the nurse and Emi returned. As soon as she walked in the door I went to her and gave her a big hug. "Emi, you look great! How's your hand? You look like you've gained weight and your color is much better! Even since just this morning!"

She had her stuffed rabbit under her arm as I escorted her to her bed. The nurse left, saying she would be back. Emi's hand was now just lightly wrapped and the swelling and discoloration had gone away. The three of us inspected it and discussed the healing as Mother explained all that the doctor had told her. She could leave tomorrow. They would give Mother some fresh supplies to wash and re-dress the wound for the next several days. She was to have the stitches removed in one week, something Mother could easily do. Emi was advised not to play in dirt or foul water. The wound was to be kept clean and dry except for an unguent applied after cleaning. If there were any complications or a recurrent infection, a fever or pain, she was to get to our local clinic right away.

I remembered the seashells and took them out of my pocket to show Emi, and gave her the one I picked up. She looked longingly at the one Bobby had given me, but that one I was going to covet. Emi whined about wanting to see the ocean and the town, but Mother explained that we would have to leave early tomorrow to make any headway home. "Besides, aren't you excited to see Father and your brothers?" asked Mom.

"Yeah, I guess," Emi responded with resolve. She didn't argue much. She was tired of being in the hospital and was ready to get on the road again, to get home. We visited for a while longer until her dinner tray arrived. Mother and I kissed her on her forehead and left her to eat as we headed back to the hotel.

"It's a shame that she can't see the ocean," I said as we left the hospital. "She's never been to one before and it's so beautiful and powerful. Couldn't I take her down there before we leave in the morning?"

Mother answered, "I'll tell you what, let's get everything together and ready to go in the morning, then see if we have a little time to take her there. Bobby and Ohm will be escorting us home and they won't want to dawdle around waiting for us," she said with a smile.

"What about James? I haven't seen him since he left us with you and Emi."

"He apparently had some other duties to fulfill so is gone now."

"I didn't know we'd see Ohm again."

"Oh, yes. He's to arrive tonight and help pack and guide us tomorrow."

"How long will it take to get back?"

"Hopefully, not longer than a day if everything goes all right, and it should. Bobby says the road is a good one and frequently traveled."

We arrived back at the hotel and after a short, refreshing nap, went about gathering and washing clothes and hanging them on hooks, knobs, bedposts and chairs around the room to dry. By the time we were done, the room looked like it was haunted by underwear, t-shirts and nightgown ghosts.

Mother had bought some new clothes for the boys and Father, and a few other items she knew we would need right away when we got home, like soap and towels. Once everything was gathered we had a fair pile of packages and knapsacks. When finished, we went downstairs to eat.

I was hoping Bobby would be there to join us, but he wasn't. I was ravenous from the day and ate everything in front of me. Mother and I had a light conversation about this and that. It was nice to have some time alone with her and catch up with each other. She mentioned that she thought Bobby was smitten with me. I just blushed and smiled. Enough said. When supper was finished, we decided to take a walk along the boardwalk. Niobe was bright, while Idris was shy in the sky. The night air was cool and slightly breezy but refreshing. The shop owners were beginning to close and lock up for the day, each proprietor bustling about behind glowing display windows, themselves on display like actors on a theater stage under the softly glowing shop lights. "Open" signs were being turned around to "Closed." Someone here is counting out his money box, separating the coins and bills, next door a woman straightening her dress racks. Another fellow is sweeping up the spilled rice and flour from the hardwood floor. Each had a story to tell, of generations of families trying to provide for themselves, to put meat on the table, to pay their taxes. Townspeople were making their way to the trolleys that would take them home, maybe away from the city, just to be back again the next day to sell their goods and make a living.

Mother and I walked two blocks then into a small park with cobblestone pathways and short, decorative iron fences. There was a statue of an angel atop a fountain in the middle of the park and a few benches scattered about. We chose one to sit o n for a few minutes and savor the bittersweet ending to our journey.

There were a couple of lovers hidden in the shadows, whispering and murmuring in alluring tones, and a man walking his furry little dog. Otherwise the park was very quiet. We could see a hill nearby with the twinkling lights from a few homes, and it dawned on me that I hadn't yet seen the famous castle. Mother said it was a spectacular sight but difficult to see from the city. She had taken a carriage ride one day and that is how she was able to view it.

Soon, we were headed back for the night. I was ready for bed by then as it had been a long day. When we reached the hotel, both Ohm and Bobby were in the lounge, sipping on whiskeys. They got up and greeted us warmly, asking us to join them. Mother knew I was ready to call it a night, and they said they had some business to discuss and would be up momentarily. I was glad for that, but before I turned toward the stairs I gave Bobby a little knowing look and smile. I hoped I was subtle enough that it wasn't picked up by Mother and Ohm.

Chapter 25

I must have fallen right to sleep because I didn't hear Mother come in or get into bed. I woke refreshed at dawn and was anxious for the day. Out the window I could see the day opening up, the clouds changing from dark gray to light gray, the sky from dense night to azure blue; then a little orange and yellow underneath, the sun pushing up from the depths, warming the earth.

Mother roused as I was getting dressed, surprised to hear me up so early. I told her I wanted to try to get Emi up and out early, so that maybe I could take her to see the ocean before we had to leave.

"Honey, that is very thoughtful and I'm sure she'd love to, but the hospital won't release her without me. I have to sign some papers."

"Well then, get up!" I teased as I tossed the blankets back, exposing her to the cool room.

"My, you *are* anxious! Okay, I'll get up. I think we have almost everything together but why don't you go downstairs for some breakfast, and I'll come down as soon as I get ready."

Although I wasn't very hungry I ordered pancakes and eggs, sausage and hash browns, coffee and juice, hoping it would hold me until our first stop, wherever that might be. I was eating and thumbing through the local Tribune when I was surprised by Bobby sitting down across from me.

"Well, you're up early, good morning," he said.

"Oh, hi. You rather startled me."

"Sorry, didn't mean to. So are you ready to get going this morning?"

I told him I wanted to take Emi to the water but had to wait for Mother to come with me to break her out of her confinement. We chatted lightly while I ate, and he ordered his food. Mother soon joined us and so did Ohm. The three of them talked about the plans for the day, what route we would be taking, how far between breaks, whether we could make it as far as Bellingham before nightfall and so on.

"I thought we'd be home by this evening?" I stated.

"Well, no, not quite," said Ohm. "Your father doesn't want us to bring you in yet. He wants the gambling games to be well over and make sure Boris and his cronies are kicked out first. He doesn't want to risk putting the family in jeopardy until he knows absolutely that it will be safe." I looked at Mother with concern and disappointment, but she just smiled and nodded.

He went on. "There's still a chance that Boris could rebel and try to stay. He doesn't want to give up the estate or the crown and he won't do it without a fight. From the communications we've been getting, he's feeling a lot of pressure to win, but is worried about his young opponent. We hope he doesn't try anything to cause a problem."

"Like what?" I asked.

"We don't know, but a person like Boris could become volatile and violent if things don't go the way he planned. He doesn't like losing in gambling, and especially won't like giving up what he feels is his birthright. If he's under the influence of alcohol and the devil, he could be dangerous." I felt Ohm was exaggerating but everyone else around the table seemed to take him seriously.

"Enough of this. Let's be on our way!" said Bobby with a thrill for adventure in his voice.

So Ohm and Bobby headed out to get the wagon and horses and to pack supplies. Mother and I brought our packages and luggage down to be loaded, and headed over to the hospital to fetch Emi.

She was dressed and just finishing her breakfast when we arrived. She was very excited to go. Mother signed the requisite papers and talked to the doctor and nurses one last time, as I helped Emi gather up the few things she had accumulated including the gifts we had made for her, some flowers and cards she had received, and her stuffed bunny. I told her I wanted to take her down to the water before we got on the road and she beamed with anticipation. She was tired of being cooped up in a hospital room. As soon as Mother was finished we left, Emi with a bounce in her step.

She was grateful to be outside and was gazing all around, amazed at the sights in this big city. As when I first arrived, she wanted to stop and look in each storefront. We went by the hotel where the men were packing up our wagon and dropped off Emi's things, then she and I headed down the road to the ocean. She was in awe as soon as she laid eyes on the sea and the beach.

"This is the most beautiful thing I have ever seen!" she exclaimed.

We took off our shoes and walked down the beach, the sand oozing softly between our toes, listening to the crashing of waves, feeling the misty water on our cheeks and picking up seashells. We didn't have much time, but Emi was in such good spirits that we lingered longer than we should have.

When we got back, the wagon was packed and the horses ready. Ohm and Bobby were finishing some last-minute details and Mother was trying to organize space for us in the back. This was a much more basic wagon than ours and didn't offer much room or comfort. It smelled like worn old wood and hay, a bit musty. And it only had one very small window. However, it was otherwise sturdy and solid.

Soon we were on our way. Mother sat in the jump seat with Ohm, Emi and I made a nest for ourselves in the back, and Bobby rode alongside. We opened the tarp in the back so as to get some air and be able to see out. As we left, Emi and I were filled with excitement and anxiety. In less than twenty-four hours, we should be back home! Emi was in rapture as we made our way through town. We passed by two parks with children shrieking and playing, by many more shops, then some beautiful homes, and through a square with large, imposing government buildings. As we made it out of town, we took a carriage road on a cobblestone street that took us up and over a hill that led us through the royal gateway of the city. Suddenly, there was the Escavaro palace looming from the hillside. It was an incredible, beautiful but foreboding fortress surrounded by huge stone walls and canals. The palace looked to be built on many levels climbing ever higher into the sky, with lots of windows, ramparts, decorative pillars, archways, fountains and gardens. It was such a marvel. I knew there were palaces such as these but I had only seen pictures or read about them. We certainly didn't have anything like this in our realm.

In a short time we had left the city and were on a dirt road with low grasses and few trees. There was sadness in watching Escavaro fade from view; the palace with its shooting spires and mammoth high walls began to look like a toy dollhouse as it receded into the distance.

Emi and I had lots to talk about, so we settled back and went to work catching up. She wanted to know what had happened after she left, where the boys and Father were, any more encounters with the Inky Dinks? I asked her about her operation, did it hurt, how was she managing without her index finger, could she hold a fork? And I asked her more about her dream of seeing Anton and receiving the bunny. She looked at me very seriously and said, "Blue, it wasn't a dream. He was there, in my room. He sat next to me in the chair and put his hand on my forearm, it was warm and he said he hoped to see me again soon, then, placed the bunny on my lap, and he left. I know it was him." It was clear that

Emi had nothing more to say about it as she nuzzled the rabbit and kissed its head. It did look a lot like Sniffles.

The day started out clear but cool and as time went on, thunderclouds began to develop and the wind picked up. I pulled out my cashmere sweater. Emiline pulled a blanket up around her. Mother came back to join us and check on Emi and her hand, which had a nice fresh bandage on it. She inspected it for any signs of swelling or redness and Emi assured her that there wasn't any pain. We talked and laughed and didn't discuss anything serious. Emi fell asleep first. Mother and I joined her in a nap as we were peacefully rocked by the wagon. The sound of horse's hooves clopping on the road, muffled by the soft dirt and the faint voices of the men, was relaxing and reassuring.

Then the wagon stopped and I heard some voices. Mother was already up and gone, Emi still slept. I poked my head out the front flap and saw Bobby and Ohm talking to some strangers. I could tell there were three men and a woman, but I couldn't discern the gender of the fifth person, who was a dwarf. They were all dressed in very colorful clothing with layers upon layers of sheers, silks, muslin and cotton. The men had on elaborate headwear, hats made of wrapped material and decorated with chains and jewels. They also wore long necklaces made of what looked like shiny heavy chain with a large amulet dangling to the waist, and they carried long, threatening- looking muskets. The woman wore the same sort of garb but more ornate, with jewels and beads, and she had little bells on delicate chains around her ankles; when she moved, they tinkled with the sweetest sound of chimes. They all wore face coverings and heavy black and purple eye makeup. They were riding bareback on very large goats!

Their voices sounded a little menacing and argumentative, and as I picked up the conversation I realized they were gypsies on the road and wanted food, drink and money. I could tell that Bobby and Ohm were trying to calmly negotiate but it was a bizarre conversation. Every now and then, the woman would swing up and onto her lap an instrument similar to a ukulele and begin strumming fast, singing in a language I didn't understand, all the while guiding her goat in circles, first clockwise then counter-clockwise. The rest of them would break out in laughter, dancing their goats around and around, laughing until they nearly lost their breath. In the middle of all that, the dwarf would climb off his goat and do a silly jig while swigging from a cask. Then as suddenly, the woman would stop playing, drop the instrument to her side, the dwarf would climb back on the goat and they'd get all serious again. They threatened to set the wagon on fire and wreak havoc if we didn't give them what they wanted. These rounds of music, laughter and seriousness and threats went on for several minutes.

By now, Emi had heard the commotion and was poking her head out close to mine. When the gypsies went to singing and laughing, prancing their goats about and making quite a scene, Mother and Ohm just looked at each other and whispered in a conspiring way while Bobby kept a wary eye on them. Every now and then, Ohm and Bobby would try to ignore them and chucked the reins to start the horses moving, but the gypsies blocked our way and only got angrier. After several rounds of their insanity, Mother reached to the back and asked me to hand her a gray knapsack. It took me a minute to locate it as I didn't recognize it, but I soon found it amongst our luggage and handed it to her. During the start of one of their serious rounds, Mother pulled from the knapsack a small piccolo, which she began to play, and then mimicked their laughter in an exaggerated way. Ohm and Bobby picked up right away and started laughing and whistling, slapping their thighs and getting truly funny. Bobby pranced his horse around in circles, first one way, then the other while the confused gypsies looked on. Emi and I couldn't help laughing out loud too. It was all so ludicrous! When Mother stopped playing, she put the instrument in her lap and we all got as serious as we could. Ohm and Bobby then began threatening them but in a way that didn't make a bit of sense. Ohm would say something like, "Now, you understand that this here little escapade of triviality and lack of morality can't suffer no more of your shenanigans or we'll call in the whippersnappers with this here noisemaker and then you'll be sorry." And Bobby would follow with, "See those little girls there?" pointing at us, which put us on the spot, "they're young witches and they have tails curled up there in the wagon with venomous fangs at the ends. We'll set them loose on you!"

This seemed to stir the gypsies a bit but yet another round of singing, laughing and dwarf dancing ensued. Mother subsequently played the piccolo, we'd laugh, get serious, and then they would do the same. Finally the rounds got mixed up like a tiger chasing its tail, and suddenly we were all laughing together at the same time, while the woman strummed her instrument and coaxed her poor goat to make more circles; Mother whistled and Bobby ran his horse around in a stamping flair while the dwarf danced in the dust of the horse and goats. When we'd all stopped laughing so hard we were crying, the woman sauntered up to the wagon and asked for an exchange of her instrument for the piccolo, with the understanding that no further negotiations were necessary and they would let us pass posthaste. An easy trade I thought, although Mother hesitated for a moment, perhaps to show a little negotiating power. The exchange was made and we even gave them a loaf of bread, just for good measure. They let us pass and we were on our way after an hour of all that nonsense. Bobby lingered to make sure we were out of danger and that they wouldn't suddenly turn and come after us again, as gypsies could not be trusted at their word, but they just continued down the road, every now and then stopping to play the piccolo and laugh and watch the dwarf dance and get drunker, then get serious and argue with each other, the men trying to push each other off their goats. They were certainly a crazy group. We had some good laughs recalling that episode for a long time.

In another hour or two, the air got a lot cooler and clouds drifted lower and became darker. Spits of rain began to strike the wagon. It appeared we might be in for a thunderstorm. We found some shelter in a grove of thick pines and boulders just off the main road. The men went about setting up camp and a fire. Mother helped put together a meal, but Emi and I stayed dry and warm in the wagon until they indicated we could come out for the warmth of the fire and something to eat. The fellows had made a lean-to out of scrub and brush and a tarp they carried, which was substantial enough to keep the now pouring rain and wind away. The plan was to keep going through the night so as to make it home by midday tomorrow. In the meantime, we enjoyed some hearty beef sandwiches and fruit. While waiting for the storm to subside enough to clean up and move on, Mother picked up the stringed instrument and started picking at the strings, getting a sense of the notes and sounds. Soon she was able to do a little strumming and humming. The thing had a very nice sound, smooth and clear. Then Ohm went to the wagon and retrieved a harmonica, and picked up the rhythm and beat of Mother's tune. Bobby used the lid of the kettle and his spoon to drum out a pattern that fit perfectly with the others, and Wilt made odd noises with his mouth that somehow sounded like a bass. Emi and I were in awe of the spontaneity of the music-making and how nice it sounded. I found myself tapping out the tune on my knees and bobbing my head, while Emi did her best to sing or hum along. It was a lot of fun, but soon the storm began to pass and without wasting any more time, we were on our way again. Back in the wagon I asked Mother where she got the piccolo and why.

"Oh, I got it in Escavaro. I was going to give it to Jeffrey, as he seemed to have a little talent blowing the whistle at the Inky Dinks. I thought perhaps he would enjoy learning the piccolo."

"I guess he'll have to learn this other instrument now?" I asked.

She smiled, "I guess so."

"Do you know what it's called?"

"No, I don't. We'll have to look into it when we get home. It's got a nice sound though, don't you think?" I had to agree.

CHAPTER 26

Knowing we would be home soon, the night became very long and I had a hard time sleeping with the anticipation. I was kept up thinking about my room in the castle, our hills and the bridge over the river, remembering some of the things I used to do like tending to the chickens and turkeys, gazing through my telescope, reading and studying, and writing, visiting with friends from time to time. My thoughts also ran to the many memories of the past several months and of all our adventures, of all the people I had met and of Anton and Bobby. It wasn't until near dawn that I finally fell into a cold restless sleep. It felt like only minutes later that I was awakened by Emi, shaking me hard and excitedly saying, "Get up! Get up! We're here!"

I popped up in a dense chill and found the windows to be frosted. We were in the town of Zap. A small town of 1,200 on the edge of our realm, it was snow- covered and quiet. Emi and I couldn't contain our excitement and were bouncing up and down on the bedding, laughing and giggling. Mother poked her head back with a big smile on her face. "Do you girls know where we are?" she asked. We both screamed, "Zap!"

"This is where we'll be staying until your father finds us and tells us when we can go home."

"You mean we can't keep going?" I asked, feeling a lurch through my stomach.

"We're only a few miles away!" Emi whined.

"Well, we're still about twenty miles from the castle, but your father wants us to remain out of sight until all is clear to return. The big playoff game is tonight. If there are any problems he doesn't want us nearby, but if all goes as planned, we'll be home by late day tomorrow. For now we'll be staying at the Hildebrandt Inn. The boys should be there by now. Everyone will be able to clean up and have a good supper tonight. Bobby and Ohm will keep me informed on the status of the games. Oh, and girls, just a word of warning. I would advise you to be very discreet while we're here and not talk much about the past eleven months. You may or may not be recognized by these townsfolk, but we'd best keep the business of our travels and what's happening at the castle between us. Be your sweet friendly selves, just don't reveal too much."

We took Mother at her word and didn't attempt to argue. It was clear that we had come this far and we didn't want to "mess it up."

By the time we pulled in front of the Hildebrandt, we had donned heavier clothes and pants, dug out coats, hats and mittens. Emi seemed happy to have a pair that was custom-made for her and with a little careful help, she was able to pull the right one over her bandage. She held them up and admired them, turning her hands back and forth before nodding her head in approval. As soon as we pulled up to the hotel we jumped quickly out of the wagon, our boots crunching on the new-fallen snow. There were a few wisps of flakes falling and swirling lightly, the air fresh and cold. Emi and I ran for the front door but Mother stopped us with a reprimand. "Not so fast, girls, help us unload some of our things."

Grumble, grumble. We were anxious to reunite with the boys and Father but followed directions. We each took two pieces of luggage and humped them to the front door. A doorman was waiting and held the door open while we dropped the items in the foyer near the reception desk. Then we ran back out and grabbed some more. Just then Phillip and Jeffrey burst out the door and grabbed us up in big hugs and happy smiles. Mother took them in her arms and squeezed them hard. We were all talking at once, the boys wanting to know how the rest of our journey was, how was Emi's hand—she held it up proudly and showed off her glove and how well it fit, then slipped it off to show them her hand as if the loss of her finger were some kind of badge of courage, which in a way, it was. We were reeled in to finish unloading the wagon and the boys eagerly pitched in. Soon the wagon was empty of all of our belongings, and Bobby and Ohm were left to finish up.

A porter had already taken our bags to our rooms. Passing by the hotel café, I could smell the chicory fragrance of coffee, bacon, fresh sweet pastries and whiffs of eggs and oatmeal. My stomach growled and suddenly I was famished. There was a warm fire burning in a fireplace in the lobby, and the whole atmosphere was cozy and comforting.

We first went to our rooms. Mother and Emi and I were in one room, the boys, and presumably Father, had a room just down the hallway. The boys said Father had left the evening before to go to the castle, so for now, they had the room to themselves. They felt important and I was a little jealous. But my moodiness quickly resolved in that I was just so happy to all be back together again and so close to home.

We washed up and headed down to breakfast. We could hardly contain ourselves and our conversations were rapid and exciting. The boys said that after I left for Escavaro with Bobby, the rest of the way was mostly uneventful except for crossing paths with a herd of large, brawny yulaks that simply wouldn't move and stood their ground on the road. They can be aggressive if provoked, especially the bulls, so all they could do was gently push them along. But one of the horses got spooked and reared up bucking and snorting, kicking up dust and frightening the yulaks, who hoofed the ground and sounded their roar as they are known to do. Their wagon was yanked upward violently onto one wheel, nearly tipping over and sending the boys flying about as if shaken like a pair of dice. Phillip got a nasty bruise on his elbow and knee. Jeffrey wasn't hurt, but anything that wasn't securely fastened down was dumped about, which was mostly soft goods. They thought for sure there was going to be an unpleasant incident, a stampede or an attack, but Father got control of the horse, the yulaks calmed down and eventually parted, and let the horses and wagon pass. As they slowly passed the herd, one of the bulls decided to show them who was boss and came running fiercely and threateningly toward the wagon, his head down, horns ready to put an end to the rolling threat, kicking up dust and blowing steam through its nostrils. Luckily, they were able to outrun the beast, and with hearts beating fast, settled into a noneventful final push toward Zap. The boys being boys just shoved everything that had tumbled into a big pile in the corner, figuring they could deal with it later.

We had lots to tell them: how much Emi loved their gifts, how she was treated at the hospital (ice cream every day!), how she learned to use utensils and hold a pencil without her index finger, the friends she'd made in the hospital. I told them all about the fine city of Escavaro, the sights, sounds, scents, shops of the city. I told them about the "used" bookstore and the books I had gotten, about the new clothes I bought, and especially about the sea and the immense, beautiful palace on the hill. Then we told them about the goofy gypsies on the road and how we got out of that. We spent a good two hours at the breakfast table while nibbling on this or that and drinking tea and coffee. After that, the boys and Emi got bundled up and went out to explore Zap. I was so tired from my lack of sleep the night before, and all the talk and excitement, that I excused myself to go take a nap. It was only noon, but I felt I'd been up since yesterday. Mother fussed around with luggage and packages as I dozed off.

I woke up midday, refreshed and ready to go out. It was obvious that Mother had rested too, as her bed covers were rumpled. I got cleaned up, put on warm clothes including my Anton cashmere, my new boots, a jacket, hat and gloves, and headed downstairs.

The lobby was quiet except for the crackling of the fire in the sitting lounge off to the side, and very soft conversations and tinkling of silverware on plates floating through from the dining room. The snow was still falling lightly and the sky was overcast, but the sun filtered through and gave the snow and everything it landed on a brilliant silver sparkle. Each snowflake that landed on my sleeve was easily identified for its individual uniqueness, until it disappeared into a tiny drop of water.

Chapter 27

The town was quaint and looked like a winter wonderland. Few conveyances were on the road and those that were, rolled slowly and quietly along. Horses' hooves were muffled, as were conversations. I began wandering and noticed that many shops were closed (what day was it anyway?), but there were Christmas trees and decorations along the street and in the square. Garlands hung from door and window frames, pretty lights were strung about. Crosses and other Christian religious symbols were placed in windows along with Christmas figurines and candles. The streetlights were lit with an amber glow. The bakery was open. I stepped in out of the cold and was offered a cup of hot cider topped with whipped cream, which I gladly sipped on while admiring the beautifully decorated pastries and cakes. From the counter was hung a string of paper gingerbread men and women with their black dot eyes, red buttons and plaid scarves, hand in hand, happily greeting customers with friendly smiles. There were bows and ribbons festively placed so as to make the shop feel and appear very homey. The scent of fresh bread, sugar and goodies was heavenly.

I took a seat near the frosted window, at a small café table bedecked with colorful holiday linen and a small centerpiece of holly, berries and sprigs of evergreen. I savored my cider, the steam rising to tickle my nose, as I watched a few people bundled up braving the cold, making their way one way or the other on the boardwalk. Then I saw Bobby and Ohm pass by. I knocked on the window and got their attention. They said something to each other, then Ohm went on as Bobby stepped through the door, tinkling the doorbell, stomping his feet on a welcome mat, and came right to my table. "Mind if I join you?"

"Not at all," I said with a smile, and gestured to the other chair for him to have a seat. As he removed his hat and coat, he was greeted by the pretty young waitress, who offered him some hot cider and said, "Can I get either of you a pastry or doughnut? We have some fresh, homemade apple strudel?" We politely declined.

"So, a bit of a change in weather…" he said, rubbing and puffing into his hands to warm them up. There was a faint bit of steam emanating from the top of his damp hair. His cheeks were rosy and his eyes bright and sharp.

"Yes, but it's oh so beautiful."

"Are you excited to return home?"

"Of course, I can't wait. The past few months have been quite an adventure but it will be so nice to be back in familiar surroundings and to sleep in my own bed again," I said in a dreamy way.

"The games will culminate tonight. Phillip, 'scuse me, your dad, will be watching from the wings, make sure it all goes as planned. The first rounds have been played and Boris has won six to three, but he tiring and he's running out of strategies."

"The odds sound pretty good for him. Isn't that worrisome? How long have they been playing?"

"They've been at the last game, Quark, for three days now. His first two opponents have been eliminated. He's all cocky now, drinking a lot."

"How can he possibly lose?"

"His newest and last opponent is a world expert. He is known all over for his skill and finesse. We have great confidence that this fellow will best your uncle, although he's planning on making it a long drawn-out game. The game is very complicated and requires a great deal of concentration. He wants your uncle to be tired, thirsty, hungry and completely confused by the end. That way he won't be as likely to fight or cause trouble when the winner is declared."

"Could there be trouble?" I asked.

"Oh, yes, but your dad and his men have taken all the precautions necessary to make sure that if there is trouble, it won't last for long."

"Could it become violent?"

"We certainly hope not, but Boris is unpredictable and as you know, can be extremely volatile. Plus he's developed some loyal followers who have been promised certain wealth, including land and livestock, 'when he wins' and becomes 'the true king of the realm.' Our boys are keeping a close eye on them."

"This all sounds extremely dangerous. Will Father be all right?"

"Sure, he'll be fine. The only ones who know he will be there are the ones watching his back. They won't let anything happen to him. If it makes you feel any better, Ohm and I will be there too."

"That doesn't make me feel any better. In fact, it worries me three times as much," I said with a sly smile. "Does Mother know all this?" I asked worriedly.

"Of course, she has been kept abreast of the plans for the past eleven months. She's fully aware of what's going on."

"Boy, there sure has been a lot of secrecy!" I said, a little incensed.

Bobby just laughed. "That was on purpose, no need to worry all of you. Well, sorry to cut this little visit short but I've got to be on my way. Ohm and I want to get to the castle early enough to meet with your father and a few others."

"Wait, I have some more questions!"

"Sorry, they'll have to wait, Blue, I've already spent too much time here. I don't want to hold Ohm up."

He stood up and put some money on the table, enough to pay for both of us. I stood too.

"Bobby, please be careful. I wouldn't mind seeing you again." And I gave him a kiss on the cheek.

"You will, Blue, I promise." He squeezed my arm, then grabbed his coat and hat, and with three long strides he was through the door, slinging his jacket on as he took off down the street.

My mind was reeling. I sat back down, finished my now lukewarm cider, and headed back to the hotel.

When I returned, I peeked in the lounge just off the foyer. The room was smallish but warm. The nice little fireplace was ablaze, the mantel hung with garlands and knitted Christmas socks. There was a card/game table, some very comfortable overstuffed chairs, a sofa and a few other small pieces of furniture, atop which were little holiday figurines. A couple of soft-lit lamps with pretty bows on the shades glowed, and placed around the room were flickering candles of white and gold, carefully seated in crystal candle holders. On the wallpapered walls were a couple of large gilt-framed oil paintings of country scenes. One was of a woman dressed in finery sitting on a divan. The floor was covered with a soft, multi-colored rug that had seen its finer days, but which tied the room all together. I picked up a hint of cinnamon and pine in the air. And there was Mother, comfortably curled up in an armchair with a book.

"What are you reading?" I asked softly so as not to startle her.

"Oh, hi Blue. Oh, this is a book I found on the bookshelf about the history of the area, some of the attractions, which include a waterfall in the foothills to the north and an ancient burial site just outside of town, plus some information about the native wildflowers and some stories and folklore of the area. It's really quite interesting. It's amazing how little I knew about Zap and yet it is so close. What have you been up to?" she asked with interest.

I sat down in a chair next to her. "Not much," I said with a shrug. "Just walking around a little."

"I sense something bothering you, Blue. Do you feel all right?"

"Yes, I feel fine. I guess I'm just a little melancholy."

"We should be able to go home tomorrow if all goes well tonight," she said, to comfort me. "I think we're all tired of being on the road, and the disruptions of our life. It will be good to get back to old routines."

"Yeah, I guess," I responded, looking downward.

Mother switched her position to face me straight on, her hands in her lap. "Tell me, Blue, what's bothering you?"

"I don't know, Mom. I guess a lot of feelings are going through my head. I can't wait to get home, but I wonder what it will really be like. Traveling has been interesting and a lot of fun in many ways. I wonder if I'll be able to pick up where I left off. I'm not sure if I'm even interested in my telescope anymore. A year ago I thought I might go to the university and study astronomy or astrology; now I'm not so sure. I'll be 18 in a month and I feel more uncertain about my future than ever. And then there's…" I trailed off.

"Others, perhaps?" she asked.

"Well, yeah."

"Honey," she said as she took my hands in hers, "I know you've got a fondness for a couple of boys. I've seen how you've acted around Anton and Bobby. It's only natural for you to have men on your mind. That's what we women do!

Especially at your age. If we didn't have these natural urges, men and women would never procreate. But you are young. You still have a lifetime in front of you. At this age you should take advantage of everything that comes your way. Go to the university. Travel more, write a book. Meet more people. Do whatever your heart desires. You are smart and lovely. People respect you, and with that power, you can go far."

"But, what about you and Father?"

"What about us?"

"You wouldn't want me taking off, traipsing around the world just for the fun of it, would you? What are your expectations of me?"

"Blue, your father and I love you very much and hope we have brought you up with good values and firm morals. We are confident you will make the right choices in life. You have not disappointed us yet and now you are an adult! It is not for us to decide your future. You must do what it takes to make you happy and fulfilled. We will always be supportive and always be there for you, as with the other children."

"Mom, I love you. You always know the right things to say. I promise I won't make any rash decisions, and the way you and Father have raised me guarantees that I'll never stray too far, or ever forget my family." My eyes were moist with happy tears and we put our foreheads together in a most loving gesture.

That evening was bittersweet. Mother, my sibs and I bundled up and went down the road to a café for some supper, which was filling, but nothing to brag about. Then we came back, got some comfy clothes on and met back down in the lounge to play some card games.

It felt to me like we were just biding time, waiting for the clock to tick toward our bedtime. The other kids didn't ask anything about the games, Uncle Boris, or what was going to happen in the morning. We goofed and teased each other but it was subdued. Mother had cleaned and re-bandaged Emi's wound with just one layer of gauze and she probably didn't even need that, but Emi wasn't ready to have it visible to the public yet. She was still self-conscious about the disfigurement and although the wound was healing well, it was still a little red and she didn't like looking at the stitches. However, she shuffled and played cards as if all her fingers were present.

It was the first time I had really noticed the changes in the boys, and how they had each grown a couple of inches in just the eleven months. Phillip was looking much more mature; his face lengthening, his jawline was sharpening and eyebrows looking darker and more bristly. His voice hadn't started changing yet and there was no facial fuzz either, but I could tell that his puberty was beginning its natural progression. Jeffrey had just grown taller, but he was still a fun-loving kid with no apparent concerns. As far as I could tell Emi hadn't physically changed at all. She had, however, matured beyond her age. There we all were, gathered for our last night on the eve of our homecoming. What did the future hold now? The mantel clock struck ten, and although we really hadn't been on any kind of time schedule for months, we all seemed to act on that chime, began putting away the cards and trundled off to our rooms.

By the time Mother had checked on the boys and returned to our room, Emi and I had brushed our teeth and were in bed, I with my book and Emi rolled over to her side, not yet asleep, whispering softly to her stuffed bunny. Mother attended to her nighttime routine and got ready for bed, then came to our bed and sat next to Emi.

"I am so proud of you two. You have made a very long, unexpected journey with more grace and maturity than I could imagine. I can't say the reason for all this was anything but horrible, but I have watched you kids navigate a world of unknowns, both good and bad, yet you've adapted, learned and moved on. All of life is full of unknowns. Now you have a good set of tools to make it in the world with very little help from others. I think this trip has brought the family together in ways that never would have happened otherwise, and I'm very grateful for that. Now, get some sleep. Tomorrow will be a big day. We should be home by early evening. Good night my loves," and with that, she kissed us on our foreheads, tucked us in and went to her own bed.

CHAPTER 28

The next morning brought a hive of activity. We grabbed a quick breakfast, then headed back to our rooms to pack up and get ready for the last leg of our journey. I was wrapped up in my own thoughts but Emi and the boys were hyper with excitement, and kept running back and forth between the rooms teasing, giggling, throwing pillows and becoming far too loud. Mother grabbed Jeffrey by the arm as he was flying by and told him and Emi to "Stop this!" and "Behave yourselves!" Phillip had eluded the reprimand. Once we were packed there was nothing much to do but wait. Mother gathered us all in the game room lounge and presented us each with a small gift.

"These are just a few things I've collected along the way. I wanted to give you kids a gift from your father and me, to tell you how proud we are of all of you and how much we love you. You can call these early Christmas gifts."

Phillip was given a chess game set, something he'd been wanting for a very long time. He was jubilant. "Wow, thanks! I've wanted one of these forever!"

Jeffery had already opened his package bearing the stringed instrument, looking at it carefully, strumming a few notes, and trying to figure out what it was.

"I don't know what it's called, honey. I was going to give you a piccolo, thinking you might like to learn to play an instrument, especially after showing your talent on the whistle, but the gypsies demanded a trade and this is what you got instead. I think it has a real nice sound, and it may be easier to learn than the piccolo."

Jeffrey seemed to be quite taken with it and was strumming out a few nonsense tunes. "Thanks, I really like this. It's gonna be fun to play."

Emi was next to open her package. She excitedly ripped off the paper and was awed by the nice new coat inside. "Oh, this is just the most beautiful thing I've ever had!" she said as she held the coat up, admiring the thick, soft, forest-green chenille with its oversized stylish buttons, finished cuffs and roll-up collar. She tried it on right away. It fit almost perfectly. It was just a little too big, but not noticeably, and otherwise looked very smart on her. "I thought it might be a little big for you, but I think it will fit you well in a few months," said Mother, smoothing down the hem as Emi twirled. "I love it, Mom! Thanks!"

Next, I opened my small package. In it was a beautifully hand-decorated book, a journal with blank pages made of thick, homemade paper. I was feeling the texture of the decoration of ribbon and colored cut pieces of paper on the cover as Mother said, "The journal you've been writing in has been looking pretty dirty and tattered, yet you seem so dedicated to writing, I thought you could use a nice new one—for your next journey or chapter in life."

"It's so lovely I'm not sure I'll want to sully it with a pencil," I said, only half serious, and reached over and gave Mother a kiss on her cheek.

The rest of the day was boring and slow. Mother insisted we stick nearby so that when the men returned we would be ready to go. We puttered in our rooms, played a couple of games in the lounge, read, nibbled on snacks, napped, took short walks. The hours ticked on. Soon it was five o'clock. Mother seemed to be getting a little worried and wondered out loud why the men weren't back yet. I didn't want to voice my concerns because I could only imagine the worst; did Boris win the games? Was there violence? Was someone hurt? Did they get in an accident on the road? I tried not to think about it and went on reading some more. Mother paced, went up to the room, came back down a few minutes later and checked the front desk for messages. She tried not to show her concern but it was hard to hide. Luckily the younger kids hadn't picked up on it, even though they pestered Mom throughout the day about "how much longer?" But suppertime came and we were hungry. They were getting restless.

Phillip broke the silence and asked, "Where's Dad? I thought they were supposed to be back by now."

"I thought so too, honey. There's been no word. I'm sure everything's okay. Maybe the last game went on longer than expected," Mother said.

"Do you think they're okay? I mean like hurt or anything?" I tried to ask without sounding alarmed. Emi's eyes were moistening and the boys looked very worried.

"No, I'm sure not. Your father and the other men are very capable and have an army of men watching out for them. I think there's just been a setback for some reason. But come on, let's get something to eat and we'll just wait."

She wasn't very reassuring and I could tell she had a lot on her mind. We ate a slow supper in the café, mostly in silence, and were just getting up from the table when Ohm and Bobby came through the door. They didn't look concerned and even seemed to have little smiles on their ruddy faces. They stomped the snow from their boots as they whipped off their hats and slapped them against their legs, ice crystals flying. Mother went to them quickly and put her arms around each of them. "Oh thank God you're back. I was so worried," she blurted out.

"We're fine, Victoria, just fine," said Ohm. "The last game was delayed because Boris kept trying to come up with tactics to stall. He really didn't have a chance of winning and knew it, but didn't want to finish the games. He wanted to appoint his mentor to take his place, but that wasn't allowed. Nonetheless, he kept arguing his point. When that didn't work he tried some other shenanigans. Finally he gave in to the taunting and chiding of the audience and sat down at the table two hours late.

"It was a fine and exciting game. The challenger did just what he planned; he acted innocent and inert. He lost the first four rounds, then won the fifth and sixth, Boris won the seventh and eighth. Boris was ahead by four; he seemed to be on a roll. The fickle crowd went from heckling to cheers. He got cocky and self- confident and let his defenses down. That's when Anton struck and…"

"Anton!?" I blurted. "Anton who? From Iznot?! How could that be? It certainly wasn't him!"

"Well, yes," responded Ohm as everyone else looked on.

"Mother, did you know about this?"

"No I didn't," and she looked between Ohm and Bobby. "Is that the same Anton we're talking about?"

"Has to be," responded Ohm. "The kid's from Iznot, 'bout 21 or 22? Does a lot of traveling? You met him?"

Mother and I looked at each other. "Yes, while in Iznot," she said. "That would explain a lot of things. He's about the only one Phillip never put a name to."

I turned and stomped off, hurt and mad for reasons I wasn't really sure of.

"Sorry if I said something I shouldn't have, ma'am. I figured by now you must know all the details, at least most of them."

"That's okay, Ohm, you did nothing wrong. I'm just glad we found out and that you're all okay."

Bobby whispered, "Is Blue all right? She seems to be mad or something."

"She'll be fine; it's just kind of personal. She'll get over it," Mother said

softly.

"Well, I knew," spouted Emi, sounding self-important. "I told you. He came to visit me in the hospital. He gave me the bunny! You didn't believe me!"

"I guess I do now, honey. Was he in Escavaro?" Mother asked of both Bobby and Ohm. They shrugged.

"Coulda been, I suppose, but I don't really know," responded Ohm.

I had gone into the lounge to sulk but could still hear the conversation. My eyes were welling up and I was shaking. I was angry. I felt I should have known. I felt left out of the bigger picture, like Father should have said something or that Anton should have told me. Didn't he trust me? If he was nearby I could have seen him. And what about my feelings for Bobby? I was so confused.

Just then Mother was at my side, putting her arm around my shoulders as she sat down on the arm of the chair. I hadn't realized their conversation had ended. "Honey, I'm so sorry. I really didn't know. Your father must have wanted to keep him secret, especially since it was apparent that you and Anton had become fond of each other. It might have jeopardized the games. I'm sure he had a good reason."

"There've been an awful lot of secrets!" Now I was weeping and whining like a six-year-old. What had come over me? Mother caressed me patiently. A comfortable time later, she rose. "We'll stay here another night and leave first thing in the morning. We should be home by midday. Take your time, come to bed whenever you want," she said gently, then stepped away.

I spent another hour sulking as the fire died out, and then went up to my room. It was after midnight. My time in the comfy lounge chair facing the warm and embracing fire had allowed me to sort through my thoughts, throwing away the trivial and unessential, the bygones and riffraff; embracing instead the memories, the people, the smells, adventures, the newness and the strange. I realized that it wasn't for me to question the wisdom of my father, and through all of this, we had remained safe and cared for. I was grateful for the many stories I would remember forever. I thought about my future, who I was and what kind of person I wanted to be. Soon I would be home. A known. No surprises, just routines. Could I readapt? Of course! I would find a way. I would make it another adventure! See life with fresh eyes! Open my heart to possibilities! I'll never be afraid to step out of my realm and explore all there is to know.

The next morning was bright and sunny, but dense with cold. Icicles hung solidly on the eaves, the boardwalks were slick, puffs of steam billowed from the mouths and nostrils of people and horses on the street; few people were out. The mood at breakfast was light, easy and happy. My own mood had improved dramatically. I too was happy and excited and found myself smiling more than I had intended. I generally wasn't a moody person but thought I wanted another day of grumpiness just for good measure. Instead I gave in to enjoying the day. The next thing I knew we were all comfortably situated in our caravan. Ohm and Bobby were in front. Mother was in the back with the rest of us. Wilt came by to bid us farewell but hadn't planned on accompanying us. Said he had some other things to attend to. We thanked him for all he'd done for us and for keeping us entertained with his stories. He shook hands with Bobby and Ohm and was on his way.

I'd forgotten how much room our old caravan had compared to the wagon that brought Mother and me to town. We were all dressed in our warmest clothes. Emi had on her new mittens and coat. The boys, looking more and more like the men in the jump seat, had on leather jackets and wool pants, and I had on my Anton sweater under a heavier coat. This morning I decided to wear the circus amulet. I didn't want it to get lost in the packing, but mostly I had come to terms with the important role Anton was playing and that indeed, it really hadn't been any of my business that he was involved in the plan to get us back home.

We loped out of town through the crunchy snow and were soon on a well-worn albeit snowy road, taking us in a full circle.

"So don't you want to know what happened, Blue?" asked Phillip.

"What do you mean?"

"You know, the end of the games. You missed the last part."

"Yeah, 'cause you were all whiny and crying like a girl," piped Jeffrey.

"Now, now," said Mother sternly.

"Well, she was," Jeffrey said under his breath.

"So what *did* happen?" I asked, directing my question to Phillip.

"Yeah, so anyway Anton was down four." Phillip got excited and animated in the telling.

"He came into the ninth round with fire and slammed down Boris with double points. Boris fought back hard but Anton played with admirable finesse—that's what Ohm said, 'admirable finesse.'" Jeffrey nodded his head in agreement and mouthed the words to himself. "And beat Boris on the tenth and eleventh rounds, securing a healthy win. But they had one more round and Boris was furious! Pounding his fists on the table and demanded an all or nothing round. There was a lot of confusion and the crowd was loud and booing, 'cause really, that last game of Quark was suppose to be the all or nothing game. Boris just wanted to add on an extra one."

Jeffrey interrupted, "Bobby said he was spittin' mad."

"So anyway, the crowd got quieted down as Anton was standing and gesturing calm. Then Anton, being all thoughtful and stuff said, 'I will agree to an all or nothing last round if when you lose, you and your men will leave here peacefully as in the terms of the original agreement. You will be expected to never return and go far from this realm.' 'Ha!' said Boris."

"Yeah, he said that, 'Ha' just like Phillip said!" Now Emi was excited about the telling of the story and wanted to add a part.

"So anyway," Phillip continued, a little annoyed at the interruptions, "Boris was angry and laughed at Anton. A big belly laugh, so much so that the crowd laughed with him. 'You will not win this round because I'm changing the rules and you can't do anything about it! For it to be all or nothing, I choose to have my mentor, Mr. Crock play in my place and I'll even play fair and let you choose someone to take your place. Take it or leave it!' There were gasps and hushes, worried looks and whispers. Suddenly the betting got frantic and people were exchanging money like they had it to spend. The stakes were high. Anton thought about it for a while, and I guess Father really wanted to come out from the shadows and offer advice, but of course he couldn't be seen so he remained hidden behind a balcony pillar under a hooded coat. So then, Anton announced that he and he only would play the last round against the mentor, all or nothing. More gasps of the crowd and more exchange of money. Now it was getting exciting!"

By now Emi, Jeffrey, Mother and even I were leaning in, wrapped up in the story. Phillip was doing a fine job of keeping our attention, and based on everyone else's reactions I got the idea that he was elaborating much more than Ohm had told it. Perhaps Phillip should consider studying journalism. He went on.

"So, Mr. Crock stepped in and took a seat with Boris hovering over his shoulder. The crowd went silent and the last round began. This part is boring 'cause the pieces and the cards kept going back and forth a lot, and it went on and on. I guess Mr. Crock gave Anton a good run for his money. Or maybe Anton was just playing him, wearing him down. That's what Bobby said."

"What does 'playing him' mean, Mom?" Jeffrey pondered.

"Shush. I'll tell you later. Now let your brother finish the story," she responded.

"Suddenly," continued Phillip, "Anton slapped down three cards, all aces, and knocked over a piece on the playing board, meaning he had won. Mr. Crock threw up his arms and shook his head in defeat. Boris grabbed Mr. Crock's neck, intending to strangle him, but others jumped in and pulled Boris off. Unc was fighting, screaming and spitting, yelling that the games were thrown, that Crock was paid off, that he wanted yet another round. The sheriff hauled him off to jail to let him cool off. The crowd went wild. Booze was poured and spilled, money was exchanged, minor drunken fights broke out, Anton was glad-handed and slapped on the back and people poured out into the night, wanting to be the first to announce the news. Father slowly emerged from the shadows and soon joined Anton on the main floor. It was just then that people recognized him and began chanting his name, 'King Hamilton, Lord Hamilton!' He was all smiles and congratulated Anton on his fine performance. Bobby and Ohm left right away to come back here, and that was that!"

"So now we have our castle back and we don't have to worry about Uncle Boris anymore!" Emi said excitedly.

It was a remarkable recap but as Phillip told it, Mother nodded in agreement. "There will be a celebration in a few days after we return. Your father and I want to thank all the people who helped us out during the year."

"Like a party?" asked Emi.

"Yes, like a party."

"Will Anton be there?" I asked hopefully.

"I imagine so. He's rather the star, don't you think?"

"I had no idea he had that kind of talent."

"You weren't supposed to know," Mother said with a wry smile.

We talked for a while longer about the whole thing and put together some of the parts of our travels that had been puzzling to me; like the mysterious meeting in the forest in Iznot, and the men who followed us out of town going to Pea, and how suddenly Walt, Ohm and Bobby and James showed up after the Inky Dinks. It all began to make sense.

We made it to the edge of our estate in no time and could barely contain our excitement. When the castle came into view, I was awed. Our home, the rolling hills, our river and bridge were all there, blanketed in fresh white snow. Someone had lit the fireplaces and the chimneys were puffing out a warm welcome.

It wasn't until we came closer that I began to see our broken down and partially burned barn, with the doors hanging on creaky hinges, slats missing from the roof and sides and trash scattered throughout the property, poking through the drifts here and there. Our cobblestone driveway was missing pieces of stone from the decorative wall and it was clear, even at this time of year, that our beautiful trees, bushes and vines had not been maintained. I could see some broken windows in the top floors on the wings we never used and were closed off, which made me wonder what on earth Boris and his minions and whores had been up to. I looked over at Mom, who I could tell was wondering the same sad thing. It was disheartening to think that our rooms and possessions might very well be in the same bad shape, or worse. But it was home and for now, that was all that counted.

Father greeted us heartily at the door and as I stepped into the stone foyer, the warmth that enshrouded me was overwhelming. I couldn't help breaking into tears of happiness. A few workers were bustling about but I caught a whiff of apple pies baking in the kitchen. Perfect for our homecoming!

Epilogue

Word travelled fast that Lord Hamilton and his family had returned in good health, putting aside any rumors of kidnappings, separations or horrible deaths. People from all the surrounding towns came to offer us welcoming gifts and food, and participate in the celebration that took place two days hence and lasted for nearly two days after. Father was obligatorily reinstated as King, and Anton was honored for making our return possible through his excellent skills and gamesmanship. He was given a bag of money and a fine horse. Many others were recognized for their help and efforts in returning the rightful owner to the realm, including Bobby, Ohm, James and Wilt. Stories abounded about how Boris tried to rule but with inadequacy and awkwardness, at which the people rebelled, making his job difficult and a joke. He apparently gave up after a few months and the people ran their towns and cities as they always had, without much disruption. Citizens continued to pay taxes, which were deposited in the local banks, essentially going into arrears with the kingdom. But Boris's minions were too inefficient to enforce collection. Once Father regained the kingdom, the whole of the taxes were fairly turned over to him, and he in turn began releasing funds for overdue repairs of streets and buildings and city maintenance.

It took many weeks, with the help of a multitude of volunteers, to clean up the mess and make the necessary repairs to get our home back into moderate shape. By spring, everything was pretty much in order. Indeed, we had lost a number of personal possessions. All of Mother's jewelry was gone, a number of paintings and furniture were broken or missing, my telescope was gone, and several books in the library had been torn apart and used as kindling. Rugs were soiled to the point of no repair and walls had been sullied with lewd markings and graphics. In one of our dens it appeared that someone had started a fire in the middle of the room, as there was a large burn mark on the floor and spent wood and ashes. Our rooms with fireplaces were obviously not vented properly; soot covered the bricks from floor to ceiling. And as expected, our closed-off wings had been invaded by partying truants who, although they had no belongings to ruin, broke windows and bottles and threw trash about. The stench was unbearable in one of the rooms. There could have been a dead body in there for all we knew.

The first week of living with this was almost more than I could bear, but at least our beds and most bedroom furniture were still in place, and what clothes weren't stolen were still in closets and drawers, albeit rifled through and stinky. Everything had to be washed or thrown away.

Spirit never returned to us and nobody ever found her, although after word had gotten out in Pea of her bolting in fright from the Inky Dinks, several people went searching for her. Alas, she was lost.

Anton surprised Emi by guiding her to the barn. "Come here, I want to show you something," and there was Sniffles comfortably nested in a warm corner of the barn, in a large wooden hutch with a mound of clean hay and straw for bedding, munching on carrots and lettuce. He had gotten fatter and seemed happy to see Emi, who scooped him up and snuggled her face in his fur. Anton admitted that he indeed did visit Emi in the hospital in Escavaro on his way to the games at the castle, so Emi was vindicated and held her nose up high.

Mother removed her stitches about ten days after our return. Her wound looked good and healthy although still puckered and slightly pink. In a few months that would all settle down and the scar would be barely noticeable. She used her hand so well that it often took a second glance to realize she was missing her index finger.

Jeffrey learned to play the instrument Mother had given him. We found out it was called a lute. He played it frequently, and when I went to our local library in Bellingham, I picked up a beginner's guide to playing the lute. He actually became quite proficient and in years to come, would be asked to play with other musicians on small stages or entertain at various gatherings. His wanderlust never waned, and he took every opportunity possible to explore our vast property or to ride to various towns with Father and Phillip.

Phillip eased into puberty the next year, his voice cracking at the most embarrassing times, facial fuzz began to show on his chin and he became taller and lankier. Plus, he began noticing girls; stealing quick glances, finding ways to stand near them, awkward and reluctant and too uncomfortable to say anything. He was embarrassed to let Mother in his room and no longer displayed open affection to the parents when in the company of his friends. Despite his physical awkwardness, he was growing into a very savvy, intelligent, inventive young man to whom Father turned for advice and opinions. He was given the tasks of riding to the kingdom's towns and cities to collect taxes and report back on any problems. That is, within reason. Mother insisted he go no further than twenty miles away and with strict instructions to be back at a given time, even if it was a day or two later. She felt Father was giving him too much responsibility and they had discussions about that. Sometimes they'd allow Jeffrey to go with him, but that only worsened Mother's anxieties.

Father stuck around while the repairs and clean-up continued, just taking day trips to check on his property and visit the towns, whereas Mother found a new interest in cooking and spent many hours helping the cooks clean out and organize cabinets, gather essential spices and prepare meals. They seemed to enjoy having her in the kitchen and even learned a few tricks from her themselves. Soon she was trying her hand at baking and made some wonderful breads and pastries. In the spring she claimed a plot of land near the kitchen service door to start her own garden. Father and the boys helped build the plot with walking paths, fencing and planters. Mother added a couple of small garden statues and Emi made her a scarecrow out of discarded goods from the house. There, she grew herbs, vegetables and flowers.

I turned 18 at the end of January and decided to enroll in the university. I loved the atmosphere of campus, the intellectual bantering and the learning. I did much better than I had when home schooled. For one thing, I was more disciplined. My grades excelled and I met lots of friends, and my adventures became a constant source of discussion and entertainment, so much so that I was asked to speak for various occasions on campus and off, which I found to be useful and fulfilling. I continued to see Anton and Bobby from time to time, and had the privilege of being wooed by other men. But, while Bobby became a lasting and reliable friend, Anton held a special place in my heart. He was always off traveling, as he had gotten a lot of offers to instruct and compete in various games around the world. And whenever he returned, he made a point to visit me at home or at the university, regaling me with adventures of sailing vast seas and experiencing cultures I'd only read about or had never even heard about. He often brought me a trinket or gifts from exotic lands.

When Bobby came around we found a great deal of interest in the fun aspects of life. We'd go horseback riding off in the countryside, stopping for a picnic or swim. He'd entice me to join him at festivals in nearby towns; we went to the theater together, and spent endless hours laughing and talking. We could hug and kiss in a friendly way, but romance was kept at an easy distance as we had such a good time just being together.

I continue to write in my journals and long ago filled up the beautiful book Mother had given me. I enrolled in journalism and writing classes at the university and I loved those the most. It is too early to make a decision on my career, but I know I want to have one—hopefully, one that will allow me to travel! And so, the sun and moons continue to rise and set, and I will never forget the dreams and experiences of the past year.

The End

64917985R00162

Made in the USA
Charleston, SC
11 December 2016